Cover Girl

NIC TATANO

Harper*Impulse* an imprint of
HarperCollins*Publishers* Ltd
1 London Bridge Street
London SE1 9GF

www.harpercollins.co.uk

A Paperback Original 2015

First published in Great Britain in ebook format by Harper*Impulse* 2015

A catalogue record for this book is
available from the British Library

ISBN: 9780008162139

This novel is entirely a work of fiction.
The names, characters and incidents portrayed in it are
the work of the author's imagination. Any resemblance to
actual persons, living or dead, events or localities is
entirely coincidental.

Automatically produced by Atomik ePublisher from Easypress

Printed and bound in Great Britain

For Myra, the best thing that ever happened to me

Chapter 1

"Men can't write romance. Their sex scenes only last one paragraph."

Keira Madison's answer to the question as to why there were no men in the standing-room-only romance-writing seminar got a huge laugh from the crowd of over two hundred women. The tall, skinny redhead, a/k/a Cover Girl, was the most powerful editor in the romance genre. She smiled as she waited for the laughter in the auditorium to die down.

But it was all she could do to avoid adding one more sentence. *"And this is why I never meet any guys in my job and I'm on my way to being a cat lady at thirty-five, even though I don't have a friggin' cat."*

The group settled down and Keira nodded at a young blonde in the second row who had her hand raised. "I'm curious if your own personal romantic experiences have an effect on the books you buy. You know, if you prefer fictional male characters who are like the ones in your life. Do you look for your *type* when you read a romance novel?"

Well, so much for holding back.

Keira pushed her mound of red tangles back from her face then grabbed the side of the wooden podium and leaned forward, her turquoise eyes getting wide. "Let me tell you something, girls. I love my job and wouldn't trade it for the world. But look around this room. Do you see one guy in here? No. This genre repels men like a Star Trek force field. Drop by the romance division where I work. All women. The highlight of my week is when a man shows up to stock the soda machine and I drop by to get a Dr. Pepper just so I can talk to someone with a Y chromosome. And I don't even drink soda. While my life revolves around romance and I've edited some of the steamiest books of all time with some of the hottest men on the covers, it is unfortunately all fiction. And since I don't go to bars I rarely meet guys. So the answer to your question is no, since the best men I've met only exist on paper. I have a great job, but if you want a career that will let you meet guys, this ain't it. If you think you'll run into Prince Charming at your book-signing, fuhgeddaboudit. While I'm in the business of selling the Mister Right fantasy, for me it is, unfortunately, still a fantasy."

Keira smiled as the crowd chuckled a bit. The clock on the wall told her she needed to wrap things up since the military thriller seminar had the place booked next. She looked at the back of the room and saw an attractive dark-haired thirty-something man peeking around the open door and pointed at him. "Hey, look, a cute guy! C'mon in, join the romance revolution!"

The crowd turned around and the man smiled. "Thank you, but I'm waiting for the next seminar."

"C'mon, we won't bite. You'll never have better odds... two hundred girls to one guy. If you've got some sort of harem fantasy, indulge!"

The guy waved. "That's okay, I'm not into a ménage à horde." He smiled, then disappeared to a lot of laughs.

"Figures. The one guy who drops by is a smart ass. See, romance is scary to them." The group turned back to face her. "Now, watch, in five minutes this room will be filled entirely with men for the military thriller talk. So if you wanna meet a guy who likes to blow things up and dream of sharing a futon in his mother's basement, stick around." She looked at the back of the room to see if the guy reappeared, then raised her voice. "Hey, youse guys out in the hallway, if male writers were a little smarter, they'd realize the market for military thrillers is stone- cold dead and the easiest genre to crack is romance. C'mon in!" She paused a moment to see if there was any reaction. "Bueller? Bueller?" Still no one. "Oh, whatever. I gave it a shot." Keira had time for one more question and pointed at a brunette in the back.

"Keira, do you think a guy *could* write a romance? I know you were joking around... but seriously, could a man do it?"

"Hey, good writing is good writing. A good writer is a good writer, regardless of gender. Every male author out there has female characters in his books, so it's not like they can't write women. And every one of you has a hero in your work, but no one ever says a female romance author can't write men. There are a few guys out there who do write romantic novels, but a manuscript from one has never crossed my desk. But sure, a man could do it. He'd have to be a special kind of guy, though. I don't think a man could write a romance unless he was a romantic soul at heart: the kind of guy who respects you as an equal but holds doors for you, who brings you gifts without occasion, who is kind enough to take in a stray kitten out of a rainstorm, who leaves little love notes on the pillow if he has to go to work early, who knows when a woman needs to be left alone and when she needs to be held, who is so damn hot every woman in the room is jealous of you, who will look at you in the same way twenty years after your wedding day and make your heart flutter. Who—"

Keira realized she'd verbalized a familiar daydream and caught herself before going any further. She looked out at the crowd and saw a room filled with dreamy-eyed women, their heads cocked to the side like puppies waiting for a treat, who knew exactly what she was talking about. "Sorry, occupational hazard. Easy when you create Mister Right on paper, huh?" The crowd chuckled as she saw a few famous thriller writers waiting in the wings offstage. "Okay, we have to clear out for the boys with their toys, so thank you all for coming and I'll be around the convention all day if you have any questions. Don't be shy. But please don't pitch your book in the bathroom like someone did to me last year."

The crowd began to disperse as Keira picked up her leather satchel and headed off-stage.

She was surprised to see her publisher, Jill Howland, waiting, on the phone, looking devastated as she ran one hand through her dark-blonde hair. But then Jill had a tendency to overreact. She ended the call as Keira arrived at her side. "What's wrong, Jill? You look like someone ran over your dog."

"It's Rose." She bit her lower lip as her green eyes welled up.

"What, is the bestselling romance author in history gonna be late for the awards dinner tonight?"

"Oh Keira, I know how close you two are. Something happened..."

As usual, Alex Bauer wore his heart on his sleeve, so trying to sneak one by his roommate Juliette Frye would be fruitless. If there was such a thing as a poker face for literary rejection, he had the opposite. And he knew he couldn't get anything past her. Juliette was like a human polygraph. His olive-green eyes could project a life force that was off the charts... or be deep pools of permanent hurt.

Which they were right now.

She studied his look as he came through the door and put his portfolio on the dining-room table. "Uh-oh. That bad, huh?"

He moved to the kitchen and grabbed a bottle of beer from the fridge. "Same old story. The market's extremely tight for military thrillers. You're a good writer, but... blah, blah, blah."

"How many people did you meet with this time?"

"Four agents and three editors." He opened the beer, took a long swig and plopped down in his leather reclining chair, stretching out his lean five-foot-ten frame. "I've actually run out of places to pitch the damn thing. Today was my last resort. So my book literally becomes the tree that fell in the forest." He looked up at

4

the ceiling as he ran his fingers through his thick black hair. Maybe I need to go back to reporting."

The petite blonde got up, stood in front of him and folded her arms. "Alex Bauer, you stop that right now. Hey, look at me." Her pale-blue eyes locked with his as he faced her. "Don't start with that again. You hate what journalism has become and that's why you spend one night a week teaching reporting ethics at the college. You want to be an author. You socked away enough money to give it ten years and you've only been at it for two."

"Well—"

"And to be honest, the newsroom has gotten a helluva lot worse since you left. The bias is off the charts and I'm thinking of leaving myself. I actually got a feeler today from a PR firm for when my contract is up next year. Good offer, normal hours, great money. Low stress."

"You'd be good at that."

"And *you're* a great writer. You have been since college."

"Thank you, but that's not translating into a sale. Geez, even the seminar was depressing. A bunch of has-been authors, who hadn't sold anything in years, basically telling us how tough it is. Probably because they don't want any new competition. I was hoping to be energized but came away even more discouraged." He flipped the lever on the recliner and put his feet up. "Funny, the military thriller seminar was right after the romance talk and I happened to get there a few minutes early. Those women were having a blast."

"Well, they usually aren't writing stories with snipers and people dying. Don't think terrorist sleeper cells and nuclear warfare are popular plot elements in a romance novel."

"You've got a point. Anyway, I'm out in the hall waiting and the woman running the thing sees me peeking around the door. Real cute redhead. I mean, seriously cute. So she invites me in, but I mean, there's not a single guy in the crowd so I duck back into the hall. But I can still hear her."

"Wait a minute… did I just hear you say a 'seriously cute redhead' gave you an invitation and you went in the other direction?"

"I know. You would think my thing for redheads would have taken over, but I was scared."

"Scared of what?"

"Being one guy in a room with two hundred women."

"I would think that would be every man's wet dream. *Author gets harem, film at eleven.*"

"Funny. Anyway, then the cute redhead said something interesting. That military thrillers are dead and romance is the easiest genre to break into."

"I would think so. Simple supply and demand. There are more romance books in the bookstore than any other genre."

"Then she says if guys were smart they'd give it a shot. Writing romance, I mean. Pretty funny, huh?"

Juliette put her hands on her hips. "Well?"

"Well, what?"

"Why don't you give it a shot?"

"Me? Write a romance novel? You mean chick lit? What the hell do I know about purses and shoes?"

"You're a reporter, do some research. And not every romance novel is about shopping. Besides, for the past ten years you've been sharing this townhouse with a woman who has been the sister you never had. I know you've always thought of me as one of the guys, but I do possess the shoe chromosome. Seriously, Alex, you could do it. Remember that creative writing class we took in college and the assignment to write a short story for someone you love? And the one you wrote for your girlfriend about the engagement ring?"

"You mean *Ring Girl*? What about it?"

"Okay, full disclosure. I never told you this because I thought you'd be embarrassed, but she-who-must-not-be-named showed it to me. It was incredibly romantic and beyond sentimental. Along with being funny as hell. It made me laugh and cry at the same time. If our relationship wasn't platonic I would have fallen in love with you after reading it. And she was blown away by it."

"Yeah, she was so blown away she broke up with me after I gave it to her."

"Because she thought you were getting too close and *she* was the girl in the story. That's how much pure emotion it had, that's how much it touched her. But you're missing the point. *You* wrote a romantic short story. Why couldn't you write a romantic novel? In fact, I'll help you get started… why not flesh out that short story *into* a novel? It was such a terrific plot and the characters were so memorable I can tell you their names today. Lexi and Jamison."

His eyes widened in surprise. "I cannot believe you remember that."

"Like I said, it was a great story. So I want you to do it."

"Seriously?"

"It was beyond clever, Alex. And since you never throw anything out I assume you still have it."

"It's on an old computer disc, but the story's still in my head."

"It's still in my head, too, which should tell you something. Alex, I read that genre from time to time, and I'm telling you, what you wrote back in college combined with the romantic soul I know you are tells me you have it in you. You can do it. You spent years in newsrooms filled with women so you know more about us than you might think. I'll help you add a little of the girly stuff. Take you shopping for shoes. I'll even let you go through my purse to see what's in there."

His face tightened as his eyes filled with fear. "I'll go shopping with you, but I'm not going in your purse."

"What the hell are you afraid of?"

"I dunno, purses remind me of that movie *Roman Holiday*."

She furrowed her brow. "Huh?"

"You know, that scene with the *Mouth of Truth* where you put your hand in it and if you're a liar the statue will bite it off. And Gregory Peck sticks his hand in there and pulls it up into his sleeve

7

so Audrey Hepburn would think the legend was true."

She shook her head. "I assure you, there are no extremity-eating monsters in my purse."

"It's just one of those places where men dare not go."

"Fine, I'll dump it out on the table. But I want you to do this. Now put that damn military thriller away, get your ass in the chair and start writing."

"Okay, but there's one major flaw with your plan."

"What's that?"

"How many editors will take a look at a romance novel written by a guy?"

"Well, that redhead you saw today sounds like she seemed open to it. And who says they have to know the author is male? Look, your first name is also a popular woman's name. Or you could use a pen name. There's no rule that says any editor or publisher has to meet you in person."

"What about book-signings? Am I supposed to dress up in drag like Dustin Hoffman in *Tootsie*?"

"You could pull it off. You've got better legs than Hoffman."

"Again, funny."

"Look, you told me yourself that they only do book tours for bestsellers these days, so I'd worry about that if you actually sell the thing and it takes off. At that point it will be a nice problem to have. Hell, you could even hire some woman to play the part." She pointed to his laptop. "Chair. Now. Find that disc with *Ring Girl* on it 'cause I wanna read it again. And you need to do the same." He bit his lower lip as the story dredged up a bad memory. "Look, I know you've been terrified of getting close to any girl ever since that incident, but maybe if you write it with a 'happily ever after' ending it will help you get over your fear of women."

"I don't know about that, but I'll write the thing."

"Meanwhile, I've got some research for you in my bedroom." She started to head down the hallway.

"What? I gotta go through your lingerie too?"

"No, I've got a bunch of romance novels and you need to read them to give yourself a guide. Get familiar with what women are looking for. You need to get acquainted with an author named Rose Fontaine."

"Who?"

"Bestselling romance author of all time. And an incredible writer. Actually, she has a snarky style that's a lot like yours."

"Okay. You promise to help me with the girly stuff?"

"Honey, when I get through with you you'll be able to get a job writing for *Cosmo*."

Chapter 2

Alex saw the email in his inbox from one of New York's most powerful literary agents, but knew it was too soon for a good-news message to arrive. Rejections always came quick from agents and editors; half the time they responded so fast he wondered if they even read his work at all. Her request yesterday to see his full manuscript after sending a one-page query letter and synopsis had surprised him, but he hadn't gotten his hopes up. Signing on with Bella Farentino was a serious long shot. Most of her clients could be found on any bestseller list. So he'd tempered his excitement, even though Juliette said her request was a major victory. Now, at six in the morning, he wasn't sure if he wanted to start his day with bad news. He clicked on the email. "Oh, what the hell. Get it over with."

Alex,

Your manuscript kept me up till three in the morning because I couldn't put it down. Ring Girl is incredible! Lexi is an amazing heroine and I cannot believe how well you write male characters! Please contact me as soon as possible (hopefully before you call anyone else) as I would like to offer you representation. I note from your address you're only a few blocks from my office, so I would love to meet you in person.

Sincerely,

Bella Farentino

He sat up straight as his eyes widened. "Oh. My. God."

"You're up early," said Juliette, yawning as she headed from her bedroom to the kitchen.

"So are you."

"Need that golden glow of the sun for this shoot. High def is not kind to those of us nearing our expiration dates." She studied his intense look as she loaded the coffee machine. "What's up? You've got that 'reporter stumbling on a huge story' face."

"You know me too well and you're right. Come look. This is better than any exclusive."

She headed toward him, then looked over his shoulder and read the email. "Ho-lee shit. You got Bella friggin' Farentino."

"Only because you made me pitch her."

"Maybe so, but you wrote a terrific book." She leaned down, hugged him and kissed the side of his head. "Congratulations, I am soooo happy for you!"

He couldn't help but smile. "Thank you. But I couldn't have done any of this without you."

"Damn, your book is as good as sold with her. Please remember me when you're rich and famous."

"Meanwhile, did you catch the last line of the email?"

"Yeah. Guess the cat is about to be let out of the bag as far as the agent part of the deal is concerned."

"I thought you said no one would ever have to meet me."

"Well, then you shoulda moved to California or used a mail drop way out of town. It's an occupational hazard for a writer living in New York City with an agent around the corner."

"So what do I do?"

11

"I'd loan you a dress and we could do the *Tootsie* thing, but I don't think you're my size."

The office of Farentino and Associates was exactly what he'd expected. The reception area something out of *House Beautiful*, with rich mahogany library paneling, deep-brown leather chairs and a huge antique oak desk in the center. An attractive thirtyish brunette with horn-rimmed glasses sat behind it, looking all business in a high-necked red silk blouse as she manned the phones that were ringing off the hook. The wall behind her featured a massive gold logo surrounded by posters of book covers from famous bestsellers.

All agented by Bella Farentino.

Alex paused at the door, tried to exhale some tension, straightened his tie and walked to the desk, arriving just as the receptionist had finished a call. She looked up without a smile, probably worn away by writers trying to sneak past the gatekeeper.

"May I help you?" she asked in an emotionless tone with a typical New York death stare.

"Hi. Alex Bauer to see Bella Farentino."

She slid her glasses down her nose and looked over the top. "Do you have an appointment?"

"I do."

The receptionist relaxed her face and smiled. "Oh. Sorry, but I have to play the part of the troll guarding the bridge."

"Do I have to answer a riddle to get past you?"

She laughed. "No, but sometimes I need a whip and a chair to keep writers at bay."

"That bad?"

"You kidding? We've had everything from phony pizza deliveries with the manuscript in the box to a query letter written on a note attached to a bouquet of flowers. Anyway, let me ring her. Sorry, what was your name again?"

"Alex Bauer."

She wrote his name on a pad, punched a button on the phone and waited a beat. "Bella, Alex Bauer is here to see you." She listened a moment then hung up. "She'll be out shortly. I'm Rachel, by the way. Have a seat. Want coffee? It's my special battery acid blend to chase writers away."

He laughed a bit. "I'm good, thank you." Alex turned and grabbed a chair next to the only other person in the lobby, a plump fortyish blonde woman with a horrible dye job who was busy wringing her hands. "Hi, Alex Bauer."

"Jeanne Terry."

"You look nervous."

"First time here. Can't believe I got a call from this agency."

"Same deal for me."

"Who are you meeting with?"

"Bella Farentino."

"Damn, you hit the jackpot. I got one of her associates, but I'm not complaining. It's a foot in a really big door."

A buzzer interrupted their conversation as a door opened and Bella Farentino made her entrance. She was more attractive in person than the photos he'd seen while doing research. If the woman was fifty-five, her face didn't get the memo as she looked ten years younger. Maybe five-six, hourglass figure, black hair and large dark-brown eyes. Obviously Italian. He recognized her burgundy Chanel suit as one his roommate wore when she anchored a newscast, a single strand of pearls the only accessory. The agent's face lit up as she locked on the woman next to him and moved toward her. Alex stood but Bella blew right past him and extended her hand to the woman. "Alex, so nice to meet you. Bella Farentino." Her voice didn't match the face, a two-packs-a-day wicked New York accent filled with a truck full of gravel.

"Pleasure to meet you, Ms. Farentino, but I'm Jeanne Terry. I'm here to see Brad Deller."

"Oh. Well, welcome." Bella, now with her back to Alex, turned toward the receptionist. "Rachel, I thought you said Alex Bauer was here."

The woman was on the phone, so she simply pointed at Alex.

Bella turned around and her eyes widened as Alex held out his hand.

"Hi, Alex Bauer."

"Excuse me?"

"I'm Alex. Author of *Ring Girl*. You wanted me to come by."

Her face tightened as she folded her arms. "Is this a joke? Did Frankie send you over here?"

"I don't know who Frankie is but I'm Alex Bauer. You know, the guy whose book kept you up till three in the morning?" He pulled his wallet out of his back pocket, flipped it open and showed her his driver's license. "See?"

She looked at it, then studied his face. "But... you're a guy."

"Last time I checked, yeah."

"You're telling me that you actually wrote *Ring Girl*?"

He nodded.

"Did you start life as a woman?"

"Nope. Never had a sex change."

Her jaw dropped as she shook her head. "Well, I'll be a sonofabitch." She took his elbow and led him toward the door as the receptionist buzzed them in. "C'mon, honey. I have a feeling you and I are about to embark on a very unique journey."

Bella closed the door as Alex sat down opposite her desk. The floor-to-ceiling windows of the corner office offered a spectacular view of both Central Park and the Hudson. She moved behind her desk, sat down, folded her hands in her lap and smiled at him. "Okay, first I need to know is how in the world a guy wrote this. You gay?"

"Nope."

"Bi?"

"Straight as an arrow."

"Then how the hell did you get inside a woman's head like this?"

14

"My best friend is a woman who happens to share a townhouse with me. I worked in television news, which is dominated by women who aren't shy about talking sex in the newsroom. And I grew up raised by a single mom while my grandmother lived with us. I will confess my roommate helped with the shopping scene."

"You worked in TV news?"

"Yeah, I was a reporter for ten years at the CBC network."

"I watch that newscast. How come I've never seen you?"

"Because I was what is known as the 'custom reporter' for the network. When affiliates wanted a live shot for their station to make it look like they had a reporter stationed in New York, I would do it. 'Reporting for Eyewitness News in Peoria, I'm Alex Bauer in New York.' Like anyone would believe a station in Peoria actually had a New York bureau. Some nights I'd do fifteen live shots on the same story. New York City is the only place I *haven't* been seen."

"Huh. I didn't know something like that existed. Learn something every day. So what's your day job now?"

"Writing, though I still do some freelance research for the network. I'm also a part-time adjunct professor teaching journalism ethics."

"No offense, but isn't that an oxymoron?"

"No kidding. That's why I left the network. Got sick of the bias and having half of my stories spiked. Anyway, I've always been passionate about fiction, was tired of TV news and had put aside enough cash to give it ten years. That was two years ago. But I was writing military thrillers."

"I don't even take new clients who write those. They don't sell nearly as well as they used to and it's really tough to break into that genre."

"Don't I know it! Anyway, I was at a writer's conference and I overheard a romance editor say this was the easiest genre to crack. I mentioned it to my roommate and she reminded me of a short romantic story I wrote in college. *Ring Girl* is the fleshed out version."

"Do you read a lot of romance books?"

"I never had until I started writing one and I was actually surprised how much I enjoyed them. I needed to get the feel for the genre."

"Well, you certainly succeeded. Alex, it's an amazing book, and as you probably know I don't take on many new clients. Maybe one a year, if that."

"So I've read. I'm really flattered you're interested in me."

"Trust me, Alex, you have no idea what you've got here and I *know* I can sell this. Anyway, here's the deal. There's no agency contract as I prefer to do things on a handshake. If you or I ever want to stop working together, a piece of paper shouldn't prevent it. It's old school and it works for me. Besides, my last name is Sicilian so no one would ever dare cross me." She flashed a sinister grin as she narrowed her eyes. "I *know* people."

"Well, a handshake is fine with me as well." He leaned across the desk and they shook.

"Okay. Now this is quite a curve ball you've thrown me this morning and I will have to use a different strategy with this book."

"In other words, you can't let editors know I'm a guy."

"Correct. I don't want any preconceived notions. Some editors wouldn't care but I know a bunch who would. And the ones who are open-minded might have a subconscious bias and look for reasons to turn it down. Or offer less money. They're buying your voice and your words, not your gender. For all they know Alex is short for Alexandra or Alexis. And as far as marketing the book, best to let readers think the same thing. A lot of women wouldn't buy a romance book written by a guy."

"What do we do if there's a book-signing?"

"Good question. To figure that out, Bella needs some time in her fortress of solitude."

"You mean like Superman?"

"Yeah, but with a loud Italian family like mine, it's basically a long hot bath with a bottle of wine and the door locked."

"So what happens now?"

"Now," she said, "I work the phones. By the way, you ever hear of Rose Fontaine?"

He nodded. "I love her work."

"Funny, when I was reading your book it almost felt like she wrote it. And I know just the person who will think the same thing."

Chapter 3

SIX MONTHS AFTER THE DEATH OF ROSE FONTAINE, NO
HEIR APPARENT IN SIGHT

By Holly Denton

"She's irreplaceable. Both as a writer and a best friend."
The words of powerhouse romance editor Keira Madison are
accompanied by a single tear. It's clear that six months after the
tragic death of bestselling author Rose Fontaine, she's not recovered from the event that turned her professional and personal life
upside down. Her famously sharp wit has been understandably
dulled a bit, the turquoise eyes surrounded by a constellation of
freckles seem less full of life. And while losing the woman she
considered her closest friend has been emotionally devastating,
Madison must put her feelings aside and focus on what seems
to be an impossible task.
Finding a writer who can capture the romance market in the
same way Rose Fontaine did. In many ways, it's like trying to
find a new best friend.
"Her voice was so unique, and her plots were damn clever," said
Madison. "Readers could never anticipate the endings of her
books. Her work was never formulaic and she always came up
with something new. So many writers do the same book over

and over while just changing the characters. With Rose, each book was unique, each one had its own formula. Every time we released one other authors tried to copy that formula, but no one ever could."

Madison and Fontaine began their publishing journey together, she the rookie editorial assistant fresh out of college and Fontaine the young author looking for her first break. Madison found Fontaine's manuscript for *Soul Mate* in what is known as the "slush pile"; a place where unrequested manuscripts go to die. Together they watched it become the bestselling romance novel of all time. Madison acquired the nickname "Cover Girl" since she came up with the concept for one of the most famous book covers in publishing history and continued to inspire Fontaine's other dust jackets. *Soul Mate* sold more than forty million copies and was developed into a hit movie, making Fontaine incredibly rich while rocketing Madison up the publishing ladder. The "Rose of Romance" as she became known now has more than 200 million copies of her books in print.

"We were both new to publishing, the same age, and had a ton of stuff in common," said Madison, voice cracking. "We just clicked and became incredibly close in a short time. Since we were both freckle-faced redheads people thought we were related, and it felt like we were. For thirteen years she was the sister I never had. I miss her terribly."

While the two shared common interests and a tight personal bond, Fontaine would never let Madison peek at her works-in-progress. "She never gave me a concept, an outline or a synopsis. She wanted me to be as surprised as the reader so I never got a manuscript until it was finished. Which is one of my problems with her last book. She had one chapter to go and I have no idea how it was going to end. I've read it three times and can't figure it out. Neither can anyone on our staff. And even if I did figure it out, I'd have to find a writer who could copy her unique voice to finish it. Good luck with that. So right now it's sitting on my desk and I doubt it will ever be completed. It would be a wonderful legacy for her because it's a spectacular book, but it's in limbo." Meanwhile, revenue for the publisher has dropped considerably without the best-selling author cranking out two books each year.

"Every day I come to work hoping I won't hear it, but someone always says it. We've got to find another Rose. And I have to resign myself to the fact it may never happen. I keep thinking of that line from Shakespeare. A rose by any other name wouldn't smell as sweet."

Gretchen Beckett, who hated her full name and insisted on being called Gretch, was the perfect assistant for a romance editor. Keira smiled as her right-hand girl entered her office and handed her the morning mail. Keira studied Gretch's face, hoping for a smile from the spunky woman who was the clearing house for gossip in the publishing office. A grin meant someone on the staff had read something wonderful and Gretch would be chomping at the bit to tell Keira first.

Alas, no smile.

"How was your weekend?" asked Keira, not really asking about her personal life.

Gretch shrugged. "Four smoking-hot men with zero personality." The curvy twenty-eight-year-old doe-eyed brunette snapped her ever-present chewing gum. "Sorta like the guys I usually date."

"Those aren't dates, Gretch, they're *exercise*."

Her assistant sat, her short leather skirt riding up on her thigh. "Hey, girl's gotta scratch an itch."

"Yeah, and you've got sexual poison ivy. So, did you read all four books I gave you already?"

"I *tried* to read them. Just like the Mets, oh-for-four. Didn't even get out of the batter's box. Swing and a miss for the golden sombrero."

"The what?"

"When a batter strikes out four times in one game, it's known as getting the golden sombrero."

"Oh." Keira looked down at the legal pad which held her notes on the books in question. "What was wrong with *Tryst in the Mist*? The synopsis sounded great."

Gretch twirled her long necklace as she blew a bubble. "Well, said tryst pretty much missed. Foreplay was about two paragraphs. The actual tryst was one. And the writing wasn't up to your standards. See Dick chase Jane. See Dick nail Jane. See both light up a cigarette. The end."

Keira ran the pencil down the pad. "How about the erotic one, *Seduction Place*?"

"If I lived on Seduction Place I'd move out due to the lounge lizards. It read like a bad porn movie from the seventies. All I needed was synthesizer music while I was reading."

"You've been watching late-night Cinemax again, haven't you?"

Gretch smiled as she shrugged. "It saves me from actually talking to my dates and it's a convenient method of foreplay. Worth the ten bucks a month."

Back to the legal pad. "The sweet romance… *Down the Aisle*?"

"I left the writer at the altar around halfway through. Big time head hopper. Honestly, I didn't know whose point of view I was reading, and it would change in the middle of the scene like one of those body-switching movies. When the priest said 'Speak now or forever hold your peace' I actually yelled 'Stop the wedding!'"

Last one. "*Man-a-holic* sounded like a funny rom-com."

"I'd be an *alcoholic* if I had kept reading. Not a single laugh in the first ten chapters. Lotta rom, no com. Sorta blows the hell out of the premise."

Keira shook her head and exhaled. "Anyone in the bullpen excited about anything this morning?"

"Nope. But I've already got the two trainees digging through the slush pile, so you never know what you might find."

"Don't I know it." Her mind wandered back to her first days at the publishing house, when she pulled Rose Fontaine out of the massive pile of manuscripts. She couldn't help but smile.

"What?"

"I was just thinking, before electronic submissions we actually had a slush pile room that was filled about six feet high with real paper manuscripts. It looked like something from one of those hoarding reality shows. One day the pile fell over while I was sitting on the floor reading and it actually buried me in an avalanche of paper." The phone interrupted her thoughts and the name she saw on her cell made her eyes widen. "Holy shit, it's Bella Farentino."

"And she only calls when she's got something good. Put it on speaker. Gretch wants to listen."

Keira sat up straight. Gretch leaned forward as she answered the call and engaged the speaker. "Hi, Bella!"

"How's my favorite romance editor?"

"I'd be better if I found the next big thing."

"Yeah, I hear ya. Seriously, how you holdin' up, kiddo? I read the article about you in *The Post* last week."

Keira's eyes misted at the thought of her best friend. "Hangin' in there, but it's tough. I keep seeing things that remind me of Rose. Still can't believe she's gone."

"You were a good friend to her, Keira. And the woman was an absolute gem."

"She was the best. So, did you just call to check on me, or have you got something that will brighten my day?"

"Like I said, I read the article in *The Post*, and I've got the answer to your prayers. No disrespect to your dear friend, but I found the next Rose Fontaine."

Keira and Gretch both sat up straight, eyebrows up. "And this person would be…"

"Debut author named Alex Bauer. The book is called *Ring Girl*. Honest to God, the best romance I've read in years. Funny as hell and will make you cry at the same time. A lot like Rose's books with the same snarky voice. Went through the whole manuscript in one shot, kept me up till three in the morning. The author has an incredible style. Anyway, I'm calling you first."

"And how many editors are you calling today?"

"One. You. I'm giving you an exclusive. You've always been fair with me, Keira, I trust you and consider you a friend. Besides, the universe and the *New York Post* tell me you need some good fortune and I need a good deed to balance out what I'm gonna tell the priest in confession this week. But I will tell ya, if you want this book, it's gonna cost ya. Because after the exclusive, you're gonna have to take a number to get it."

"If you found the next Rose then money is no object. How long do I have?"

"Till close of business Thursday. If you don't want it or your offer isn't acceptable to the author, I'm sending it out Friday. And then I guarantee it will go up for auction. If you want it, you gotta pre-empt it. So you've got four days. But guess what, Keira?"

"What?"

"You're only gonna need one of those days." Keira heard a keyboard tapping. "Okay, it's on the way to your inbox. Enjoy."

"Bella, I can't thank you enough. I really appreciate you thinking of me."

"You'll be thinking of me tomorrow, honey. And when you do, be thinking of a big number that will knock my socks off. Tell Jill to open up the vault. Operators are standing by."

"I'll start reading right now. Bye, Bella."

"Talk soon, kiddo. And smile. God and Bella love you."

Keira hung up, quickly flipped open her laptop and clicked on her email as Gretch got up and moved behind her. She looked up at her assistant. "Gretch, I can forward it to you."

"Nah, we gotta read the first part together. I wanna see the look on your face that you had when you found Rose."

Keira smiled as she maneuvered the mouse over the email attachment from Bella. "Ready?"

"Let's rock."

The manuscript opened and page one filled the screen.

By page ten, both women were beaming.

"So who was that?" asked Alex.

"The number one editor in romance, Keira Madison. She's the one who discovered Rose Fontaine." Bella reached behind her and pulled a New York tabloid from the credenza, flipped it open, then handed it to Alex. "Here's an article about her that was in *The Post* on Friday. It'll help you get familiar with her, since I think it's a stone-cold lock she'll buy your book."

Alex looked at the paper and studied the photo above the article. "Hey, this is the editor I saw at the writer's conference. The one who said romance was the easiest genre to crack. She's indirectly responsible for the book. What a wild coincidence."

Bella reached for her candy jar, grabbed a Hershey kiss, unwrapped it and leaned back as she popped it in her mouth. "Small world. Serendipity is a beautiful thing."

"She single?"

"Why?"

"I've got a thing for redheads. And she seemed pretty cute from a distance." He looked at the photo again. "Looks even better here."

Bella rolled her eyes. "Ah, so that's why your heroine is a tall, skinny redhead and looks exactly like Keira. *Ring Girl* is your own personal fantasy."

He shrugged. "It's fun creating Miss Right on paper. Anyway, is this Keira available? When I heard her talk she went on this funny rant about how she never meets men in her profession. I listened to her for a few minutes and she sounded like she had a lot of spunk. Also my type."

"She wrote the book on spunk. Well, let me ask you this… is the male love interest in your book based on you? Emotionally, I mean."

"Pretty much. Why?"

"I've known Keira a long time. And what you've written

describes her perfect man."

His eyes widened. "Really."

"Yep."

"You didn't answer my question. Is she currently seeing anyone?"

"Had lunch with her a few weeks ago, and she's still spending Saturday nights with a bubble bath, a book and a bottle of wine."

"Terrible waste of an attractive redhead."

"Huh. I always thought she was kinda plain."

"She's my type. All men have a type, you know."

Bella put her palms up. "So, you want me to fix you up?"

"I wouldn't mind meeting her. You know, see if there's any chemistry beyond the initial attraction. Since, you know, you think I might be *her* type."

"Hmmm, let me get this straight. You want me to play Jewish mother with a woman you can't meet because she has to think you're a woman despite the fact that the qualities of the male character in your book are basically yours and those she has conveyed to me that are necessary in her dream guy. Please explain how I am supposed to make this happen."

"Yeah, I guess that might be a problem. This sounds like a romance novel in itself."

"So, you want a date with the redhead, figure out a plot twist."

Keira looked at the clock, saw it was ten minutes till six and hoped her publisher hadn't left for the day. She dialed the extension and drummed her fingers on the desk while it rang.

"Keira, I was just about to leave—"

"Jill, hang for sixty seconds. I'll be right there."

"This important?"

"Extremely."

"Okay, but hurry. I've got a dinner date."

Keira hung up and bolted out of her office, dashed down the long hallway that led to the corner office occupied by the publisher. The door was already open and she saw Jill Howland looking at the skyline. "Thanks for staying," she said, out of breath.

The forty-year-old publisher turned to face her as Keira leaned over and rested her hands on her knees. "Sweetie, you gotta get out of your office and work on your cardio."

"Later. Anyway, I found her."

"Found who?"

She stood up straight. "The next Rose Fontaine."

Jill's eyes widened and she plopped down into the chair behind her desk. "Seriously?"

"Bella Farentino sent the book over this morning. We've got an exclusive for four days, but you'll want to pre-empt this. It's incredible. I spent the entire day reading it. Didn't even go to lunch."

"*You* didn't have lunch?"

"Okay, I demolished that box of chocolates you gave me."

"Ah, your sweet tooth rears its ugly head."

"Anyway, I just emailed the manuscript to you. It's called *Ring Girl*. Debut author named Alex Bauer. Seriously, Jill, you need to stay up all night if you have to and read it. You'll need a cold shower when you're done."

"That steamy?"

"That's the amazing part. There are no sex scenes. It's a sweet romance but an incredible turn-on. The hero is off the charts. He's everything women want in a guy, and more. And the chemistry between him and the heroine is smoking hot. Plus, just like Rose's books, it has an ending no one will ever see coming."

Jill studied her face and slowly nodded. "First time I've seen you smile since..."

Keira bit her lower lip for a moment as her eyes welled up a bit. "Yeah, I know. But even Rose would admit this writer has an amazing voice. And the book has a really clever plot, just like her books did. Look, Bella gave us four days and I trust her, but I want to lock this up as soon as possible just in case this rookie author goes rogue and does something crazy like switch agents and hire an uncle. I want to present our best offer first thing in the morning."

"You're *that* sure?"

"Gretch read it too and she was all flushed like she usually looks after a Chippendales show. She just left for the bar downstairs to find the nearest breathing male she could ravish."

"And… how does the good Catholic girl know how Gretch looks after a Chippendales show?" Jill raised one perfectly plucked eyebrow. "Hmmm?"

Keira blushed. "I, uh, ran into her one Saturday night when she was leaving the club. I happened to be out for a walk. On, you know, my way to confession."

"Uh-*huh*." Jill chuckled a bit. "Okay, I'll read it tonight, but let me make a call first."

"Jill, please don't call the CEO. You know he's a cheap bean-counting sonofabitch and doesn't understand romance."

"I wasn't calling him. I'm breaking my dinner date."

Chapter 4

Jill handed Keira a contract and a check. "You think this is enough?"

Keira looked at it and smiled. "Yeah. No debut author is gonna turn down this amount of money and a three-book deal. Bella would never let that happen." But one worry still ran through her mind. "You clear this with the CEO?"

"Nope. Thankfully he's on vacation on a cruise ship the rest of the week and for whatever reason I was unable to reach him." She shrugged as she flashed a wicked grin. "Those satellite phones are *so* damn unreliable. And, you know, since I'm in charge when he's out of pocket…"

"This is exactly why I love working for you. He thinks there's still a glass ceiling in this place and has no idea we broke it and installed a trick circus mirror."

Jill's face tightened. "Stop. The thought of him looking even fatter than he is will kill my appetite for the whole day." She sat opposite Keira. "Well, when this book hits he won't have a problem. You're right, it's incredible. So what time does Bella get in?"

"Nine. I already emailed her and told her I would have an offer at nine-oh-one."

"Okay. Let me know how it goes. And look, if you need to sweeten the pot a bit, go ahead. You can go twenty percent more if you have to. More than that, call me."

Alex Bauer looked at the grandfather clock in Bella's office. The pendulum seemed to be swinging in slow motion.

Bella shook her head. "Will you stop checking the time? Trust me, when Keira says she'll have an offer at one minute past nine, she's not kidding. She's as much a deadline nut as you TV people are. And by the way, don't *ever* miss a deadline with her."

"Never missed one in TV. Not about to start doing it now."

"Good. Now please try to relax. Your life is about to change in an amazing way when that phone rings in two minutes."

Alex released his white-knuckle death grip on the arms of the chair opposite Bella's desk. "Sorry. I've been waiting a long time for this."

"Trust me, I've seen that look before. And you can actually hear it over the phone if the sale isn't done in person. Making the call is the best part of my job."

"I can imagine. I'm sure it's like playing God."

"In some ways. I mean, I have helped change lives in a big way. But it's still the author who has to put the words down on paper. Without the unique voice to sell, I've got nothing."

"Can I ask you something?"

"Shoot."

"How do people change when they suddenly become bestselling authors and millionaires?"

Bella leaned back in her chair and folded her hands in her lap. "Interesting question. That's one I've never had asked of me by a writer."

"Well, I am a reporter."

"True. Anyway, it runs the gamut. I've had some authors become huge egomaniacs and impossible to deal with. Some don't change at all. A few turned out to be one-hit wonders, blew all their money and are back where they started. A writer can fall off the mountain a lot faster than it takes to get up there. So don't go out and spend your advance on a Maserati."

"Who the hell wants a car in New York City?"

Bella smiled and nodded. "That's the attitude I need to hear. So, you figured out a plot twist to meet the redhead?"

"Well, actually—"

"Hi, Bella!"

Alex saw Bella's eyes widen and turned around to see who had interrupted him. His eyes matched those of his agent.

It's her!

I'm not ready—

Oh my God, she's even cuter up close...

Bella shot Alex a quick look as she stood and moved around the desk to greet the editor. "Keira... I, uh, didn't know you were actually coming by."

"I figured for an offer like this I'd bring it by in person. And you know I'm an old-school face-to-face gal."

Alex stood up and turned to face her.

Keira looked at him and smiled. "Bella, sorry if I interrupted a meeting. Rachel buzzed me in. I told her you were expecting me."

"Not a problem," said Bella.

Keira stuck out her hand toward Alex. "I'm Keira Madison, Senior Editor at Starstruck Books."

And I'm star struck.

Think fast!

"I'm, uh, the author's cousin, *Alexander* Bauer," said Alex, as he shook her hand.

"Nice to meet you," said Keira. "Is she not coming?"

Bella raised her eyebrows as she looked at Alex and folded her arms as if to say, *okay, let's see you wiggle your way out of this one.*

His plan wasn't completely formulated and his heart slammed against his chest, but he used his considerable television skills to wing it. "Well... she's, you know, incredibly shy and actually borderline agoraphobic. Plus she, uh, weighs about four hundred pounds and is real sensitive about her appearance, so it's all I can do to get her to leave the house." He caught Bella rolling her eyes in his peripheral vision. "We share a place in the city."

Keira shrugged as if it were no big deal. "Well, shy authors are nothing new. So, you two are Alex and Alexander?"

"Our family has a fondness for the name and all its incarnations. Alex, Alexander, Alexis, you name it."

"Ah, so that's why the heroine is named Lexi."

"Uh, yeah. In any event, I always represent my cousin in business matters and she trusts my judgment."

"Good to know," said Keira, whose spectacular turquoise eyes locked with his for a moment and sent a bolt of electricity through his body. Her warm smile was accented with dimples and freckles, her face framed by shoulder-length red tangles. Overall it made her look like a little girl. She was tall, about his height, maybe five-nine or five-ten, and skinny, with not much on top but a great pair of legs shown off in a knee-length emerald-green dress. Not stunning by any means, but beyond girl-next-door cute. What Bella saw as plain, he found irresistible.

Definitely his type.

And the look she was giving him told him he might be hers.

"Well," said Bella, taking a seat behind her desk, "what sort of gifts does my favorite editor come bearing?"

Keira sat in one of the seats opposite the desk as Alex took the other, then reached into her satchel and handed Bella some papers in a blue cover that Alex recognized as a legal document.

A contract.

This is it!

Keira leaned back in her chair and crossed her legs, rocking one shoe on her toe. "Well, you were right. We want this badly, Bella. And I hope this is the number you had in mind that will knock your socks off." She turned to Alex. "And those of your cousin. It's a three-book deal, so we're looking to build a brand. I assume she's working on the next one."

"Absolutely."

Bella looked at the contract, smiled, and nodded. "Keira, this is extremely generous."

She handed the contract to Alex and it was all he could do to keep his jaw from dropping as the dollar amount jumped out from the legalese. "I, uh, would say that's more than fair."

"You think she'll be happy with that?" asked Bella.

Alex nodded. "I feel certain she'll accept. In fact, I know it."

"Good," said Bella, who got up. "Let me give her a call and make it official." She shot Alex a wink.

"You want me to wait outside?" asked Keira.

"Nah, you two get acquainted." Bella smiled at Alex as she pulled out her cell phone and headed out the door. "Be right back."

Alex looked at the contract and tried to sort through it. Keira slid her chair next to his a bit, bringing with it a hint of floral perfume. "If you have any questions about all the legalese, fire away."

He tried to concentrate, but the perfume was very distracting, as was the glimpse of her legs visible over the top of the contract. "So, uh, do you have a ballpark publication date for the book?"

"I'd like to fast-track it, so about nine months. That's actually lightning-quick for publishing as we often move at the pace of continental drift. But I'll be editing it personally and I've got a great idea in mind for the cover, so I'll get with our art department later today. Assuming of course, your cousin accepts."

"She'd be crazy not to."

"Good. I'll look forward to working with her."

Time to tap dance.

Like Richard Gere in *Chicago*.

"Well, you'll probably be working through me a lot. But don't worry, I'm intimately familiar with the book."

She raised her eyebrows as she leaned back and folded her hands. "Really? You read romance?"

"I know, I should turn in my male membership card, but I got hooked a while ago. There are some terrific writers in the genre. Anyway, I've read *Ring Girl* several times. Even did the proofreading."

"Well, my compliments. I hardly saw any typos or grammatical errors. If you ever wanna be one of our freelancers, let me know. By the way, what do you do for a living?"

"Used to work as a TV reporter. Now I teach journalism at a small college."

"Oh, that's interesting—"

"Deal's done!" said Bella, as she blew back into the office and extended her hand to Keira, who stood to shake it.

"Excellent!" Keira let out a loud exhale. "Whew. Now I can relax. I was so nervous I couldn't eat this morning."

Bella's jaw dropped. "You couldn't eat? Stop the presses."

"Smart ass."

Alex saw an opening. "I didn't have anything either. I, uh, would be happy to take you guys to breakfast."

"Thanks, but I already ate," said Bella, obviously getting the message. "You two go."

Keira turned to him and smiled. "I'd like that."

"Uh, okay, great. So, I gotta ask… why were you nervous?"

"Long story. Feed me something sweet and I'll be happy to tell it to you."

Bella laughed and turned to Alex. "You will shortly discover that the way to Keira's heart is through her stomach. With sugar."

Keira sat up straight and smiled as she watched Alexander make his way through a Denver omelet. The Greek diner was a throwback: a hundred things on the menu, huge portions, a jukebox selector at every booth. He'd offered to take her to an expensive restaurant, but she loved this place. The dozens of different smells that wandered by every time a waitress passed their booth, the classic oldies that filled the air. It offered comfort food; something she'd needed a lot lately.

But it all took a back seat to what had fallen in her lap in the past twenty-four hours.

A sure-fire bestseller.

And the fact that she'd be working with a very cute single guy while putting it together. Who ever thought that buying a book written by a morbidly obese author who wouldn't leave the house could bring a bonus?

She took a bite of her pancakes that she had turned into a maple-soaked sponge and let the sugar flow into her veins. Not that she needed a rush because the man sitting across from her was sending her pulse up a good bit.

Down, girl. Breathe.

Jill, I got your cardio workout right here.

Fifteen minutes into her conversation with the man, she knew *something* was there. Something she hadn't felt for ages. Something she hadn't seen across a dinner table in, like, forever.

Something right out of a romance novel.

He was about her height, dark and slender, with terrific eyes. A lean face with dimples running the length of his cheeks. A bit nervous, but that might be chalked up to intimidation, as she'd seen the same body language from most rookie authors who walk on eggshells around their first editor. But he was funny as hell. Not at all classically handsome but boy-next-door cute. Very much her type. It had become obvious that the author had used her cousin Alexander as a template for the hero in *Ring Girl*. The men in her romance novels actually existed. Who knew?

But was Alexander the richly drawn character in the book or simply the physical version of the heroine's love interest?

And was he attached? Surely a guy like this with a great personality had a girlfriend.

Inquiring minds wanna know.

"So," he said, washing down a bite with a sip of orange juice, "you were gonna tell me about why you were nervous this morning. I thought authors were the only ones who had that problem."

"I guess Bella never told you about Jennie Dunway."

"Who?"

"Exactly. But that's the end of the story."

"What's the beginning?"

Keira dabbed her mouth with her napkin, folded her hands and leaned forward. "Okay, so one day Bella calls me up with this terrific novel. Sorta like she did yesterday, but *Ring Girl* is much, much better. Anyway, I read it that weekend and wanted to buy it so I headed over to Bella's office on Monday with an offer. But by the time I got there the author had dropped her as an agent."

"Someone dropped Bella Farentino? What writer does that?"

She put her palms up. "I know. Whoda thunk it? Anyway, apparently over the weekend the author goes to a barbecue and her Dutch uncle tells her there's no way an agent should get fifteen percent and that he can represent her for nothing."

"Was he an agent?"

"No, he was a retired longshoreman."

"Huh?"

Keira put up her hand. "Patience! The story gets better. And you can't make up stuff this good even if you write fiction for a living. So she agrees to let Uncle Longshoreman pitch her book."

"But she already signed with Bella."

"Ah, but as you know, Bella operates on a handshake so there's nothing in writing. So the author dumps Bella, who had already told her I was the editor that wanted to buy the book."

"Which means Bella could've filed a lawsuit if you'd bought the book, since she'd done the legwork."

"True, but that was never gonna happen for reasons I will explain shortly. So the Dutch uncle contacts me and starts to play hardball. I have no intention of buying the book because I'd never screw Bella, but I let the guy ramble on just to mess with his head. He wants double what I was going to offer and a laundry list of perks. National book tour with first-class airline tickets, hotel suites, limos, you name it. The book was good, but it wasn't *that* good. Anyway, after I turned him down the guy was like a bull in a china shop and no editor wanted to deal with him. So the book went unsold."

"Why didn't the author go back to Bella? Or find another agent?"

"She tried both, but by that time the story had gotten around and no one wanted anything to do with her. And, if you cross Bella once, you're basically dead to her. Publishing is a very small, closed group, and gossip moves at the speed of light. Gossip between agents and editors went *viral* way before the internet existed. Bella knows everyone. Everyone knows Bella."

Alexander nodded. "So that's why you were nervous."

"Yep. Bella says there's always a possibility of *Dutch uncle deja vu*. Which is why both of us like to make quick deals. And why I showed up at one minute after nine." She offered him a soft smile. "Of course, now that I've met you I realize I obviously had nothing to worry about."

"Nope. Never worked as a longshoreman." He returned the smile, which sent a warm feeling through her body. "Obviously I have nothing to worry about with you either."

She furrowed her brow. "How do you mean?"

"Oh, you know. There are all these tales on the internet about ball-busting editors and those who change the story completely and drive writers crazy. Bella had already assured me you were the perfect editor for the book, that you could actually make it better without changing the plot. But, you know, a person always worries until they actually meet someone."

"So we *both* have nothing to worry about."

"Apparently."

They both went back to their meals and then it hit Keira. One thing was definitely different about this guy.

He actually listened to her.

Keira beamed as she walked into her office.

Gretch was bouncing up and down on her heels. "You got it?"

"Signed, sealed, delivered."

"Yessss!" Her assistant threw her hands in the air, then studied her face. "Wait a minute... you got that look."

"Yeah, I just bought a bestseller."

She shook her head as her eyes locked with Keira's and looked closer. "No, there's more. You got that look you get when you meet a nice guy."

"It's that obvious?"

"You're all flushed like you're ready to lay back and light up a cigarette even though you don't smoke. What, did Bella get a hot new male associate?"

"Nope. But get this… the author is a four-hundred-pound agoraphobe."

"A what-a-phobe?"

"One of those incredibly shy people afraid to leave the house."

Gretch grew a worried look, bit her lower lip and took Keira's hands. "Oh, sweetie, if you're getting turned on by an antisocial morbidly obese woman, this is a cry for help."

Keira couldn't help but laugh. "No, Gretch, I've not given up on men. But, you're right. I met one."

"So if it's not someone in Bella's office, who is it?"

"The author's cousin. Apparently she's so terrified of being out in public, he acts as her intermediary. And you'll love this part… he's exactly like the guy in *Ring Girl*."

"Excuse me?"

"The hero. Jamison. Obviously the author wrote the character with her cousin in mind."

"So what's his name?"

"Alexander Bauer."

"And the author's name is Alex Bauer, right?"

"Right."

"So let me get this straight because I'm getting confused… a writer named Alex, who is a very large woman that never leaves the house, uses her cousin Alexander as the template for Jamison?"

"Sure seems that way. Anyway, he took me to breakfast after we did the deal at Bella's office. And it turns out I'll be working closely with him on the book."

"You're gonna work with a *guy* on a romance novel?"

37

"He said he was intimately familiar with the book. Just to be sure, I asked him about a few obscure facts that were in it and he wasn't kidding. He knows it like the back of his hand, and even served as the proofreader. And he reads the genre. Big fan of Rose. Anyway, I think there's some chemistry there."

"With Jamison."

"No, Alexander, who I think is based on Jamison. Wait, I got it backwards. Jamison is based on Alexander."

"Who was written by Alex. Who is a woman."

"Right."

Gretch shook her head. "I'm gonna need a scorecard on this… ménage-à-whatever. Considering one of those involved is fictional. So why do you think there's chemistry?"

"He played one of my favorite songs on the juke box. Bobby Darin. *Mack the Knife.*"

She rolled her eyes. "Oh, for God's sake, you went to that Greek diner to celebrate a six-figure deal?"

"You know I love that place."

"And because you two like the same golden oldie you think he's interested?"

"That was just one little thing. When I was talking he was actually paying attention instead of the usual guy-tuning-me-out bobblehead. But at one point he locked eyes with me and gave me this look that went right into my soul. Anyway, you'll meet him tomorrow morning. I invited him to the office to give him a tour and meet the team."

"You sure that's safe with a floor full of women who are working in the equivalent of dating Guantanamo?"

Keira narrowed her eyes, folded her arms, stretched to her full height and looked down at her assistant, who was about six inches shorter. "Hands off, Gretch. I saw him first."

"Fine. Does that mean you're going to finally get over your phobia of relationships and actually go after a guy? I mean, it has been two years, since, you know…"

Keira bit her lip, felt a demon start to dance in her head, then quickly shoved it aside. "We'll see."

"Sorry, didn't mean to bring up old wounds, but it's about time for you to rip the band-aid off. You're way overdue." Suddenly her eyes widened. "I just realized something."

"What?"

"Well, you said this Alexander guy seems to be the Jamison character. Remember what you said about the heroine when we were reading the book yesterday?"

"Yeah. It sounds…" her eyes widened to match Gretch's. "…like me."

"Tall, skinny, girl-next-door, smartass, freckle-faced redhead chocoholic. If that's not you, I don't know who it is."

"So if the writer based her male character on Alexander—"

"Maybe she knows him so well she based the heroine on *his* type."

Keira shook her head. "Nah, that's too much of a stretch."

"Did he say anything that indicated he was interested?"

"He mentioned that my hair was such a pretty color."

"There ya go. You're livin' it, honey."

"Living what?"

"The book. *Ring Girl*. You're Lexi to his Jamison."

"We'll see. So, you wanna go out to dinner and celebrate tonight?"

"We're not going back to the Greek diner, are we?"

"Nah, I think the company can spring for something a little more upscale."

"While your loyal assistant is flattered you want to celebrate with her, don't you want to spend the evening with a man? C'mon, we'll go down to the bar and I'll be your wing girl. Find someone hot you can ravish."

Keira shook her head. "Not interested."

"This guy really shot an arrow into your heart, huh?"

She shrugged. "Maybe. In any event, I can't wait for tomorrow."

Chapter 5

Keira nearly choked on her champagne. "Oh my God!"

Gretch's eyes grew wide. "What?"

Keira leaned forward and lowered her voice. "He's... here."

"Who?"

"Jamison. I mean Alexander. *Him.* Mister Right from *Ring Girl* at three o'clock."

Gretch looked to her right. "Where? All I see is a fat bald guy."

"Sorry, my three o'clock. Your nine. At the table in front of the big fountain where the waiter is standing." Gretch whipped her head one hundred eighty degrees. "Gretch, don't be obvious!"

She spotted him and nodded. "Whoa. Damn, you weren't kidding. He really is the guy in the book and definitely your type." She craned her neck to get a better look. "Who's he with?"

"Can't see. Waiter's in the way." The waiter finished taking the order and moved on, leaving both with a clear view of Alexander's dining partner. Keira's face dropped. "Sonofabitch. Check out the smoking-hot blonde."

"Her? Eh, she's okay."

"Stop trying to soften the blow. She's stunning."

"Fine, she's hot. But you said he worked in TV news and that business is loaded with peroxide babes. Maybe she's a co-worker."

The blonde reached across the table and patted Alexander's

hand. "Shit, they're together."

"Will you stop it? For all we know she's a relative."

"Yeah, right. A four-hundred-pound cousin and a supermodel sister? Damn, she's gorgeous."

Alexander turned his head and spotted Keira, smiled and waved. "Shit, he saw me!" she said, talking through a clenched smile as she waved back. She felt her pulse spike as he got up, grabbed the blonde by the hand and headed in their direction. "And he's coming this way. Sonofabitch."

Gretch sipped her wine and leaned back in her chair. "Relax, maybe we'll find out the deal with the blonde." She pointed at the beads of sweat forming on Keira's forehead. "You're glowing, sweetie."

"Dammit!" Keira quickly ran her hand across her face as Alexander and his companion arrived. She stood to greet them as she wiped her damp palm on her dress.

"We've gotta stop meeting like this," he said.

"New York is a small town." Keira smiled at him before giving a quick glance at his petite date, who was even more spectacular up close. The woman was flawless. "Hello, I'm Keira."

"Juliette."

Keira gestured at Gretch. "And this is my right-hand girl, Gretch."

"Short for Gretchen. Everyone calls me Gretch."

Keira turned back to Alexander. "So, out celebrating?"

"Yeah. My, uh, cousin told us we had carte blanche tonight considering the big check you dropped today."

"Couldn't get her out even on a day like this?"

Alexander shook his head. "Nope. But I had a lobstergram sent to her."

"That's nice."

"Well, just wanted to say hello and thank you again. Tomorrow morning at ten-thirty, right?"

"We'll see you then."

The blonde flashed a warm smile and actually seemed sincere. "Nice meeting you both."

They turned and headed back to their table. On the way he put his arm around her shoulder.

"So much for me living the book," said Keira, watching the couple as they sat and Alexander flagged down a waiter. "Good God. Look at the body on that woman. She's not just hot, she's 'stripper hot'. And her skin was like porcelain."

"Hey, we still don't know the deal about the blonde. There was no ring on her finger."

"Thank you for checking, but I don't think it matters." Keira grabbed a bread stick, disgustedly took a bite and talked through the dry crumbs. "Sonofabitch. I can't compete with a girl who looks like that."

"Not always about looks, sweetie. For a girl who edits romance, you're supposed to get that part. And you're extremely cute."

"Hot trumps cute every time." Keira picked up the wine bottle on the table to get a refill and found it empty. "I need another round." A waiter carrying a bottle of champagne in a silver ice bucket was heading in their direction and she waved at him. He arrived at their table and smiled. "We're gonna need one more bottle. Who knows, maybe two."

The waiter laughed as he placed the bucket on the table. "Good timing," he said, then pointed at Alexander. "From the couple seated next to the fountain." He popped the cork on the bottle and poured the champagne into two fresh glasses.

She looked at Alexander as he and his companion raised glasses in their direction. She and Gretch smiled and did the same as the waiter placed the bottle back in the bucket and moved on.

Gretch turned back to Keira. "Class act."

"Only makes it worse."

Juliette studied Alex's face as he sipped his wine. "You're flushed. You like her."

"You can tell?"

"Pffft." She waved her hand like she was shooing a fly. "I know your type and I've seen that expression you're wearing."

"What expression?"

"The quivering lip, the little wobble in your voice that only I notice. You're scared of her. Which means you like her. Luckily you had your 'safe date' on your arm or you would have been a shuddering lump of flesh. You're smitten. And from the way she looked at you, I can tell the feeling is mutual."

"You think so?"

"Yep. But the way she checked *me* out means you need to clear up something right away."

"What's that?"

"She thinks we're a couple."

"Why would she think that?"

"Duh-uh, you're out to dinner with another woman. What the hell else is she supposed to think, especially with you putting your arm around me on the way back to the table?"

"Oh, shit. Why the hell did I do that?"

"Because, you clueless idiot, you love me like I love you and you're an old-fashioned protective Boy Scout. But no big deal. Just make sure you let her know you're unattached and we're best buds. Or, if you want, I can time my trip to the ladies room when she goes. I can talk you up."

He put up his hands. "Nah, then it sounds like a fix-up."

"Don't you want to be fixed up?"

"Yeah, but I don't wanna scare her away. Besides, she might think there's some sort of 'conflict of interest' thing since we'll be working together."

"Okay. But, seriously, when you get together tomorrow morning, make sure she knows I'm a platonic friend."

"Suppose she doesn't believe me?"

"Why *wouldn't* she believe you, Alex?"

"Not too many guys have platonic friends who look like you."

Juliette smiled and blushed a bit. "See, that's the sweetness in you that women love. Trust me, she'll trust you. And if not, I've got a backup plan I *know* will work."

Keira looked up from her desk and saw Gretch's disapproving expression. "What?"

"The first guy to ever work on a romance novel is coming in today, he's got that 'boy next door' thing going you can't resist, he was classy enough to send over a bottle of champagne last night, and *that's* what you're wearing?"

She looked down at her gray suit. "What's wrong with it?"

Gretch sat on the edge of the desk. "What's *wrong* with it is that you wear it here all the time. It *screams* corporate. Hell, it almost screams cat lady. All that's missing is a pair of horn-rimmed glasses on a chain." She tapped Keira on the head with a knuckle. "Earth to Keira! A man who you're interested in will be here in an hour and a half—"

Keira pointed at Gretch's ultra-conservative navy-blue dress, which was very out of character. "*You're* not dressed to the nines. And I don't think I've ever seen you with a hemline to the knee or something buttoned up to your neck. Did you go to an Amish festival?"

"Funny. Gretch is dressed in the dowdy collection because she is your loyal and trusted assistant who wants Alexander to notice *you.*"

"Where'd you get that thing? I know you didn't buy it."

"Borrowed it from a friend who works in a library. Highly unflattering, don't you think? Anyway, my natural hotness doesn't need to be a distraction, hence it remains under wraps."

"I appreciate that, but c'mon, Gretch, he's obviously off the market. What's the point in getting all gussied up?"

"Because, McFly, as we discussed last night, the blonde might not be his girlfriend. Or even someone he dates."

Keira shrugged. "Doesn't matter. He's out of my league."

"Bullshit. I saw the way he looked at you, and you said you felt some chemistry at lunch yesterday."

"Yeah, but—"

"Yeah but nothing." Gretch got up, grabbed Keira's arm and pulled her out of the chair. "Get your skinny ass home and put on that killer royal-blue dress you wore to the wedding last month."

"That's kinda fancy for work, don't you think?"

"Have you *seen* how the rest of the office staff dressed today since they found out a man is coming by? It looks like the cattle call for the 'Tits and Ass' number in *Chorus Line*. Now, you live around the corner so you have no excuse for not going home and getting dolled up." Gretch put her hand on Keira's back and pushed her toward the door. "Go. Don't come back until you look as hot as possible. Do something with your hair. And when he gets here I'm gonna clear up the mystery about the blonde first thing."

"How are you gonna do that?"

"Trust me, boss. I know how to get information out of men."

"Yeah, but we don't have a bed in my office."

"Very funny." She pointed at the elevator. "Home. Now. Gussy up."

Juliette ran her hands down the sleeves of his gray wool window-pane suit and patted Alex on the shoulders. "I pronounce you ready." She looked up into his eyes. "However…"

"However…what?"

"You look nervous. You already got the check and can buy any midlife crisis convertible you want, so relax."

He exhaled. "It's not the book deal. It's this whole deception thing. I just feel like it's going to come back and bite me in the ass."

"They bought your work, not your equipment. Trust me, when the publisher makes a fortune off the book they won't care if you're a cross-dressing hermaphrodite."

"Still, it worries me. And…"

She nodded and smiled. "Ah, the redhead. I forgot how

powerless you are around them. I do remember what you called them in college."

"Kryptonite girls."

"Well, relax, I could tell she likes you."

"She looked at me more businesslike last night than she did at breakfast."

"Because you had *me* on your arm. You tell her we're platonic friends and the barrier will fall like the Iron Curtain."

Keira watched the staff all snap to attention, smile and stand up straight like they were in Catholic school. The horde of short skirts, low-cut tops and stiletto heels parted like the Red Sea as a smiling Gretch led Alexander through the babe gauntlet to her office and left a dozen hanging jaws in their wake. Keira's heart got caught on her tonsils as she stood to greet them. "Right on time," she said. "We like people who respect deadlines."

"When you work in TV, you can never be late," he said, as he shook her hand.

"Can I get you anything?" asked Gretch. "We've got coffee, soda, and some killer cheese Danish this morning. Unless my boss ate them all."

"Hey!"

He laughed. "I'm good."

"Then I'll leave you two to talk." Gretch headed for the door, then stopped and turned back to face him. "Oh, Alexander, before I forget…"

"Yes?"

"This is probably a stupid question for a guy, but do you happen to know where your girlfriend got that dress?"

Keira's eyes grew wide as her pulse spiked.

He furrowed his brow. "Girlfriend?"

"Yeah. The girl you were with last night. What was her name… Juliette?"

His face relaxed. "Oh, she's not my girlfriend. We've known

46

each other since college and worked together at the network. She's actually my best friend. But it's strictly platonic."

Gretch smiled and shot her an *I told you so* look at Keira. "Oh. I just assumed she was your significant other."

"Nope, we're just great friends. As for the dress, I have no clue. But I'll ask her for you."

"Great, thanks. Oh, Keira, after you guys are through, don't forget to put in the paperwork for *that raise* you promised me." Gretch playfully batted her eyes at her boss.

"Yeah, I'll take care of it." Gretch left the office and closed the door behind her. While her assistant had cleared up the situation with the hot blonde, it still didn't shed any light on whether or not Alexander was attached.

"She must be a good assistant if you're giving her a raise."

"You have no idea."

Chapter 6

"For such a smart guy, sometimes you can be a complete idiot."

Alex furrowed his brow as he took off his necktie and looked at Juliette. "What'd I do?"

"You failed to tell her you didn't have a girlfriend."

"I just told you I did, or were you acting like a man and not listening? Her assistant asked me about you and I said that you and I are platonic friends."

Juliette shook her head as she rolled her eyes. "Duh-uh! That still doesn't tell her you're *available*. Just because you aren't dating *me* doesn't mean you aren't dating one of the other four million women in this city."

"Oh. Right."

"Alas, the light bulb goes on."

"You know how nervous I get around women I'm interested in."

"Well, luckily you'll be spending lots of time with her, so you need to clear that up." Juliette pointed at her mouth. "Read my lips and repeat after me. *I'm not dating anyone.*"

"I'm not dating anyone."

"I can't HEAR you!"

"Okay, okay, I get the point. But how do I do that without being so obvious?"

"Since I cannot trust you to take care of a simple task, why don't you call your agent and have her do it? She told you she knows the editor very well."

Gretch folded her arms as she stood in front of Keira's desk. "I don't know *why* you continue to doubt your assistant. You should know by now that my romantic radar is always spot-on."

Keira leaned back in her chair. "Fine, you were right about the blonde. Thank you for clearing that part up."

"See, you got all frazzled for nothing. Now aren't you glad I sent you home to dress up?"

"Yeah, but he still might be attached."

"I'm betting no."

"And to what do we owe this bit of intuition?"

Gretch took a seat across from her. "The way he looked at you. I could tell he wants you. I caught him checking out your legs."

"He could be one of those guys who wants anything in a skirt. If you'd worn your quarter jeans instead of something dowdy we might know the answer to that question."

"My *what*?"

"Those lacquered-on jeans you have. If you put a quarter in the back pocket I could tell if it's heads or tails."

"Very funny. Fine, I'll sleaze it up the next time he's in, stick my boobs in his face and I'll bet he doesn't even notice. Perhaps *you* noticed he didn't pay much attention to the rest of our staff that was dressed in the Miley Cyrus spring collection."

"Well, anyway, I can't exactly ask him out on a date. I mean, how would that look?"

"Oh, I'm sorry, I forgot to look at your calendar and see that it's 1850. I guess you'll have to wait for the Sadie Hawkins dance and you can invite him to the hoe-down."

"Stop it, Gretch."

"Hey, I'm trying to help things along here. I've got it… how about doing it the back-door way? Work late with him and then, you know, sort of invite him to continue things over dinner since you're on a roll or something. Then it's not really a date, but you're in a more casual one-on-one setting than you would be in the office."

Keira shrugged. "I don't know…"

"Good God! For such a kick-ass editor you really amaze me."

"What?"

"You take no prisoners at work and act like one when it comes to real men. Have you forgotten how the women in Rose's books always took charge romantically? And that's how the heroine in this new book acts as well?"

Keira said nothing, knowing Gretch was right.

"Trust me, Keira, it'll work. Get him out of the office and let him see you with your hair down a bit."

"We already had breakfast out of the office."

"Big friggin' deal. No one ever got laid after pancakes. Things are different at night. It might not be an official date but it will have the same effect. Finish up the work over appetizers and then you've got the rest of the dinner to get to know each other better."

"But all this might be a waste of time if he's already got someone."

"Well, you've gotta eat dinner anyway, may as well do it with Alexander. You need to take a shot either way. Even if he is dating someone else he might like you better.·And looking at your face, I can tell you're a bit smitten with the guy."

"Fine, I'm smitten. But I've never asked a guy out before. Or even tried your 'back-door' method."

"Good God, Keira, you're not asking him to marry you. You just want to find out if he's available."

"So, oh great and wise dating oracle, how do I do it *without* asking him out? What's in that dating database you keep in your head?"

"The *Book of Gretch* suggests the use of a matchmaker." She pointed at the phone. "Why don't you let Bella find out for you? She's not apprehensive about asking anyone anything. She makes me look shy."

Bella Farentino's phone buzzed at one minute past nine. "Yes?"

"Two calls," said Rachel. "Keira Madison on line one, Alex Bauer on two."

"Tell Alex to hold for a minute and I'll pick up on Keira."

"Got it."

She punched a button that connected the first line. "Hi Keira, how you doin' this morning?"

"Very good, Bella, you?"

"Not in my body yet. Ask me around noon. So how'd your day with Alex... Alexander go?"

"Gave him the nickle tour and went over some notes for the author about my suggested edits, along with a few ideas. He'll be back this afternoon and we're going to get started."

"Think you'll be okay working with him?"

"Sure, Bella. Speaking of which... I was wondering if you might do me a favor."

Her phone buzzed, the automatic reminder she had another person on hold. "Hang on a minute, Keira."

"Sure."

She punched line two. "Hi, Alex."

"Hi, Bella, how arc you this morning?"

"Fine. How'd things go yesterday?"

"Very well. She gave me the tour, I met most of the staff. We discussed a few changes and we're gonna start when I go back today."

"Sounds like you're off and running."

"Yep. Listen, I wonder if I could ask you a favor?"

"Everyone wants favors today. But sure. Waddaya need?"

"Well, I hate to even ask, but—"

The phone buzzed again. "Hang on, Alex, be right back."

She punched Keira's line. "Sorry to be playing call-juggling with you. I've got an important client on the other line."

"Not a problem, Bella. I know how busy your days are."

"So, what's the favor and what's it gonna cost me?"

51

"It's not gonna cost you anything, but I was hoping to make use of your wonderful Sicilian information-gathering service."

"I can't get anybody whacked, if you wanna take out your CEO. Though I might do it as a public service since we all hate the tight ass."

She heard Keira laugh. "No, not that. But I wouldn't complain if he went away."

Bella heard the editor exhale deeply. "Just spit it out, Keira."

"Geez, this is going to sound so unprofessional and I cannot believe I'm doing this, but Gretch is making me."

"Oh, this oughta be good."

"I was wondering if you could find out if Alexander is dating anyone."

Buzz. "Hang on a minute, Keira." She switched lines. "I'm back, Alex, what's your favor and make it quick."

"Can you, in some casual, backdoor way, let Keira know that I'm unattached?"

"Seriously?"

"Sorry, Bella, I know that's not in your job description."

"Why don't you just ask her out yourself?"

"Well, I get the feeling she's interested, but thinks I'm dating someone. I think if she knew I was available she'd send clearer signals that she's receptive to a date."

"Lemme get this straight. You were a network reporter and you're afraid to ask a girl out? How the hell did you ever interview women?"

"The microphone and camera gave me license to do it. Otherwise I could never approach women I didn't know."

Un-believable.

Buzz.

"Fine. Hang on, Alex." Bella put him on hold, held out the phone and looked at it, shook her head, and said, "Do I look like friggin' match-dot-com?" She switched lines. "So Keira, all you need to know is if he's attached?"

"Yeah."

"He's not. It came up in conversation."

"Oh. Really."

"Yes. Really. And… he's interested in you. That also came up. So does that make your day?"

"Yeah, very much so."

"Fine. Look, I think he's a little shy with women, so send him some signals, grab his ass, do whatever to let him know the feeling is mutual, *capische*?"

"Got it, Bella. Thanks."

Buzz. "Later, Keira." She switched lines. "Okay, Alex, I'll take care of it. By the way, she's interested."

"Oh, really. How do you know?"

"She mentioned it when I talked with her earlier."

"Terrific."

"Fine. So ask the woman out. Go, have fun. And remember she's a chocoholic. Anything else?"

"No Bella, thanks so much. Talk later."

She ended the call and looked up as Rachel entered her office. "What?"

Rachel backed up, eyes wide. "I just came in to see if you wanted coffee."

"Yes, sorry I snapped at you."

"Everything okay?"

"Yeah. I think."

"You think?"

"I also think I might be playing with fire."

Keira looked at the lunch selection as she waited for the barista to fix her coffee. The paninis looked appealing and made the prospect of eating at her desk more bearable. Her lunch meeting with an author had just fallen through, too late to make another appointment with anyone else, and Gretch had already taken off on an errand. Besides, *Ring Girl* was demanding her immediate attention and Alexander was coming by at one; it was almost as if Rose was calling her from the great beyond, acting as a guardian angel, telling her to get this book out as quickly as possible.

And setting her up with her soul mate.

"Keira!"

The barista's yell interrupted her train of thought. She raised her hand. "Right here."

The twenty-something peroxide walking ad for body piercing handed her the large Styrofoam cup with her name on it, spelled wrong as usual. "Anything else?"

Keira pointed at the counter. "I'll take that prosciutto and mozzarella panini."

"Half, right?"

"No, I want the whole sandwich."

"Skinny thing like you gonna eat it all?"

"Yep. To go, please."

The girl frowned. "Damn, you got the last one. I was hoping it would make it through lunch so I could have it."

"Them's the breaks. Guess you guys need to make more of 'em."

The barista grabbed the sandwich, wrapped it, put it in a bag, handed it to Keira and hit a few keys on the cash register. "Eleven-forty-three."

Keira swiped her credit card, waited a moment for approval, signed, and grabbed the receipt. "Thanks."

She quickly turned and ran right into a very tall man. The plastic lid on the cup flew up and the coffee shot out like it was being launched, covering his shirt.

The guy screamed. "Ow! Dammit!"

"Oh my God! I'm so sorry." Keira grabbed a stack of napkins from the counter and started to pat the guy's previously white starched shirt and red tie, now obviously ruined beyond repair.

The guy gritted his teeth. "Sonofabitch, that's hot."

"Dear God, are you burned?"

"Don't think so. But it sure woke me up."

54

A young guy with 'manager' written on his shirt ran around the counter. "Sir, you okay?"

"I think I'll live. Don't worry, I won't sue you for making hot coffee." He looked down at his shirt and his face tightened.

"Sir, I'll be happy to loan you one of our barista shirts and pay for the dry cleaning. Lunch is on me as well."

"Thank you, that's very kind."

Keira noted the guy wasn't mad at all, taking the whole thing in stride.

She also noted he was off-the-charts gorgeous. Maybe early thirties: thick, dark hair, Carolina-blue eyes, at least six-foot-four, maybe taller, and from the look of the wet shirt stuck to his body, a ripped torso.

Ah, the old spill coffee on the hot guy trick. Sounds like one from Gretch's playbook.

She reached out and took his forearm. "I'm so sorry. God, I'm such a klutz. Let me make it up to you. Buy you a new shirt and tie."

He smiled as he undid his sopping-wet tie. "That's not necessary. Plenty more at home." He looked at the tie, still dripping coffee. "I was tired of this one anyway."

"Well, geez, I ruined your day. I feel like I owe you something."

He smiled and locked eyes with her. "Tell you what, if you really feel the need to apologize…"

"Yeah?"

"I'd rather have your phone number."

Gulp.

Her jaw hung open as his request hit her from out of the blue and sent her brain into meltdown. *I've just given a gorgeous man a hot-coffee bath and he wants my phone number and I just met Alexander, who is interested in me and I haven't had a date in two years and now I have to meet two guys in the same week… this isn't fair.* "Uh…whuh…"

"Cheaper than a new shirt and tie."

"What is?"

"Your phone number."

"Uh… yeah."

He gestured to an empty table. "And have lunch with me? Add that to the list and we'll call it even."

"Uh-huh."

"Great."

The manager returned holding a pale-blue button-down oxford and handed it to him. "I think this should fit, it's an extra-extra large. You can change in the back room. Follow me."

He turned to Keira and pointed to an empty booth. "Grab that and I'll be right back."

"Yeah, sure."

The guy followed the manager behind a curtain while Keira sat at a table for two in the corner, keeping her eyes locked on the curtain, which didn't close all the way. The guy pulled off his shirt.

Gulp, again.

Oh. My. God.

He's a real-life romance-novel cover.

She stared at his chiseled body and absentmindedly licked her lips as he changed into the barista shirt. Massive shoulders, cut pecs and a well-defined six-pack. The man was seriously ripped. He thanked the manager and shoved the curtain back. She quickly turned her head and looked out the window so he wouldn't see her staring. He pulled out the chair and she turned to face him. "Maybe I can moonlight serving coffee and get a kickback from the men's store across the street."

He laughed and extended his hand across the table. "Dash Riley."

She shook it. "Keira Madison."

He studied her face. "I've seen you before, right?"

"I don't think so."

He shook his finger. "No, no, I never forget a face. And I'd remember one like yours."

"Like mine?"

"Got a thing for redheads with freckles. My mom says it's the

Irish genes. Give me a minute." His eyes widened. "Got it. I saw an article about you recently in *The Post*, right? You're that publisher."

"Editor. But yeah, that's me. You have quite the memory."

He turned serious. "That was a touching story about your best friend."

She bit her lower lip, the image of Rose flashing through her mind.

His eyes locked with hers for a moment. "Sorry. Didn't mean to—"

"It's okay. I think of her every day. It's gonna take a while to get over it."

Their gaze was interrupted as the manager slid a sandwich and soda in front of him. "Here you go, sir. And I do apologize. Sometimes our baristas don't put the coffee lids on tight enough."

Keira laughed. "Hey, not your fault, I'm the clumsy one. You didn't give him a latte bath."

"You two enjoy your lunch. If you want anything else, dessert, whatever, let me know. On the house."

Keira lowered her head and her voice. "Tell him you want tiramisu."

Dash smiled. "I guess the lady wants tiramisu."

"Coming right up," said the manager, who spun on his heels and headed toward the kitchen.

Dash turned back to Keira. "So, editor. I imagine that's a fun job."

"Depends on the day and what you're reading. But I love my work. Getting paid to read and discover great talent is something really special. So what do you do?"

"Political media consultant. Currently working on Senator Bradley's re-election campaign."

"That sounds interesting."

"It is, though working with some politicians makes you want to take an hour-long shower at the end of the day. But Bradley's a good guy, so I'm enjoying this election cycle."

"Well, from what I've read, your candidate has a good shot."

"As long as some unexpected shit doesn't hit the fan." He grabbed his sandwich and took a bite. Keira unwrapped her panini and did the same, not taking her eyes off him.

He looks so familiar…

"So, Dash, have I seen you somewhere before?"

He shrugged. "Don't think so. I'm always behind the scenes. And I've never been in the paper."

Then it hit her.

Ho. Lee. Shit.

He looks exactly like the guy on the cover of Rose Fontaine's first novel. The *Soul Mate* hero was real.

And she instantly knew she'd been lying every time she made a speech at a writer's conference.

The best men I've met only exist on paper.

"Excuse me, aren't you Alex Bauer?"

Alex turned and found himself looking at a perky brunette behind him in the drug store checkout line. "That's me."

Her huge ice-blue eyes beamed. "I knew it."

"I don't usually get recognized in New York. How do you know me?"

"I just moved here from Texas. Used to watch you on Channel 4." She extended her hand. "I'm Lauren Hale."

He shook it and smiled. "Alex Bauer."

"Yeah, I already figured that part out."

"Right. So, Texas, huh? How do you like the Big Apple?"

"Love it. Never want to leave. Not wild about the cold, but I've gotten used to it. So what channel are you on here? I haven't seen you on the local news."

"I left television two years ago. I'm a writer now. Just sold my first book. It'll be out in nine months."

"Wow, that's terrific. Great American Novel?"

"Don't laugh, but it's a romantic comedy."

"Why would I laugh? I love a good rom-com."

"Men don't usually write those."

She shrugged as she flashed a smile. "Just tells me you're a romantic guy, and there's a serious shortage of those around here. Actually there's a shortage everywhere."

The woman was beyond cute; one of those girls with a sweet, innocent face. But the body was anything but innocent. Maybe late twenties, about five-seven and seriously stacked with dangerous curves wrapped in a dress that matched her eyes, gentle curls that ended in the middle of her back, and a soft, devastating drawl. She was still locked on to him with those eyes.

"So, Lauren, what do you do?"

"Struggling actress. Which is redundant in this town."

"Have I seen you in anything?"

"If you've been to Jensen's restaurant, you've seen me pitch the overly pretentious specials of the day, which, I must say, I deliver like Meryl Streep in a highbrow British film. I've gotten great reviews on fine-dining websites." Her statement wasn't typical New York sarcasm, didn't have any frustration in it. She stuck her nose in the air. "This evening our chef has prepared a delightful honey-braised free-range capon stuffed with organic barley couscous, accompanied by gently sautéed chestnuts in broth accented with a hint of coriander."

He couldn't help but laugh. "What exactly is that?"

"Chicken 'n' rice with a bowl of really weird soup."

"Well, you make it sound delicious."

"You should hear the fifty-word description of what amounts to chocolate cake."

"I'll bet. I can certainly see you as an actress."

"Thank you. I've had a lot of callbacks lately, so I feel like I'm making progress. Just a matter of time."

"Seems like you have a good attitude. I'm sure something will come along."

"That's what I keep telling myself. Of course in this town, a lot of your success depends on who you know, and I don't know anyone."

"Very true."

She lightly touched his forearm and sent a charge through his body. "Though now I know you."

"Next!"

The cashier's yell made Alex turn around. He saw everyone in front of him had checked out and he was ten feet from the counter.

The plump, middle-aged cashier glared at him over half glasses. "Buddy, this ain't e-harmony-dot-com."

"Sorry," said Alex, who blushed as he placed his items on the counter while Lauren followed.

Lauren put her items behind his. "So, if you're a writer, I assume you work at home?"

"Most of the time. I also teach journalism two nights a week, but otherwise I'm pounding the keyboard."

"So you can work whenever you want."

"Right. Very flexible schedule."

"Which means you're free for lunch. Like, now."

He turned and found her smiling at him with a look that went right into his heart. "Uh… yeah, sure."

Her eyes beamed. "See, I knew there was a good reason to shop here."

They clicked.

Alex hadn't felt it in a while. A long while. And now he'd felt it twice with two women in the same week. The exponentially cute Southern gal sitting across from him seemed totally in tune. It wasn't just that they had a lot in common. The conversation flowed easily and her tendency to play footsie with the cuffs of his slacks sent a definite message. Sweet and innocent girl next door, well… maybe.

Alex knew what Juliette would say: *Two women? You? Ha!*

His cell on the table clicked with a text just as he took his last bite of dessert, lighting up with Juliette's face. Lauren took a look and her eyes went wide. "Wow. She's gorgeous."

"Excuse me a minute." He read the text and tapped a few keys. "My roommate."

Her face dropped. "Oh."

Juliette's words flashed through his brain. "*For such a smart guy, sometimes you can be a complete idiot.*"

Clear it up. Now. Before yet another girl thinks you're already off the market.

But am I, after meeting Keira?

Why do I have to meet two nice girls at the same time after a long dry spell?

Not fair.

"Juliette and I worked together at the network. We're best friends. Strictly platonic."

"Ah." The smile returned. "So, Alex… what does your *girlfriend* think of you having a platonic friend who looks like that?" She pointed at the phone.

"Don't have a girlfriend."

"My, my. This day just keeps getting better and better."

Chapter 7

"Keira, where the HELL are you?"

Gretch's call jolted her back to reality. She looked at the clock on the restaurant wall and saw it was twenty minutes past one. "Oh, shit! I lost track of time. Be right there."

"Problem?" asked Dash.

Keira stood up and put on her jacket. "Forgot I had a meeting with a new author at one. Please forgive me for leaving so abruptly."

"Hey, no problem. Uh, I'd still like your phone number. I know I put you on the spot earlier, but I'll certainly understand if you don't want to—"

She whipped a business card out of her purse and handed it to him. "Here you go."

"Great. Keira, I really enjoyed meeting you."

"Same here. And again, sorry about ruining the shirt and tie."

"It was definitely worth it. By the way…"

"Yeah?"

"You know those guys who say they'll call and never do? I'm not one of them."

She moved closer, close enough to get a whiff of his cologne, looked up and locked eyes with him. "I'll look forward to you proving it, Mister."

The elevator door opened, revealing Gretch standing with her arms folded, tapping her foot and glaring at her like an angry parent. "Alexander has been here a half hour. What the hell happened?"

Keira power-walked out of the elevator and headed to her office with her assistant in hot pursuit. "Where is he?"

"In your editing cave. I've been keeping him busy going over your suggestions. Luckily your irreplaceable assistant knows your taste. Also lucky your irreplaceable assistant can be trusted with a guy you want."

"I owe you one, Gretch."

"So where were you?"

"I met a guy."

Gretch stopped and grabbed Keira's forearm. "Excuse me? Did you say you *met* someone?"

"Long story and I'll fill you in later. Bottom line, I spilled coffee all over this guy who looks like the cover model for *Soul Mate* and we ended up having lunch. We really hit it off—"

"Whoa, am I hearing you right? Is Keira Madison cheating?"

"How can I be cheating?"

"I don't mean *regular* cheating, I mean Keira's brand of cheating. You already want Alexander and before you even go out on one date you're already interested in someone else? Keira Madison doesn't date two people at once."

"I'm a big girl. I can play the field. And stop talking about me in the third person."

"Where the hell did this newfound confidence with men suddenly come from?"

Keira shrugged. "What can I say? It hit me about an hour and a half ago. There are two cute guys who like me."

"Whoa, *this* just hit *me*. Back up a minute… the man you met looks like the guy on the *Soul Mate* cover?"

"Dead ringer for our computer generated hero. After I spilled coffee on him the restaurant manager gave him a clean shirt. I caught a glimpse." She licked her lips. "It's the *Soul Mate* cover boy, though unlike the virtual version this one is actually real."

"Hell, you don't have two cute guys. You've got one cute guy and one fantasy."

"Whatever. They're both nice."

"This is getting too weird. You meet one guy who looks like the hunk on the first book you discovered while your life parallels the novel you're about to edit."

"Yeah, stranger than fiction, huh? Maybe one will actually be my *real* soul mate."

Gretch took her shoulders and turned her so they were face to face. "Keira, this isn't you. You've never done the 'playing the field' thing."

"Maybe it's time for me to broaden my horizons."

"Well, if you are to proceed without getting burned you'll need the rules."

"Rules?"

"The *Book of Gretch* has rules for the care and feeding of multiple boyfriends. If you wanna do this right, you need to be able to juggle relationships like a circus performer."

"I thought *you* weren't doing that anymore."

"Hey, I'm still a *recovering* skank. I just keep missing the meetings. And I'm only on step three."

Keira nodded as she ran her eyes up and down Gretch's outfit, a short black-leather skirt and tight red gathered top. "Yeah, I see you're back to your party girl collection."

"I wore this on purpose, for Alexander."

"Excuse me?"

"To prove my point. And guess what, dear boss? The man didn't even notice. He only has eyes for you."

I was afraid of this.

She wants to change my book.

Alex shook his head as he went over Keira's notes that were spread out across the round table in the small room along with his printed manuscript. The red pens sticking out of a coffee mug in the center of the table may as well have been swords dripping with blood. His pulse spiked a bit as he saw his vision being changed. Then he took in the fact that the walls were lined floor-to-ceiling with books, many of which were bestsellers.

Breathe, Alex. You knew this was coming. Every author goes through this, even the famous ones. And for what she paid you—

Don't get upset with her.

He looked up as she opened the door. Keira's apologetic look with those spectacular eyes and a slight pout sucked the stress from his body.

She was one of those women at whom it was impossible to be mad. With the red hair and freckles it would be like getting angry with the Little Mermaid.

"God, Alexander, I am soooo sorry I've kept you waiting. Honestly, I am never, ever late. I got stuck—".

"Not a problem. It happens in New York. Gretch has been keeping me busy going over some of your proposed changes."

Keira grabbed a chair, sat, and slid it in to the table. She offered a soft smile, reached over and patted his hand. "Thank you for being so understanding."

"Hey, forget it. No biggie."

She pointed to the legal pad that contained her notes. "So, I trust you've got some thoughts on my suggestions for the opening of the book."

His face tightened. "Yeah, and Gretch explained your thinking on them."

"Okay. I can tell from the look on your face you're not thrilled. So let me start by saying nothing I suggest is written in stone. I'm not a dictator and the whole editing procedure is a give-and-take process. My job is to make this book the best it can be, but I want the author to be comfortable with what I'm suggesting. So if there's anything you or your cousin don't like, or something you guys absolutely hate, don't hold back. We're a team, Alexander, and it's always important for you to remember that. I have no desire to change the basic story, which is fantastic."

His body relaxed. "Thank you for saying that. I know it will put her at ease."

"Speaking of your cousin, I was wondering if we could get her on the phone and put her on speaker while we work."

His shoulders tensed up a bit. "I would, but she's at the doctor getting some tests run today."

"Is she okay?"

"She's fine. She's just a hypochondriac. Every time she sees a TV commercial with some new drug that cures something nobody ever heard of, she thinks she's got the disease. The restless-leg syndrome thing drove her nuts. Anyway, how about I have her call you later?"

"That works. You sure we can't meet face to face?"

He shook his head. "I asked, she said no. Not right now. But I'll keep working on her. Give it time."

"Well, don't push her. I've worked with plenty of authors I've never met." Keira pointed at her notes. "So, tell me your thoughts on what I've done so far."

He snatched the first page of the manuscript. "Okay. This particular line you circled. Gretch said you want to move it. I think it's a great line for the first page of the book. And I don't quite understand why you want to move it or where you want to move it. I thought the reader has to be grabbed by the first page."

"This is true, and the first page definitely grabs the reader. It sure as hell grabbed me. But there are already three great lines and that one goes a bit too far."

"I don't think so."

"Look, Alexander, one problem with this working situation is that you're a guy and this is a book which will be read by women. So you see things differently than we do. There's a fine line between a heroine being snarky-funny and coming off as a bitch. And that line could be taken two ways. I would venture to guess you don't see her as a bitch when she says that, right?"

"Right. I just think she's funny."

"She is, but you always want the reader to root for the heroine from page one, and I don't want to turn them off right off the bat. So I thought it best to not throw that line away, but use it later in the book after we've established that Lexi is snarky instead of bitchy. By then the readers will be rooting for her and be familiar with her attitude. They'll cut her some slack. Make sense?"

He had to admit, it did. "Yeah."

"You think your cousin will understand my thinking on this?"

"Once I explain it to her like you did."

"Well, I'll be happy to go over everything when I talk to her. You think you can get her to call me tonight?"

His pulse spiked as he forced a smile. "Uh… yeah, sure."

Now he had to find someone to play the voice of his nonexistent cousin. Which made his pulse spike again.

And then it got even worse.

Juliette. Hands on hips.

Not looking happy.

"Let me get this straight. You want me to get on the phone and pretend to be the author of your book who happens to be a four hundred pound agoraphobe so that you can continue this ruse with a girl you're interested in who happens to be your editor, and, oh, by the way, you met another girl today and you're interested in her as well, so you also want my advice on dating two people at the same time while you're lying to one of them."

Alex shrugged. "That about covers it."

"You do realize you're playing with romantic nitroglycerin and this whole thing could blow up in your face."

"I know."

"What are you gonna do if I say no to playing your nonexistent cousin?"

"There is no plan B."

She threw up her hands. "Fine, I guess I have no choice. My curse for loving you like a brother."

"You know I'd do it for you."

"You'd pretend to be an obese woman who's afraid to go out in public for me?"

"I'm already doing that, in a weird sort of way. Just not for you. Anyway, I can't thank you enough."

"Well, you can thank me if we somehow pull this off. I've heard of burning the candle at both ends, but you've got a flame in the middle as well. You may get one hell of a waxing. And let me tell you, when it's pulled off, it hurts like hell."

"Trust me, I didn't intend for this to happen when I wrote the book. Your idea, remember?"

"Don't remind me. So I'm supposed to call Keira in an hour?"

"Yeah." He handed her a flip phone. "I got this burner phone in case Keira ever calls you and I'm not around. Or there might be a situation where I'm at her office and she wants to call you. So if it ever rings, remember to answer it as Alex the author. But don't use it for anything else."

"No problem."

"And…"

"And what?"

"Today didn't go well. I didn't care for some of her suggestions and things got a little… well, I got upset at some of the changes."

"Alex, you knew this was coming. And she's the editor, she knows a helluva lot more about the genre than you do. You never even read a romance until a few months ago."

"I know. Anyway, I started getting too defensive, acting like it was my book."

"Probably because it *is* your book. You didn't piss her off, did you?"

"No. I think she was cutting me some slack."

"Good. Don't forget you're interested in her romantically."

"I know. Anyway, you need to sound very receptive to her

ideas tonight."

"Hey, I give good phone. But look, I've read your book and am familiar with it but how am I supposed to have a discussion with her about all this editing stuff?"

"Put the call on speaker. I'll sit next to you with my laptop and you just repeat what I write."

"You really think this is gonna work?"

"What other choice do I have?"

"Uh… tell her the truth?"

"Not an option right now."

"She already bought the book, why not?"

"The sale has already been announced in *Publisher's Weekly*. Word could get out about the true identity of the author and that could hurt the release. Bella wants me to keep it under wraps till after the thing hits the book stores."

Juliette shook her head. "And I thought the news business was weird. Meanwhile, what's the deal with this gal from Texas who caught your eye? I thought you were smitten with the redhead."

"I am. I mean…"

Juliette rolled her eyes. "Men. In this case you want to have your cake, eat it too, and run away with the baker."

"Right on time," said Gretch as Keira's phone rang.

Keira smiled as she glanced at the clock in her editing cave. But when she looked at her cell phone she saw a different name than the one she expected. "It's not Alexander."

"Oh."

"It's the *Soul Mate* cover boy."

"Ah."

She hit the speaker button. "Hello, this is Keira…"

"I told you I was one of those guys who calls when he says he will."

"Well, Dash, I must say I'm impressed. And you didn't waste any time."

Her phone beeped with another incoming call.

Alexander.

Sonofabitch.

Gretch looked at the phone, saw who was calling, raised one eyebrow, smiled and mouthed "slut."

"Keira? You there?"

"Yeah, sorry, Dash, I got distracted by my assistant." She glared at Gretch. "I'm still at the office."

"Aren't you the dedicated one. Anyway, you free for dinner Friday night?"

"Uh… sure." She heard background noise that told her he was at an airport. "You heading out of town or coming back?"

"I'm going to Chicago but I'll be back for the weekend. Anyway, if you'll be so kind as to text me your address I'll pick you up at seven."

Alexander's call was still available. The phone taunted her.

Accept?

"That sounds great. Listen, I gotta run."

"Me too, my flight is boarding. See you then. Bye."

"Bye."

Alexander's call disappeared and went to voice mail.

"Shit!"

No men interested in me for two years, then two in thirty seconds. Life is not fair.

She punched a button on the phone to call Alexander back.

Gretch leaned back, folded her arms, and started to laugh. "Nice problem to have, huh boss?"

"What?"

"Two men. Keira's a bad, bad girl."

"Leave me alone." She flashed a naughty grin.

"And Keira *likes* being bad. Who knew?"

"Stop talking about me like I'm not here."

"That's because the real you *isn't* here. Third person Keira is juggling men, not you."

Juliette sat up straight and pointed at the phone. "She's calling back."

Alex took a deep breath and slid the laptop closer. "You ready?"

"Yeah." She pointed to the bag of potato chips and glass of soda atop the dining-room table. "You really sure we need these… accessories?"

"You need to eat while you talk. We gotta sell you as obsessed with food."

"Not exactly a stretch. Let's rock."

He answered the cell and put it on speaker. "Hi, Keira."

"Hey, Alexander, sorry I couldn't pick up earlier, I was on another call."

"No big deal."

"Is our author there?"

"Right here," said Juliette. She shoved a couple of chips in her mouth and talked through the crumbs. "Nice to meet you, Keira."

"My pleasure. I look forward to meeting you face to face sometime. Of course, when you feel the time is right."

Juliette took a sip of soda, then continued to munch on the chips. "Might be a while."

"Not a problem," said Keira. "So, have you guys gone over my proposed changes?"

Juliette leaned forward and read what Alex had typed on the laptop before the call. "Uh-huh. At first I was a little apprehensive, but once he explained your reasoning, I agreed. It's obvious you're going to make my book better." Alex patted her on the back as she sucked the remaining soda and made the gurgling noise with the straw.

"Great. I forgot to go over one thing with him. I wanted to discuss the first scene in chapter two, specifically where your heroine meets her first love interest. I personally think he's a little too perfect and might be a bit more interesting if you gave him a few flaws."

Juliette whipped her head toward Alex, widened her eyes and

put her palms up. He quickly typed and she read along. "Uh... you're probably right. Though I do think... uh... he needs to be her dream guy... ya know... in order to throw off the readers a bit."

"I understand. Maybe just a small flaw, then. Would that be acceptable to you?"

Alex nodded and gave her a thumbs-up. "Sure," said Juliette.

"And how about this?" said Keira. "Instead of the usual chance face-to-face meeting, perhaps they spot each other from afar, then run into each other later."

Alex quickly typed.

"Hmmm." Juliette paused a moment to let him catch up. "How about... the first time they see each other... having my heroine blow him—"

Alex stopped typing, turned his head and sneezed.

"Excuse me?" said Keira. "This is a sweet romance. You can't have an erotic scene with oral sex—"

Alex quickly typed.

"A kiss! Blow him a kiss!" said Juliette, rolling her eyes as Alex buried his head in his hands.

Keira laughed. "Oh. I was wondering where you were going with that."

An hour later Keira hung up and looked at Gretch. "That had to be one of the strangest calls I've ever had with an author."

"No kidding. I mean, if you can get past the fact the woman can't stop eating to talk on the phone... just the *way* she talks. With those... short, clipped sentences. It's like having a conversation with Captain Kirk. Can you imagine her on a book tour? *So... I'm signing... this book... for...?*"

"So, beyond her being the poster child for weird author syndrome and having the speech pattern of William Shatner, waddaya think?"

"Liked her idea about having the heroine hit her knees with the hot guy in chapter two."

"Stop it, Gretch. Though, looking back, I will admit that was pretty damn funny."

"No kidding. Seriously, while this is a very strange working situation going through her cousin, the author seems very receptive to your ideas so far."

"More so than Alexander. God, he fought me tooth and nail on every little thing."

"Yeah, but you still like him, right? I mean, romantically speaking."

"Sure. Gotta admire someone who stands up for what he believes. But geez, he's so attached to that book. It's like he wrote the damn thing."

"He's just being protective. You like men who are that way."

"Don't we all?"

"Yeah, but the white knight thing is a big plus for you. Keira, we have worked with some seriously bizarre people before and a lot of authors who are beyond difficult. So if she's agreeable to most of what you're suggesting, I wouldn't complain. *She's* the author, not him. It's *her* book. And she sounded like she'll be easy to deal with."

"True. The words on the page are the most important. But we still have one major problem."

"What?"

"We both know this will be a major bestseller. The announcement of the sale has already created some buzz and with this kind of advance the CEO is going to demand a tour. Eventually we're gonna have to find some way to get her out of the house."

"Sounds like we might not be able to fit her through the door, much less out of the house. Why not market her as a recluse? Sort of adds to the mystery."

"*You* wanna pitch that to our bean-counting boss? Cause I sure as hell don't. You do realize how many sales we'd lose without a book tour?"

Gretch nodded. "Yeah, I know. But we've got nine months to

figure this out. Sorta like being pregnant, huh?"

Chapter 8

Keira saw him leaning against the front desk, looking cooler than Sinatra, chatting with the doorman as she headed toward the lobby.

Dash. Perfect name for him. Must be short for Dashing. He fills out a suit like a model.

Her heel clicks on the white marble floor announced her arrival. Dash turned and smiled, giving her knee-length, long-sleeved Kelly-green dress with a single strand of pearls the quick up-and-down once-over. "You look terrific, Keira. Very classy."

"Thank you, kind sir, so do you. Much nicer without the coffee accessory."

"Well, I was gonna wear the barista shirt, but I had to give it back. Anyway, you hungry?"

"You will shortly discover that is a useless question with me. I'm always hungry."

"Right. I forgot how you demolished that huge sandwich the other day."

She playfully slapped his arm. "Hey!"

"I like a girl with a good appetite. Nothing worse than buying a date an expensive dinner and having her eat half of it in an effort to prove she's watching her weight."

"You'll never have that problem with me. Let's just say I believe it's a sin to waste food. As mom used to stay, kids are starving overseas. I would ask her where and she would say *Somewhere. Just eat.*"

"Anyway, I've got reservations so we need to roll. Our driver is right outside."

He stuck out his elbow and she looped one arm through it as they headed toward the door. Two women in their twenties walked into the building, spotted Dash, and practically tripped over their tongues staring at him. Their jaws hung open like a couple of trophy bass.

She smiled at them and gave Dash's forearm a gentle squeeze, her newfound confidence suddenly soaring.

The best-looking man she'd ever met was interested in *her.*

"Come on in. You're about to find out why I wanted to meet you at the restaurant instead of having you come here." Lauren closed the door behind Alex and he took in the sparse furnishings of the tiny one-bedroom apartment. A couch, a small table with two chairs, an old tube TV sitting on four cinder blocks, a couple of Broadway show posters taped to the walls. "Can't afford much on a waitress salary."

"Hey, I lived in one of these when I was starting out. At least you're in a safe neighborhood."

"True. Worth it to have a doorman. You know, to keep those ne'er-do-well single guys with bad intentions at bay."

"So how do you explain me getting past them?"

She flashed a devilish smile. "I make exceptions for certain intentions. And certain men."

"Ah. Oh, almost forgot. Speaking of improving on your waitress salary…" He reached inside his pocket, pulled out a business card and handed it to her. "I called a friend of mine who produces national television commercials. Turns out he's looking for a woman with a Southern accent about your age for a couple of spots. He said local actresses trying to fake the accent didn't sound authentic, and the ones that actually were from the South didn't have the right look. I described you and he said you might fit. Anyway, he's expecting your call."

Her eyes went wide as she stared at the card. "You did this for me? We just met. You don't even know me or my work. That's incredibly nice of you."

"Hey, it was a five-minute phone call to a friend, and you said you didn't have any connections. Now you've got one in the acting world."

"Do you know what the commercial is for?"

"Some new brand of sun block." He also knew his friend wanted a woman who could fill out a string bikini, and he had no doubt about Lauren's ability to do so, but he left that part out. As the guy had put it, *I need a girl who has the face of an angel with a body designed by the devil who sounds like she wants to do evil things to your body.*

She moved forward and took his hands. "God, Alex, thank you so much."

"You can thank me if you get the gig. Anyway, you ready to roll?"

"Sure." She grabbed her purse as they headed for the door. "By the way, how did you describe me? To your friend who makes commercials?"

He blushed a bit. "You're really trying to get inside my head, aren't you?"

"A girl's gotta know what the guy she's with is thinking."

"That's not really fair, is it?"

"Alex, women from the South don't play fair when it comes to men who interest them."

Dash commanded Keira's attention. Not because he was off-the-charts gorgeous (though that didn't hurt), but the fact that he was so damned interesting. It wasn't typical first date small talk; none of the discussion hit on favorite movies, likes and dislikes, how one grew up. Instead Keira listened intently to his inside stories of political shenanigans, amazed at some of the questionable tricks elected officials played to keep their jobs. The setting was spectacular as well; an outdoor rooftop restaurant with an amazing view of what was shaping up to be a beautiful sunset.

Dash pointed at her empty plate. "I've been doing all the talking. You need to let me catch up. Or I can order you another entree."

She noted he was only halfway through his dinner. "Sorry, I eat fast and food always tastes better when you dine alfresco."

"Alfresco?"

"Outside. For whatever reason the fresh air does something to food. Anyway, your stories are fascinating. When you get done with politics you ought to talk with one of our editors in the non-fiction division. This stuff would make a great tell-all book, and those tend to sell very well."

"I'd end up at the bottom of the Hudson if what I told you ended up in print. Anyway, enough about me, I want to know about you and that fascinating job of yours. Not many people get paid to read for a living. Though I'm sure there's a lot more to it than that."

She grabbed her wine glass, leaned back and took a sip as he went back to his entree. "You have no idea. There's editing, promotions, coming up with just the right cover... a ton of stuff that goes into every book."

He sliced off a bit of his rare filet mignon. "So what are some of those famous authors like to deal with? I gave you some inside stuff about politicians, now I want some dirt about writers."

"Well, Rose... you know, my best friend who you read about in that article, was what we call a dream author. She was worth a kazillion dollars but you'd never know it. Treated the interns the same as our CEO and her absolute favorite food was macaroni and cheese. She grew up without much and never really changed, appreciated the simple things in life. She used to say there were only so many lobsters you could eat when people asked her about being rich. As for the rest of our authors, it's pretty much a mixed bag. Some are easy to deal with, others... well, sometimes the editing process is the literary version of getting a root canal. A few were so difficult we let them go after their contracts were up."

"So, it's not all bottom line?"

"A lot of it is, but there's a point where some authors aren't worth the trouble, especially the ones that misbehave in public. Jill Howland, our publisher, is old fashioned. She likes decent people in our stable of writers. Doesn't want to be associated with those who end up on the police blotter. Or are rude to readers at a book-signing. When someone drops twenty-five bucks for your hardcover, the least you can do is be pleasant. And we've had a few authors we let go since they constantly missed deadlines. Then there are the quirky ones."

"Quirky?"

"One still writes on a typewriter because she's terrified of hackers getting into her computer and stealing her book. She calls it her old-school firewall. She keeps the original and sends me the carbon, and I didn't even know carbon paper still existed. We have to pay someone to transcribe it to a computer file. Another will only do book signings after six in the evening. Oh, but this latest one we just signed is shaping up to be a real jewel... very talented but she's an agoraphobe."

Dash swallowed and furrowed his brow. "A what?"

"You know, one of those incredibly shy people who is terrified to leave the house. And apparently she's morbidly obese, which might be part of the reason she doesn't want to go out in public. Get this, I'm working with her using her cousin as an intermediary, and the cousin is a guy."

"You're working on a romance novel with a man? Isn't that strange?"

"Yeah, first time for everything. But he knows the book like the back of his hand, acted as the author's proofreader as well. Anyway, he passes on my suggestions to her, then we all talk on the phone."

"So how are you going to do a book tour if the author won't leave the house?"

"Haven't figured that part out yet. And it's a stone-cold lock this one will be a huge bestseller. It's an amazing book."

"Do that many people buy books at a signing?"

"Yes, but there's also the goodwill involved. Meeting a famous author who's friendly... well, word gets around with readers. It also can go viral if an author is rude or a diva. So I've gotta be careful who I send out in public. When people stand in line for an hour to meet an author, they don't want to be brushed off. A pleasant word and a smile are worth a lot. A successful romance author really needs to realize that she's nothing without loyal readers, and creating good PR is a part of that process."

"Sorta like politics, in a way. Except your authors don't have to kiss a lot of babies. Or lie through their teeth."

A waiter came by and refilled her wine glass as a gentle breeze blew through her hair. Dash ordered dessert for both of them as she took in the view.

And then she saw him.

Alexander Bauer, talking to the maître d' at the front door.

With a brunette on his arm built like a Barbie doll.

Keira's eyes went wide as that newfound confidence deflated like a pricked balloon.

Dash noticed. "Something wrong?"

"Just saw someone I work with, that's all."

Lauren smiled as she handed the menu to the waiter, then waited for him to leave. "Nice to be waited on for a change."

Alex nodded. "So, how did our waiter do presenting the specials of the day?"

"Not bad, but I don't think he'll get nominated for an Emmy. Besides, the specials here aren't nearly as pretentious, so he doesn't have a great script to work with."

"I tended bar in college, but I imagine waitressing can be exhausting. And as for dealing with the public, ugh."

"You have no idea how people treat me. But what really

surprised me are the tips."

"That good?"

"That bad. You would think rich people who pay two hundred bucks for dinner would be good tippers, but noooo. Guess that's why they're rich."

"Well, it's not forever."

"Yeah. I could be slingin' hash at a greasy spoon back home. Which I have actually done. Nothing like having rednecks leer at you all day and picking cigarette butts out of coffee mugs. Then there were the men who spit tobacco juice into a cup before hitting on me. Not exactly the clientele I have up here. Back home you could get arrested for driving without a gun rack."

Alex laughed a bit. The girl was a natural quick wit. "That's funny."

"Would be if it weren't so true. You know the definition of foreplay back in my hometown?"

"No."

She dropped her voice to a masculine tone. "Get in the truck, bitch."

"Well, I can tell you're not exactly pining for home. So what was the final straw that made you decide to pack it up and move here?"

"Final straw?"

"Given a camel, there's always a final straw."

She glared at him. "You calling me a camel?"

"Of course not. I'm sorry—"

"I'm kidding! You obviously aren't familiar with my sense of humor yet." She lifted her wine glass and took a sip. "Anyway, as for the aforementioned final straw... besides the very shallow dating pool... I'd been doing okay in local productions and dinner theaters, paying the bills, but you're never going to get discovered in a small town. And I was always typecast."

"As?"

She pointed to her face. "Do I look like I could play a bad girl? With this face? I always got the Sandy from *Grease* type roles.

81

And when I did play Sandy the director told me I couldn't pull off the last scene."

"You mean when Olivia Newton-John comes out in black spandex?"

"Yeah."

A quick image of what Lauren might look like in a lacquered-on outfit whipped through his head. "I, uh, would guess you'd look good in that."

"You're sweet, but it wasn't about the costume. He said I had a really hard time looking trashy, or bad, or bitchy, or anything other than Miss Goody Two Shoes. So I figured casting people in New York might be more open minded and consider me for other types of parts. There was also no place for me to take acting classes back in Texas, and I enrolled in one the minute I got here. It's expensive but I think it's worth it."

"So have you tried out for bad-girl roles?"

"I got a rookie agent who sent me out on some things and I got a couple of callbacks, which is encouraging. My acting coach says I'm making good progress. Wanna see my naughty- girl look?"

"Sure. Hit me."

She narrowed her eyes a bit, then slowly slid her tongue over her ruby-red lipstick, at the same time running the toe of her shoe up his leg, stealing his breath. "So… am I convincing as a bad girl, Alex Bauer?"

"I, uh… think you'd impress Steven Spielberg."

Her smile and innocence returned.

And then everything in the restaurant stopped.

Check that, every woman in the restaurant froze. All staring at the front door.

Alex followed their gaze. And then he saw what had grabbed their attention.

Keira leaving the restaurant.

On the arm of a man so incredibly handsome every woman in the restaurant looked like she wanted to devour him.

Lauren also noticed and her eyes widened a bit. She cocked her head toward the front door, though she didn't have the same longing look as the rest of the women. "That guy somebody famous?"

"Don't think so."

She acted as if the man escorting Keira was just another guy. "That girl he's with…"

Alex sat up straight. "Yeah?"

"Can't see her face but her hair is gorgeous. I'd kill to be a redhead. I'm stuck with boring old brown."

He relaxed. "Lauren, I don't think you need to change a thing."

Chapter 9

Keira's eyebrows did a little jump as she licked her lips and made eye contact with her assistant. "Alexander will be in at three this afternoon."

Gretch carried two cups of coffee into Keira's office and set one in front of her boss. "And a good Monday morning to you too. So I guess that means your date with the *Soul Mate* cover boy didn't go well?"

"No, it was terrific. Good conversation, nice guy. Perfect gentleman. Great restaurant. Cheesecake was to die for."

Gretch plopped down on the chair in front of Keira's desk. "If you had a date with a guy who looks like a romance novel model and the dessert is the most important thing in the post-mortem, something ain't right. That's like someone trying to fix you up with an unattractive guy by saying he has a wonderful personality."

"No, we had a really nice time. But the cheesecake was killer."

"And yet here you are looking like a starving woman and counting the minutes until the guy who is merely cute gets here."

"I saw Alexander that night. He was at the same restaurant."

"That seems to be a trend. So, did he send over a bottle of champagne?"

"He didn't see me." She bit her lower lip and looked down.

"What?"

"He was with a girl."

"I assume it wasn't his smoking hot blonde friend?"

Keira shook her head. "Brunette this time. Couldn't see her face but built like the proverbial brickhouse. I'm surprised she didn't tip over. Probably hasn't seen her feet since she was fourteen."

Gretch waved her hand. "Eh, probably another silicone news babe he knows from TV."

"I dunno. They sure looked like they were on a date."

"That was the case with the blonde the last time. You thought they were on a date and they weren't. And may I remind you, dear boss, that *you* were on a date as well. There's a line about eating cake that would apply here."

"I know."

"And you were with a guy who you've told me looks like one of those computer generated men we put on our covers."

Keira nodded. "Gretch, I wish I had my cell phone video rolling. The man literally stopped traffic. You should have seen the hungry looks from all the women."

"So, let me get this straight. You were the one on the arm of the guy who looks like a Greek god, and yet you're jealous because the other guy you like, who is merely cute, is out with another girl."

"I'm not jealous. I'm… I don't know. Confused."

"So, Mister *Soul Mate*, what's his name? Dash? How did the date end?"

"Like I said, perfect gentleman. One really long goodnight kiss."

"Roman hands and Russian fingers?"

"Nope."

"Sparks?"

"Not sure if they're the right kind."

Gretch leaned back and folded her arms. "Okay, now *I'm* the one who's confused. What the hell does that mean? Sparks are sparks. They're all the right kind."

"I'm not sure if I felt something because he's so gorgeous and I haven't been kissed in forever or because I like him a lot. Or both.

Or maybe I was thinking about Alexander when I was kissing him."

"You were making out with the Greek god and you were thinking of someone else?"

"I don't know. Maybe. We were walking home and all I could think of was that stacked girl he was with."

"Good God, Keira, you need help. Or a roll in the hay. Maybe both. I could kill two birds with one stone and find a psychiatrist to sleep with you."

Keira turned and looked out the window. "I wonder what the deal is with that woman Alexander had on his arm."

"This is like high school all over again. You want Gretch to find out during algebra class while you go shop for your prom dress?"

She turned back to her assistant. "Bite me."

"So, basically, you want to date sexy cover boy and don't want any other women to date the other man you want to put on your dance card while you figure out how to deal with more than one name on said dance card for the first time in your life."

Keira shook her head and exhaled, then looked at the legal pad on her desk. She threw up her hands. "Whatever. Can we change the subject? We gotta get some work done."

"This is a helluva lot more interesting."

"Work. Now."

"Fine."

"So, what's the deal with the books I gave you to check out this weekend?" She ran her pencil down the notes on her legal pad. "*Dating Doctor Sexy*?"

"Literary malpractice. *Grey's Anatomy* it ain't. I'd rather play that *Operation* game I had as a little girl."

"So we're oh-for-one. How about the erotic book, *You've Got Male*?"

"Do you wanna read about a Meg Ryan lookalike dressing up like a slutty librarian and turning tricks to make up for lost sales in her independent bookstore?"

"Not really. So we're oh-for-two. That historical one set in Rome had a good query letter."

"*Caesar's Mistress*? I kept hoping for Brutus to stab *her*. *Et tu*, you little harlot."

"So we've already got the hat trick." Keira looked at the final entry on her list. "I'm almost afraid to ask about the paranormal romance."

"Pffft. Already wished it into the cornfield." Gretch shot her a serious look.

"What?"

Gretch looked to the side for a moment, then back. "Can we drop the supervisor-subordinate thing for a moment so I can give you some personal advice?"

"You've never been shy before. What, my mouthwash ain't makin' it?"

"No, not at all. But since these two men have come into your life, you... well, you need that take-no-prisoners thing going after hours. I mean, you still have it in the office, but when it comes to romance, the real-life kind, you have to channel your business persona. I'm impressed that you're actually considering dating two guys at the same time, but you need to let your hair down a lot more. Am I making any sense?"

"You saying I'm acting like a lovesick schoolgirl?"

"Yep. You need to kick ass and take names when you're out in the dating world, just like you do behind that desk. Keira the editor and Keira the single girl are two very different people right now, like that episode on Star Trek where Shatner gets split into good Kirk and bad Kirk."

"Soooo, let me get this straight... I'm bad Kirk at work?"

"You're bad-ass Kirk. You fire phasers and ask questions later. When you're on a date you're the opposite. You've got your shields down and if you're not careful someone's gonna fire a photon torpedo up your ass when you're not looking. Look at it this way... *you* have *two* great guys interested in you. *You* have the upper hand. Sweetie, it's the simple law of supply and demand here. There are two men in the supply and you're the only girl in demand. I'm not telling you to play games, cause that's not your style. But you need to be less—"

"Desperate?"

"I didn't mean—"

"No, you're absolutely right. It's been so long since I have been in a relationship. I guess—"

"You just want to be loved."

Keira nodded. "Don't we all?"

"Yeah. Just make sure it's on your terms. You're Keira Madison, for God's sake, the most powerful woman in romance literature. You *take* what you want. Sit up straight. Give me that gunslinger look."

Keira straightened her back and narrowed her eyes. "Better?"

"Yeah. Dash and Alexander need to see that girl."

"It won't scare them away?"

"It's the real you. Guys like girls with spunk. And any guy that doesn't isn't the right guy for you anyway."

"Very true."

"Hey, remember that old slogan Barney's department store had?"

Keira nodded as the memory of the vintage radio commercial popped in her head. "Select, don't settle."

"Sooooo?"

"I didn't shop there."

Alex got up as Juliette wheeled her suitcase into the apartment. "Welcome home. How was the trip?"

She parked it near the door and tossed her purse on the kitchen table. "Uneventful." She reached into her pocket and tossed him a pack of airline pretzels. "Didn't feel like eating dinner on the plane so I brought you a to-go bag."

"That's it for a five-hour flight from San Francisco?"

"Yes, along with the incredibly cheerful demeanor of the flight attendants. I swear to God, they must recruit people from the Department of Motor Vehicles. *Here's your pretzels. Sit down and shut up*."

"Well, I figured as much so I made you lasagna. It's in the oven."

"That's why you'll make someone a great wife. Speaking of possible significant others, how did your date go with Miss Texas?"

He smiled. "Very nice. Quite the tease. Flirted with me all night, then she was all over me when I walked her to her door."

"She invite you in?"

"Nope."

"Interesting, but it *was* a first date."

"True. Meanwhile, Keira was at the same restaurant. With a guy who could make Brad Pitt look average."

"Maybe it was another author."

"She doesn't have any male romance authors, remember?"

"Oh, right. So did you go over and say hello?"

"Didn't have the guts. She didn't see me anyway."

Juliette took his shoulders. "Okay, important question. Were you still thinking about Keira when you took the other girl home?"

He looked away. "Uh…"

"Ah, we're jealous. Better get a move on with the redhead. Unless, of course, you're smitten with the Texas girl."

"Maybe so."

"*Maybe so* you're smitten with Miss Texas or *maybe so* you're gonna get your ass moving with the redhead?"

"Maybe both. I dunno. Anyway, I'm heading over to meet with Keira at three."

"You guys want me to send out for a couple of beds?"

Keira looked up from her notes and saw Gretch standing in the doorway to the editing cave. She looked at her watch and saw it was nearly seven. "I had no idea it was that late. What are you still doing here?"

"My date works down the street and I didn't see any point in making him go all the way to Staten Island to pick me up. So I read some of the slush pile to kill some time."

Alexander leaned back from the table and stretched. "Anything interesting?"

"Couple of possibles. Listen, my aforementioned date had to give me a rain check at the last minute and we had a reservation at a really good restaurant… you two guys wanna use it?"

Keira looked at the stack of papers. "We still have a lot of stuff to go over before I get on a plane tomorrow."

Gretch locked eyes with Keira and shot her a wide-eyed look which told her that her assistant was playing matchmaker and she needed to get with the program. "You guys could keep working over a nice dinner. You do have to eat anyway, and Alexander doesn't need to see how cranky you get when you've missed your nighttime feeding."

Alexander laughed a bit. "That bad?"

Gretch nodded. "Like a vampire on a bloodlust bender. She can demolish anything in her path. She's got a roll of quarters in her desk for the snack machine. If you're smart, you'll never let her near your fridge."

Keira rolled her eyes. "Oh shut up. But you're right, I am hungry."

Gretch whipped out a slip of paper and handed it to her. "It's for seven-thirty so you'd better get a move on. Reservations are under my name."

Alexander stood up. "That's very thoughtful of you, Gretch."

"Hey, shame to let a great dinner go to waste. Takes forever to get reservations at that place. It's like the hottest restaurant in town. Supposedly it's gorgeous and the food is terrific."

Keira got up and stacked up her notes, maintaining eye contact while sending an unspoken message. "Thanks, Gretch."

"Don't mention it, boss. And remember to enjoy dinner while you're working."

The maître d' pulled out a chair for Keira as Alex took a seat opposite her at the table for two. Gretch wasn't kidding, the place was beautiful; though much too romantic for a working dinner. The antiques and classic paintings that were set off by candlelight made for a setting that was a far cry from the editing cave and gave Keira an almost angelic look as the flickering light made her hair shine like polished copper. The maître d' handed Keira a leather-bound menu, then gave one to Alex. "Someone will be along to take your order in a moment."

Alex nodded as the maître d' left the table, then turned to Keira. "Damn nice place."

"No kidding. Poor Gretch missed out on something good."

"The guy she's dating certainly has good taste."

"*Guys*. Plural. Gretch plays the field."

"Hey, she's young. Why not?"

Keira cleared her throat and raised one eyebrow. "You implying I'm old?"

"Absolutely not. I hope I didn't—"

"I'm kidding, Alexander. I love my thirties."

"Huh. I thought you were about twenty-seven."

"Nice save, mister. But I'll take it."

They were interrupted by the arrival of a waitress. "Well, hello there, Mister Bauer! Look who's dining at my table!"

Alex looked up and felt the color drain from his face.

Lauren.

Shit. How the hell did I not remember that she worked here?

"Hey, Lauren. I forgot this was your restaurant."

She looked around and lowered her voice to a whisper. "Hopefully not forever, thanks to you."

Alex looked at Keira, who was staring wide-eyed at Lauren. She had her hair up and wore horn-rimmed glasses, giving her a totally different look. "Oh, I'm sorry. Lauren, this is Keira Madison. She's the senior editor at Starstruck Books."

Lauren stuck out her hand and Keira shook it while giving Lauren's form-fitting red dress the once-over. "Nice to meet you, Keira."

"Likewise."

"Are you working on that book he told me about?"

His pulse skyrocketed as his eyes widened. The realization that he could get busted right here and now hit him smack in the face.

Oh shit.

Dear God, I told her I was the author—

Keira nodded. "I am."

Change the subject, quick!

"This is a really beautiful restaurant, Lauren."

Keira turned to Alex, studying his face as she folded her arms. "So, how do you two know each other?"

"We met in the drug store when she recognized me from TV."

"I just moved here from Texas," said Lauren. "I used to watch him on our news all the time." She turned back to Alex. "Anyway, I called your friend the TV producer and I'm going in for an audition tomorrow!"

Dear God, don't hug me. And don't call me Alex. "That's great, Lauren. I'm sure he'll like you."

The maître d' cleared his throat and Lauren saw him glaring at her. "Ah, the master beckons. May I take your drink order?"

"White wine for me," said Keira.

"Make it two," said Alex.

"Great. I'll be back to tell you about our special." She leaned down toward him. "Y'know, chicken 'n' rice and stuff like that."

Lauren headed for the bar. Alex turned and found Keira staring at Lauren, head propped up on one hand. "So, she an actress or model or something?"

"Struggling actress, like every waitress in New York. She mentioned she was having trouble getting parts and I put her in touch with a buddy of mine who produces commercials. He needed a Southern girl with an accent."

"God, she's really adorable. And I love her voice."

He shrugged, attempting to play it casual. "Seems like a nice person and you know how tough it can be in New York. Just trying to help her get started."

Keira looked back at him. "Aren't you the nice guy."

"Hey, it was a five-minute phone call to an old friend. No big deal."

"I'm sure it's a big deal to her."

"It will be if she gets the part. Anyway—"

Lauren returned and placed the two glasses on the table. "Here's your wine to get you started." She pulled out a small pad, then turned to Keira. "Before I tell you about our special, Keira, I have to tell you that your hair is such a gorgeous color. I am soooo jealous."

Keira couldn't help but smile. "Thank you."

"And I can tell it's yours from the freckles."

"Yeah, they're a dead giveaway. You want the red, you gotta play connect the dots."

"Always wanted to be a redhead. Alas, such is the life of a boring brunette." She looked around and noted her boss was not within earshot. "Anyway, tonight's pretentious-sounding special is fresh Chilean sea bass gently sautéed with organic truffles in Mediterranean chipotle lime butter topped with a bacon shallot cream sauce."

Alex chuckled a bit. "And what exactly is that?"

She wrinkled her nose and dropped her voice. "Fried fish with white sauce. Stick with the filet mignon and baked potato. Of course, that's not what it's called on the menu."

Keira laughed. "Sounds good to me. Medium rare."

Alex closed the menu. "Make it two. Medium rare for me as well."

"Excellent choice!" Lauren wrote the order down on her pad. "Two seared medallions of tenderloin gently topped with madeira demi-glace, hold the madeira demi-glace." She winked at Keira and headed toward the kitchen.

Keira chuckled as she watched Lauren walk away. "God, what

a personality! She's a pistol. I can certainly see her as an actress."

Alex picked up his wine glass and took a big sip, his heart still pounding while his shirt grew damp. "Yeah, she's certainly animated."

"Oh my God!" Keira turned back to him, eyes beaming. "You know what else I can see her as?"

"No, what?"

"The girl on the cover of your book! She has such an expressive face. She'd be perfect!"

Oh, shit. You gotta be kidding me. "Uh, the heroine is a redhead."

"So we'll put a red wig on her or Photoshop the color. I'm telling you, Alexander, she's perfect as Lexi."

"Well, along with the wrong hair color, Lexi is, you know, tall and thin. And Lauren is… uh…"

"Stacked? No shit. But it's a face I know can sell a lot of books. Besides, we can always do a little editing and give Lexi a padded bra. Or write her with a little more on top."

"I think our fictional heroine would need more than a little."

"Minor alterations, editing-wise. Trust me. I'll run it by your cousin, so don't worry. It's really not a big deal. And don't forget, covers sell books. And her face could sell a ton of books."

"Uh… okay."

Keira wore a huge smile. "How about that? I've been going through hundreds of stock photos, searching for the girl who should be the face of your cousin's book, and we find her in a restaurant. And it's someone you already know! Talk about serendipity."

"Yeah, what a coincidence." Alex quickly drained his glass, hoping to calm down. *Should have ordered a whole bottle.*

"Give me a call and I'll set things up for some test shots." Keira handed Lauren a business card as they got up to leave.

Lauren beamed. "Wow, that is so nice of you, Keira. This is the best tip I've ever gotten working here. But you should know I've never done any modeling."

"Not a problem. You've got the look I need, and the photographer I'm going to set you up with is very patient. Just remember, it's not like being live on stage. Digital film is pretty cheap. And you won't be alone when I find the right guy for the cover."

Lauren nodded, then turned to Alex. "Looks like something good happens every time I see you. You're like my guardian angel." She saw the maître d' staring at her again. "Thank you for dining with us, Mister Bauer, Miss Madison."

Alex exhaled as he dodged another bullet. "Good luck, Lauren. Let me know how it turns out."

Juliette leaned back on the sofa and folded her arms. "I feel like lately every conversation I have with you starts with *let me get this straight*."

Alex shrugged and shook his head. "I know. You can't make up stuff like this."

"So, let me get this straight. You already had a date with Miss Texas, who you like and who gave you a tonsillectomy at her front door, and are out having dinner at a romantic restaurant with the redhead, who you also like, and Miss Texas turns out to be your waitress and though she doesn't blow your cover the redhead takes a liking to her and wants to put her on the cover of your book that she thinks was written by your non-existent cousin played by your roommate who is giving an Academy Award performance as a morbidly obese agoraphobe with a potato chip obsession."

He nodded. "That about sums it up."

"You remember that third *Die Hard* movie, where the terrorist has that bomb made up of two liquids that are inert, but when you combine them they create a huge explosion?"

"Yeah, the binary thing. What about it?"

"That's a metaphor with these two women you like. And now that they've met, it's only a matter of time before the whole thing blows up in your face. Bada bing. I'll be scraping parts of you off the wall."

"So, do I come clean with Lauren and tell her not to call me Alex in front of Keira and not to say anything to Keira about me being the actual author?"

"Oh, what a tangled web we weave."

"Be serious, Juliette. I'm in a real bind here."

"If you tell Miss Texas the truth you'll be admitting you're lying to the redhead. Which might chase Miss Texas away since she'll see you as a guy who isn't honest. And then she might be so pissed off she'd tell the redhead. Which might chase *her* away. Wow, that's a new one… lose two women by telling the truth. You're right. You can't make this stuff up."

"So what do I do? I feel like I'm in too deep."

"Beats the hell out of me. We're in uncharted territory here. And, by the way, speaking of my faux three-hundred-pound weight gain, if there's another phone call coming up, we're out of potato chips."

Chapter 10

Gretch turned on her Jewish-mother accent, with the little uplifting lilt at the end of each sentence. "Sooooo? How did our dinner go with that nice young man?"

Keira leaned back and smiled. "Very well, Miss Matchmaker, thank you very much. He's terrific. But I already knew that. We had a really nice time."

"Ah, so good conversation is not the first thing on the dating post-mortem. Tell me more, tell me more—"

"What, are you the chorus from *Grease*?"

"Hey, I was home alone last night, so I need to live vicariously through you. Until tonight, anyway."

"I see."

"Besides, you owe me since without my suggestion you would have sat here editing with him till nine and sending out for pizza."

"Fine. And thank you for setting things up. That was a wonderful gesture. You missed a great restaurant. Sorry your date canceled on you."

Gretch furrowed her brow. "What date?"

"You said the guy you were supposed to go out with canceled at the last minute and gave you a rain check."

Gretch raised one hand and made a whooshing sound as she sailed her palm over her head. "Way over your head, sister. You

97

know, boss, for someone who works in the romance division sometimes you truly are clueless about dating in the real world."

"What?"

"You don't even know when you're being fixed up. *I* made the reservation for the two of you. I never *had* a date. Why do you think the reservation was in my name?"

Keira cocked her head to the side, bit her lower lip and gave her assistant a soulful look. "You did that for me?"

"Your loyal assistant knows you need a GPS when it comes to men who are not fictional."

"You're something else, Gretch. I can't thank you enough."

"So, dinner, details. Before you head out to the airport, preferably."

"Well, first of all, the waitress was a girl that Alexander knows, a wannabe actress who was waiting tables. Anyway, she's got the perfect look for the cover of *Ring Girl*."

"Wow, that's great! None of the tall skinny redheads on those stock photos did anything for me."

"Well, she's not skinny, or a redhead. She's a brunette who could actually be the poster girl for Hooters."

Gretch furrowed her brow. "Ohhhh-kayyyyy…"

"If she turns out to be as photogenic as I think she'll be, we'll use a wig, Photoshop, whatever. She's got the perfect features, great big eyes and an underlying sweetness. Too bad we don't need audio because she's got this beautiful Southern accent. Anyway, I'm sending her over to Bryan West to do some test shots and I'll need you to be there… make her comfortable, give her an idea of what we're looking for."

"Sure, no problem." Gretch licked her lips. "And I assume you want to see how she looks with a shirtless hunk."

"While I know you have ulterior motives for that suggestion, the answer is yes. Though we're going to have to do a search for the perfect guy as well."

"Happy to take care of that search, boss. Meanwhile, back to our regularly scheduled dating recap."

"Well, we didn't get any work done. That kinda went by the board considering the romantic setting of the restaurant. We're just really in tune. We were there so long talking they actually had to kick us out because the place was closing."

"And after dinner?"

"Since the restaurant, was, you know, two blocks from my place he walked me home. I tell ya, Gretch, I felt definite sparks."

"Sparks because he's cute, because you like him, or because you were thinking of Dash?"

"Hell, at this point I don't know."

"So, you invited him in?"

"It was late."

Gretch rolled her eyes and playfully slapped the side of her face. "Oh, I forgot, it was a school night."

"Stop it. Anyway, we didn't even kiss. He simply took my hands, told me to have a good trip and looked forward to seeing me soon. I got the feeling he might be worried about some sort of conflict of interest thing. But he gave me a look that went right into my soul and gave it a hug."

"Why didn't *you* kiss *him*? Let me guess… it was late."

"It wasn't the right time yet. Patience."

"Patience, my ass, you were scared to make the first move. Geez, you're still using the cat lady playbook. You're a New York woman, take the initiative."

"Maybe he's just shy."

"Fine, then lead. Trust me, and I know from experience, shy men *want* to be led. Meanwhile, where does this leave you with cover boy Dash?"

"I like him too and he asked me out for this weekend. But there's something about Alexander."

"And there's. something about Dash, too. Right?"

"Well… yeah. But it might just be physical."

"Your problem being?"

Keira threw up her hands as she stood up. "My problem being that I'm interested in two men and I have absolutely no clue how to deal with this and if what I'm feeling about one has something to do with the other or vice versa and I wish I could just combine the two of them into one guy and why does my love life have to be so damn difficult?"

"You know, when a woman goes into hysterical run-on-sentence mode that tells me one thing."

"What's that?"

"You're falling for someone."

"Yeah, but who?"

"That, dear boss, is something only you can figure out. But two men is still a nice problem to have."

Alex didn't recognize the phone number on his cell, but knew the area code.

Texas.

He figured it was Lauren calling. "This is Alex…"

"Hi, Alex, it's Lauren. I hope I'm not bothering you."

"No, not at all. What's up?"

"I had the audition with your friend this morning, and… I got the job!"

"Wow, that's terrific! I'm so happy for you!"

"We start shooting for real tomorrow, and it's one of those national commercials where I'll get residuals every time it runs. So if it really catches on I could be out of that studio apartment."

"Well, don't let the money burn a hole in your pocket."

"Oh, I won't. I'll still be waitin' tables. There's always that fifteen minutes of fame thing. But seriously, Alex, I cannot thank you enough for setting this up for me. And your friend is such a gentleman."

"Yeah, he'll treat you right, Lauren. So when will the spot hit the air?"

"A couple of weeks. I cannot believe how quickly this is

happening, but apparently the client wants to fast-track the commercial. I'll let you know when I get an actual schedule. But wait, there's more! There's also going to be a print ad! I'll be in a bunch of national magazines. Basically I'll be the face of the new product!"

"Wow, you hit the jackpot on this one."

"All because of you, Alex. So listen, I wanted to thank you in a special way and was wondering if I could cook you dinner this weekend."

"Sure, that would be great."

"Okay. Saturday at seven. Come hungry."

"Great, Lauren, see you then. And congratulations!"

He ended the call and within a few seconds it rang again.

His producer friend. "Hey, Roger, how's it going?"

"Going better since you sent me Lauren. Damn, I was having a heckuva time finding a girl for this spot, but she's perfect. And that accent is so authentic."

"Well, she actually *is* from Texas. I thought you'd like her."

"I may like her, but the camera loves her. And my God, what a body on that girl. They're gonna sell a boatload of that sunblock. She was born to wear a bikini."

"That good, huh?"

"Oh, you haven't seen her at the beach?"

"Just met her, Rog. But she filled out a dress very well, so I'm not surprised."

"You dating her, Alex?"

"We've had a lunch and a dinner."

"Well, you need to take her to the shore. Hell, if things work out you should move there and keep her in a bikini every day. Tell you what, I'll send you a clip of the audition tape. Enjoy, my friend. You lucky bastard."

"Okay. And hey, thanks for giving her a shot."

"Believe me, it was my pleasure. If I wasn't married… well, gotta go. See ya. Video coming your way. And don't watch it on your phone. You need a bigger screen for this one. It's gonna make your computer melt."

The call ended and Alex moved to his laptop just as Juliette walked into the room.

"So who's burning up your phone?"

"Lauren."

"Who?"

"Miss Texas, as you call her. And Roger called. I sent her over to him to audition for a spot and he hired her. She got a national commercial and a print ad."

"That's nice. Takes care of your good deed for the week. You've made a deposit in the karma bank. And I'm sure she'll be more than grateful."

"Maybe so. Anyway, he's sending me some video of her tryout. She's gonna be the face of a new product."

Her eyes lit up. "Ooooh, I wanna see the other girl who turned your head. Keira's competition." She looked over his shoulder as he turned on his computer. Alex logged into his email and saw the video had already arrived. He clicked on it and waited for the video to load.

His jaw slowly dropped as the video rolled. He stared at Lauren, filling out a red string bikini perfectly. The girl who seemed so sweet and innocent added a pout to smoky, smoldering eyes that made her look like a vixen from a men's magazine. She leaned back, shook out her long hair, then dipped her head and stared seductively into the camera through long eyelashes. Her gaze was almost hypnotic.

Juliette's eyes bugged out. "Ho-lee shit. *That's* Miss Texas? *That's* your idea of the girl next door?"

He slowly nodded, still riveted to the screen. "Uh-huh."

"Maybe if the girl next door was a porn star. Damn, what a body! And that look on her face… she's sexy as hell." Juliette leaned closer to the screen as the video cut to a shot of her bikini top, which seemed to be straining to keep her boobs in check. "Are those real?"

Alex shrugged. "Who cares?"

She slapped his shoulder as the video cut to a wide shot of Lauren turning around. "Typical man. But seriously, the girl is built. Look at those abs. Geez, you could bounce quarters off her ass. She's got an amazing body. I gotta get to the gym."

Alex kept staring.

She slapped him on the shoulder again. "You're supposed to say, *Juliette, you don't need to go to the gym.*"

He responded in a robotic monotone. "You don't need to go to the gym."

She rolled her eyes. "Very sincere. Hey, an alien just landed on our balcony."

"Uh-huh. That's nice."

"I'm taking all my clothes off right now and am planning to have my way with you."

"Uh-huh."

Juliette shook her head. "Men."

The video ended, Alex exhaled and leaned back. "Whoa."

Juliette ran her hand across his forehead and through his hair. "No shit, *whoa*. You're sweating."

Alex blushed as he leaned back and looked up at Juliette, who was laughing at him. "What?"

"Just funny seeing your reaction. You need a cold shower. I thought you said she looked cute and innocent?"

"She didn't look like that when I was with her."

"I think she's gonna be a little bit more than the *face* of the product. Hey, wait a minute... this is the girl who Keira wants for your book cover?"

He nodded. "Yep."

"But she doesn't look anything like your main character... and she's a brunette. The Lexi in your book is a tall, skinny redhead."

"They're gonna change her hair color. Photoshop or a wig. Who knows, maybe they'll dye it."

"Uh-oh. If that girl becomes a redhead, it's game over for you."

"Waddaya mean?"

"Hell, Alex, watching that video you needed a drool guard for your laptop like the ones they have in Chinese restaurants. Just think of what will happen if she becomes a Kryptonite girl. You'll be putty in her hands. Well, a part of you won't be putty."

"Very funny."

"But here's a question… were you thinking about Keira while you were watching that video?"

"Uh, no."

"Guess the candle is burning a little hotter at one end."

"Call me Gretch."

Lauren smiled and shook her hand. "So you're Keira's assistant?"

"Yeah. She'd be here but she had to go out of town. She sent me to make you feel comfortable."

"I'm going to feel uncomfortable?"

"You might since photo shoots for romance novels can get a little risqué. Some of the outfits we're gonna put you in aren't exactly from Catholic school. And you'll be working with another model."

"Oh, is another girl trying out?"

"It's a guy. This is a romance novel, remember? I assume you've seen some of the covers?"

Lauren began to blush. "Yeah. So the cover would feature me and—"

"A shirtless guy who looks like he was computer generated. Except he'll be real."

"Those men actually exist?"

Gretch smiled. "They do, and you're about to meet one in the flesh, accent on the flesh since he's not exactly Stephen Hawking. Anyway, I want you to remember that we can take as many pictures as we need, we're not in a hurry, and you're under no pressure. Keira just wants an idea of how the camera sees you, because not all attractive people are photogenic. Though I can certainly see for myself that in person you'd be perfect for this book."

"Thank you. I can't believe all this is happening. I just got a national commercial and a print ad. Before yesterday I'd never done any modeling."

"Well, consider yourself discovered."

Gretch looked at the monitor of the photographer's first shots and saw a face that jumped off the screen. It was clear that Lauren, despite the wrong hair color and a body type more suited for a stripper pole, had the look that would sell books. Her cell rang and she saw it was Keira. "Hey, boss."

"Just checking in on our photo shoot. How's it going?"

"You sure know how to pick 'em. She's really cute in person, but on camera… Keira, I've never seen a transformation like this. She looked like a girl in church one minute and the next she comes out of the dressing room oozing sex."

"Huh. I thought she had an innocence about her."

"She does, but still… it's hard to describe unless you see it. She's like the girl next door who looks like she wants to devour any man in her path. I'll have the photographer email you some shots when he's done."

"Have they done anything with the male model yet?"

"No, but they will shortly."

"Who'd you get?"

"Your favorite blonde six-foot-three hunk of beefcake."

"In other words, *your* favorite."

"Hey, he's reliable and always on time."

"Uh-huh. And that's always your top criteria."

"Plus, I think he's up to a seventh-grade reading level. I, of course, will be very thorough in briefing him."

"Yeah, I'll bet. Though with you 'briefing' has a double meaning."

"Why, Keira, do you think your trusted assistant would mix business with pleasure? Would I go fishing off the company pier?"

"Hell, Gretch, you've got a fully stocked tackle box. Anyway, email some shots when you're done."

"No problem, boss. I think we've found our *Ring Girl*."

Gretch looked over the photographer's shoulder as Lauren ran her hand across the male model's washboard abs, slid her pinky under his waistband and stared up into his eyes. Suddenly the photographer stopped shooting, turned to Gretch and whispered. "She's glowing. You wanna put some powder on her, or is this what you're looking for?"

Gretch noted Lauren's face and body were slightly damp, as it was obvious she was turned on by the male model. "Nah, this is perfect. And so natural. Usually you've gotta mist the models. She's obviously enjoying this."

"I was thinking the same thing."

Gretch noticed something else and dropped her voice. "And considering the fact that he's enjoying this as well, you'd better shoot above the waist."

Amazingly, Lauren emerged from the dressing room having returned to her innocent look, like some superheroine stashing her cape. She thrust out her lower lip in a pout. "I know, I was horrible."

Gretch couldn't help but smile. "Lauren, you were terrific. The camera loves you. The pictures came out great and I think Keira will be very pleased."

She exhaled and put her hand over her chest. "Seriously? I was worried I looked too nervous. My heart was going a mile a minute when I was with the other model."

"Ah, you enjoyed that part."

Lauren bit her lower lip as her face flushed. "That's putting it mildly. It was not exactly unpleasant. My goodness, that boy is seriously ripped. His muscles have muscles."

"Part of the fantasy we're selling with romance. Only he's real."

"Gretch, I thought I was gonna lose it when he picked me up

like a bride and I had my arms around his neck. He looked like he wanted to kiss me and carry me away."

"That's because he probably did."

"Oh, please, I'm sure a guy like that can get any girl he wants. A lot prettier than me."

"Don't sell yourself short, Lauren. You've got a special quality."

"Thank you, you're very kind. When do you think you'll make a decision?"

"I'll talk to Keira later today, but I know her taste and I think she'll love what she sees."

Lauren took her hands. "Thanks. And thanks for being here today."

"Not a problem."

"Well, off to my day job. But I think I'll need a cold shower first."

"You and me both, sister."

Chapter 11

"You do realize," said Gretch, "that you're about to throw a potential monkey wrench into your possible relationship with Alexander."

Keira leaned back in her chair. "How's that?"

Gretch pointed at the photos covering the table in the editing cave. "Uh, you're showing him the cover girl for his book."

"We do that with all our authors. What's the big deal?"

"The big deal is that she's incredibly hot. It's someone he already knows and she ain't exactly in the waitress uniform he's used to seeing her wear. It's not like some stock photo or a model we picked out of a portfolio."

"So, what, I shouldn't show him these?"

"It'd be like buying him a subscription to *Playboy*. He might see her in a different light and all of a sudden he's interested in her. You can just say you're going to use her and let him see the cover when it comes back from the art department. Besides, you haven't picked the guy for the cover anyway since you said the one I picked was all wrong."

"I suppose you're right—"

"Hey, you two." Keira looked up to see Alexander standing in her office doorway. He noticed the photos sprawled across the table. "Oh, you got the test shots with Lauren."

"And that barn door has officially sailed," whispered Gretch, using her favorite malaprop.

Keira stood up and extended her hand toward the table. "Uh, yeah, take a look." Alexander moved toward the desk and his eyes grew wide. "That's… Lauren?"

Gretch nodded. "Yeah. She's uh, very photogenic."

Alexander picked up one photo and stared. "Wow."

Keira sat down. "Yeah, that's what I said. I was expecting sweet and innocent and got… well, you can see what we got. She really comes across as very sexy."

Alexander looked at some of the other photos. "So you're not going to use her?"

"Oh, we're going to use her. You can still see that innocent quality come through, but there's a definite sexiness to it."

"Sorta like an R-rated Snow White," said Gretch, "with dwarfs named Horny and Sleazy."

Keira shot a look at Gretch and shook her head. "By the way, that's not the guy we're using. And we'll make her a redhead."

Alexander kept staring at the photos. "Wow."

"Yeah," said Keira, frowning as she looked at Gretch. "Wow."

Alex stretched out on the couch after the huge meal just as Lauren handed him a glass of wine and sat next to him. "Excellent dinner."

"Thank you, Alex. Glad you enjoyed it. And the least I could do for the man who got me that commercial."

"Hey, don't forget me when you're famous."

"God, I cannot believe all this is happening so fast. The commercial, the print ad. And I'd never even done any modeling."

"Speaking of modeling… I'm looking at the girl who will be on my book cover."

Her eyes widened. "Are you kidding me?"

"I was saving it for a surprise. Keira told me today and I asked her if I could break the news."

"Oh my God, Alex, that's incredible!" She leaned over and gave

109

him a strong hug. "I couldn't catch a break, and now all this." She broke the embrace and leaned back.

"So what's it like? Modeling, I mean."

"It's not exactly hard having your picture taken, though considering what I was wearing I felt a little nervous. I mean, very revealing stuff. The print ad for the sunblock was a lot easier than the book-cover shoot."

"Really? How so?"

"Well, I had to work with another model for the book. This guy who's apparently been on a lot of romance covers. The photographer had him lift me up and I had to look longingly into his eyes. He was really strong, held me up like I weighed nothing for like fifteen minutes. The man was huge, about six-three, incredible washboard abs, massive shoulders and a chiseled jaw, like what you'd expect on a romance cover. Seriously ripped. Is that what the male character looks like in your book? Perfect?"

The image of the photos he'd seen flashed through his mind and sucked the confidence out of him. He knew he was physically no match for the model, who had obviously made an impression on Lauren. "Uh… no." He looked down at his glass. "My character isn't, you know, perfect."

"Huh. I guess they put incredibly gorgeous men on all the book covers. Anyway— oh my God…" She reached out, took his chin and lifted it so he was looking at her. "Alex, please forgive me. That was really rude of me to talk about another man like that. I'm so sorry."

"No, really, it's okay."

She gave him a soulful look and it was clear she could see his hurt. "No, it's not. And I can tell it's not." She leaned forward, took his head in her hands and gave him the softest kiss he'd ever had. "Better?"

He offered a slight smile and nodded. "Yeah."

"Good. More where that came from."

"Earth to Keira?"

She looked across the table to see Dash studying her face. "Sorry, I've, uh, got a lot going on at work."

Liar. You were thinking about Alexander's reaction to seeing Lauren's photos and wondering if he was turned on and no longer interested in you and might be moving on to her now that he knows what she looks like without most of her clothes on and you're jealous of them even though you're sitting across from a Greek god… dammit, hysterical run-on-sentence syndrome again.

"Hey, I carry my work home too, Keira. Very soon you'll see me not listening to you like a typical man. If you even see me at all. That just means we're getting close to the election."

"Ah, so you're not a typical man and actually listen to women from, say, December to June?"

"Something like that. There's a lot of downtime in my line of work. Go like hell for six months, then become a couch potato until the next candidate comes along. I'm about to enter the 'go like hell' period. So if I don't call for a while, I'm not blowing you off."

"Hey, I understand. We both work in a high-pressure deadline-oriented business. So what's it like to be a freelancer? Do you ever worry you'll be unemployed?"

"There will never be a shortage of rich people who want to hold public office. And I'm pretty good at what I do."

She nodded and sipped her wine. "I have no doubt. Did you ever think of running for office yourself?"

He shook his head. "Nah. I like being behind the scenes. You can often get more done that way. I have a lot of friends in high places."

"So what do you do between elections?"

"Oh, travel, read a lot, binge-watch all the stuff I missed on Netflix. And, you know, after the first week of November I'll have more time to get to know you better."

She couldn't hold back a smile at the Greek god, who seemed to be locked onto her.

Keira wouldn't have to explain to Gretch why she didn't invite Dash in, since they were headed to his place. Supposedly he had some rare bottle of wine he wanted to share; while this would have constituted a red flag with any other guy, the fact that he was so devastatingly handsome trumped all. She felt special; a man who could have any woman, who was stared at by every woman at dinner, wanted to spend time with *her*. It was a teenage infatuation; she knew it, and yet she didn't care. She wanted to be Gretch for one night, throw caution to the wind, but Alexander was still sitting on one shoulder like some romantic Jiminy Cricket. Dash wrapped his arm around her shoulder as they headed into his building, her heart racing at his touch. They walked past the doorman into the elevator, then rode to the top floor and made their way to the end of the hall.

Dash opened the door and extended his arm. "Welcome to my humble abode. Excuse the mess."

Keira's eyes widened as she took in the living room, which looked like a political campaign headquarters. Dozens of signs from his candidate leaned against one wall; a dining-room table covered with brochures, buttons, bumper stickers, and a mountain of papers; the floor littered with a ton of newspapers and magazines while a map of New York State featuring a bunch of colored pins was taped to the wall. "You take your work home with you as well, I see."

"Occupational hazard. It looks disorganized, but I actually know where everything is. And I do have a maid come in once a year, whether it needs it or not."

"I've seen worse bachelor apartments. At least you don't have underwear hanging off the lamps and pizza sticking out between the couch cushions."

"Well, at least this place has a well-stocked bar. I do have my priorities. Make yourself at home. Relax, take off your heels."

"Best suggestion I've had all day." She kicked off her shoes and walked through the living room, stopping at a wall filled with framed photos, most of them showing Dash with famous politicians. But one featuring what looked like a very young Dash jumped out. "Hey, is this you in a previous life?"

"They're all me. Which one are you talking about?"

She pointed at a framed photo from a magazine of a very young man alone in an expensive gray suit. "I mean this one that looks like an advertisement."

He moved toward her and looked over her shoulder. "Oh, blast from the past. I put myself through college modeling for a menswear catalog. It's a well-kept secret. My sister framed that as a Christmas present years ago and insisted I hang it up."

"Huh. Well, you look better now."

"Thank you. Ready for that wine?"

"If it has aged as well as you have, bring it on, barkeep."

She followed Dash as he headed into the kitchen, reached into a wine cooler, pulled out a bottle with a faded label, opened it and poured two glasses. She noted the date on the label was from the 1960s. He handed one to Keira and held his up. "Cheers."

She hesitated. "No toast?"

He shrugged. "You want one?"

"Always. Especially if this is some rare vintage."

"Okay. To new relationships."

"Excellent." She clinked his glass and took a sip. The red wine was perfect; somewhere between sweet and dry. "Wow. You weren't kidding. This is fantastic."

"Whew. I was worried you were thinking the wine was a clever ruse to get you up here."

"You didn't need a ruse for that, Dash. And I'm honored you cracked open a fifty-year-old bottle for someone you hardly know."

He shrugged and shot her a smile that went right to her heart. "You seem like you're worth it."

The wine was strong, the alcohol going straight to her head. She was only on her second glass, but she'd had two at dinner. She steadied herself on the arm of his couch. "Whoa."

"You okay, Keira?"

"The curse of being skinny. When you're a tall drink of water you can't have too much wine."

"So it wouldn't cost much to get you drunk."

She wagged her finger at him. "Naughty, naughty." She walked around his apartment, stopping in front of the map. "So what are all the pins?"

He followed her. "Green are districts we've got locked up, yellow has a lot of swing votes, reds are areas we can't possibly win so we don't waste our time there. By the time a campaign is officially launched we've already got our preliminary polling done, so we can map out our strategy."

"Huh. And what sort of questions do you ask in the typical poll?"

Dash moved behind her and whispered in her ear. "Do you really want to hear about a boring topic like voting demographics?" He took her shoulders, turned her around, took her empty glass and set it on the table. "Personally, I hate talking about focus groups when I have a beautiful redhead in my apartment."

She melted at his words, her inhibitions way down from the alcohol. "I see. Do you have beautiful redheads here often?"

"You're the first."

Dash gently took her face in his hands and kissed her, softly at first, then with more passion. Without her shoes on she had to get up on her tiptoes. Keira couldn't stop, her hands with a mind of their own, sliding up his chest and around his neck, enjoying the feel of his rock-hard muscles under his shirt. Their lips finally parted and she went back down on her heels. She found herself craning her neck to look up into his incredible eyes. "Mister, you are awfully tall."

"I can fix that." He crouched down, placed his hands under her hips and effortlessly lifted her. She wrapped her legs around his waist, locking her ankles. "Better?"

"Much."

"Wouldn't want you to get a stiff neck."

She began to kiss him with a hunger she'd long since forgotten. Finally Keira came up for air and leaned her head on his shoulder, breathing in his earthy cologne as she ran her hands across his back. "You're right. This beats talking shop."

"I certainly agree."

The wine, the incredibly attractive man holding her… if he wanted to take her right now she was powerless to resist. She would deal with the Alexander situation later. "I assume you aren't going to carry me around all night and have a destination planned."

"I was thinking the couch might be good. I like to take things slow, Keira. If that's okay with you."

Any tension she might have had left immediately disappeared. She leaned back and smiled at him, somehow disappointed and relieved at the same time. "That's wonderful with me."

Alex gently turned the key and opened the door, hoping not to wake his roommate at this hour. But he was surprised to find her still up. "Hey, figured you'd be asleep."

"Well, look what the cat dragged in." Juliette looked at the clock. "My, my, out past your curfew. Must have had a good time with the, uh, 'girl next door.'"

"Yeah, that initial description may have been off base a bit."

"Well? So where are we with bikini girl?"

Alex reached into his pocket, pulled out a bunch of photos and handed them to Juliette. "Well, she now has more in her modeling portfolio. Test shots for the book cover."

Juliette's eyes went wide. "Hot damn."

"She looks great, huh?"

"Sweetie, I wasn't looking at her. Who's the guy?"

He shrugged. "Beats me. Some model."

"Some model? Uh, what am I, chopped liver? Have you forgotten your roommate is on the market? Do some research, will ya? Get me in on these photo shoots."

"Fine, I'll find out who he is. Though he's not the guy who's gonna be on the cover."

She looked at the photo again and licked her lips. "Damn, I don't know why."

"But he's part of the reason the date went so well."

"Ah, she worked up her appetite at the photo shoot and had dinner at home?"

He blushed a bit. "Well, thanks to that guy things did heat up a bit. She was going on and on about how hot he was, noticed me looking a bit inadequate and basically apologized for a few hours."

"Ah, your wounded doe look, I know it well. So how far did this... apology... go?"

"As far as the couch. So to answer your next question, Keira is still in the picture."

Keira bit her lower lip and looked down at her desk. "Alexander is coming by for dinner."

Gretch dipped her head to get a better look at her face. "And why are we wearing our 'I need to go to confession' face?"

She looked up and was unsuccessful holding back a smile. "I had a really good time with Dash this weekend."

"Ah, and the Catholic guilt rears its ugly head. Do you actually *have* to go to confession?"

"Considering the amount of lust I expended, I'd have to find a priest who is free for an hour."

Gretch took the chair opposite Keira's desk. "Details. Spill."

Keira shrugged. "Went back to his place after dinner—"

"You little tramp."

"No, we didn't end up in the bedroom. We just made out like teenagers on the couch."

"Well, for you, that's major progress."

"He said he likes to take things slow."

"Sounds perfect for you. A romance at the pace of continental drift. For an engagement gift I'll get you an AARP subscription.

116

Meanwhile, in light of said makeout session, I'm surmising you feel guilty about seeing Alexander today."

"Well, he's not coming by for editing or anything else. He simply asked me to dinner."

"Aha!"

"What, *aha*?"

"*Aha* he's making a move on you."

"You think?"

"Taking you to dinner for no reason other than he wants to spend time with you. I'd say that's a move. Anyway, I've been meaning to tell you… you really need to bring Dash by so I can check him out with my foolproof bullshit detector."

"Speaking of which, I assume Alexander didn't set it off."

"Nah, no red flags. He's a good guy. You'd be lucky to end up with him. However…"

Keira sat up straight, eyes wide. "However?"

"He's not an open book. It might take you a while to peel back the layers."

Chapter 12

Keira couldn't stop smiling when Alexander held the door for her as they left the restaurant.

Two nice guys. Confusing, yet fun. Like Gretch said, nice problem to have.

I could get used to this.

She started heading up the street when he suddenly took her shoulders and swapped places with her, leaving her on the inside part of the sidewalk. "You're on the wrong side, young lady."

"There's a wrong side of the sidewalk?"

"My mom taught me that when a man is walking on the sidewalk with a woman, the man walks on the outside."

"Really? Why?"

"Well, if a car jumps the curb, it will hit the man first and the woman will be saved. And during the winter you won't get splashed with slush. Or rain during the summer. Either way, the woman is protected. Anyway, that's what mom said. She's very old-fashioned and I think it's a New York thing. She'd let me have it big time if she saw me walking on the inside."

"Hmmm. I'd never heard that, but I kinda like it." She looped one hand around his elbow and rested it on his forearm. "Very chivalrous. Kinda like Jamison in *Ring Girl.*"

"Uh, yeah. Guess so."

"Your cousin oughta put it in her next book."

He nodded. "Yeah. Excellent idea. I'll tell her."

"She *is* working on it, right?"

"Oh, absolutely." Suddenly he slowed down a bit.

"You forget something in the restaurant?"

He put his hand on her forearm. "Hang on a minute." He stopped in the middle of the block and squinted straight ahead. The sound of police sirens grew louder, blending with a few screams.

Then Keira saw them.

Two men running toward them in the middle of the street, with guns. Chased by four cops.

One turned around and fired at the police.

She became a deer in the headlights, frozen by the scene taking place, when she felt his hand grab her by the collar and shove her to the ground.

Several shots rang out as Alexander dove on top of her, covering her face with his arms. Glass shattered above them and shards rained down. Her heart rate rocketed. She tried to turn her head to see what was happening but Alexander held her down. "Keep your head down, Keira!"

More shots, more sirens. Then, suddenly, it all stopped. Dead silence on a New York street. Finally, after what seemed like an eternity, a cop yelled, "It's all over, folks."

She felt Alexander get up and she did the same, brushing herself off. The two gunmen were dead, lying face down in the middle of the street, blood beginning to pool around their heads. "Oh, my God!" Her heart slammed against her chest as the bile rose in her throat. She put her hand over her mouth and started shaking.

Alexander turned her head with his hands and looked her right in the eyes. "Hey, it's over. Breathe. You okay, Keira?"

"That was unbelievable." She put her hand over her heart but it didn't downshift.

He took her shoulders, giving her a serious look. "Are you *okay*?"

She saw his forearms were scraped and bleeding a bit. "Me?

119

Look at you."

He shrugged as he held them up. "Just a few scratches. Are *you* all right?"

"Yeah. But you scraped the hell out of your arms on the sidewalk." She noted small pieces of glass covered his back and a few were in his hair. "And you've got broken glass all over you."

He ran his hands through his hair, shaking out the bits of glass, while she brushed off his back. "I'm fine." Incredibly, he was perfectly calm.

"You're bleeding."

He took out a handkerchief and wiped his arms but it didn't stop the blood from oozing. "Well, I'm not going to the emergency room for this."

"Fine, but you need attention and my place is just up the street and we need to wash your arms with peroxide and get them bandaged up because you could get an infection and God knows what germs are on the sidewalk—"

He put one finger on her lips. "We need to get you away from this. Now. You're safe, Keira. Breathe." He took her arm and led her up the street. She couldn't help but look back at the bodies in the street.

And then it hit her like a lightning bolt.

He would have taken a bullet for me.

"Hold still." She grabbed one of his wrists and held his arm over the bathroom sink. He jerked while she poured the peroxide on his forearm.

"Sorry. It stings like hell, Keira."

"I know. But we have to do this. Stop fidgeting."

"Yes, Nurse Ratched."

"Funny." She cleaned the scrapes with a washcloth, put ointment on them, then wrapped his arm in gauze. Trying to focus on her task while the image of the shootout kept replaying in her mind. "Okay, one down, one to go. Next arm."

"Yes, ma'am."

"Don't call me ma'am, I'm not old."

"Okay. Miss."

He held his other arm over the sink and grimaced as she poured the peroxide. The second arm was worse, the cuts deeper. She gently picked a few flakes of gravel out of the wounds with a pair of tweezers, causing him to wince each time, then set about cleaning the arm. But the scene in her head was on an infinite loop. Every time she saw the shootings she kept coming back to that one thought.

He would have taken a bullet.

She applied the ointment and started wrapping the arm with the gauze. "Almost done."

"You're quite the Florence Nightingale."

"My college roommate was a nursing student. I picked up a few things." She looked up and saw him smiling. "I need to ask you something, Alexander. What the hell were you thinking?"

"What do you mean?"

"I mean, the bullets started flying and you got on top of me like a human shield. You could have been shot."

"So could you."

"You're missing my point."

"Look, as a reporter I've been in some dicey situations. Self-preservation takes over. It's instinct. You have to hit the ground when something like that happens. You're not used to seeing stuff like that, I am. You froze and I got you out of the line of fire, that's all."

She bit her lower lip, felt her eyes well up as the words grew thick in her throat. "You don't understand." Her voice cracked. "What you did was not instinct. You covered me up. You *protected* me. If a bullet came our way it would have hit you, not me. You risked your life for mine and we hardly know each other."

"We know each other well enough. Any man would have done the same."

"Like hell! Half the guys I know would have hid behind *me*. Alexander, you act like what you did was no big deal."

"It wasn't."

She finished wrapping his arm as a single tear ran down her cheek. He noticed and brushed it away with his thumb. "Well, it sure was to me." She locked eyes with him, then leaned forward, took his head in her hands and kissed him, soft and long.

And as soon as their lips parted, she knew she'd made a mistake.

"Oh my God, Alexander, I'm so sorry."

"Sorry for what?"

"That was really unprofessional. I mean, we're working together and—"

He put one finger on her lips as he smiled at her. "I cannot believe you."

"Like I said, I'm sorry—"

"Keira, I cannot believe you're apologizing for giving me the best kiss I've ever had."

Her lips began to quiver and she felt the waterworks about to blow. Alexander noticed, took her into his arms and gave her a strong hug. The tears started to roll down her cheeks. "You risked your life for me. I will never, ever forget that."

He gently stroked her back, broke the embrace and wiped her tears. "Now you know why men walk on the outside of the sidewalk."

Keira doodled on her legal pad as she tried to sort out the puzzle.

"Ah, my boss is deep in thought. And you left your coffee on my desk." Gretch entered the office and set a cup of coffee in front of Keira, then sat down and began to sip her own. She studied Keira's face. "What's wrong?"

"That's the problem. Nothing."

"Ohhhh-kayyyyy…"

"Nothing at all. And it's becoming a bigger problem."

"Y'know, you get more and more confusing the longer I know

you. So please explain because I forgot my Keira Madison decoder ring."

Keira looked out the window. "Everything's wrong because nothing's wrong. Don't you understand?"

"Hang on, let me call the IT guy and get you rebooted. You're obviously locked up and have been taken over by Skynet."

She turned back to Gretch. "Alexander and Dash. Both guys are great. Gentlemen. Sweet. Decent. Fun. Terrific personalities. Easy to talk to. My type with a capital T. And last night…"

Gretch's eyes widened. "Ah, so you and Alexander—"

"No. Did you see the news last night? The story about the shootout?"

"Yeah, like the Wild West in Manhattan. It's on every front page. What does this have to do with your love life?"

Keira picked up a remote and pointed it at a flat-screen television hanging on the wall. "Someone captured the whole thing with a cell phone. Pay close attention to the background, what's going on in front of the luggage store." She hit the play button and the video of the newscast rolled.

"I still don't understand what this has to do with your date." Gretch got up, moved toward the screen and squinted. "What am I supposed to be seeing?"

Keira backed up the video and paused it. "The couple in front of the luggage store. Look familiar?"

Her eyes widened. "Oh my God, that's you and Alexander! Geez, Keira, you guys were there? You could have been shot!"

"Here's why I wasn't. Watch closely." She hit the play button again, then activated the slow-motion feature. The video showed Alexander shoving her to the ground and getting on top of her as the bad guys and cops ran past, guns blazing, a bullet shattering the window above them and raining glass down on Alexander.

"Ho-lee shit! Damn, Keira, he—"

"Protected me. With his life." She paused the video. "He would have taken a bullet for me. He risked his life for me and he barely

123

knows me."

Gretch moved closer to the screen, then turned to Keira. "Sonofabitch, you got yourself a real-life old-fashioned white knight. His stock just rose quite a bit."

"No kidding. But…"

Gretch turned back to the television. "But what?"

"I may have made a huge mistake. He got his arms all scraped up when we hit the ground, so I took him back to my apartment to get him cleaned up."

Gretch whipped her head around. "Why was that a mistake?"

"Because it led to—"

"You slept with him?"

"No! I got real emotional about him protecting me and… I kissed him."

"Oh, the horror! Let me call the Cardinal at Saint Pat's and see if I can get you special dispensation."

"Stop it."

"Sorry, still waitin' for the mistake in this story."

"I shouldn't have kissed him. It was too forward of me. But I immediately apologized, so hopefully that served as damage control."

Gretch frantically waved her hands. "Whoa, hold on. You kissed him and then *apologized*? Who *does* that? I'd hate to know what you do after sex."

"You don't understand. It was the wrong time."

"What was his reaction?"

"He smiled and said I had no reason to apologize for the best kiss he ever had."

"Please tell me after hearing that you kissed him again."

"No."

"Please tell me he kissed you."

"No, because I started crying, so he held me."

"Keira, what the hell is wrong with you?"

"Look, a man just saved my life and I saw two dead people shot

124

in the head and I was emotional and…" Keira heard a commotion in the office and glanced through the window looking out over the office. "…and meanwhile, guess who just arrived to take me to lunch and make me even more confused?"

Gretch turned around and saw Dash being swarmed by the staff. Her jaw slowly dropped. "Wow. *That's* Dash?"

"Uh-huh."

She licked her lips as she stared at him. "So you got one guy who saves your life while thinking you're a great kisser and another who looks computer generated. You're right, sweetie. Nothing's wrong. Damn, you really do have a hell of a problem."

Keira elbowed her way through the horde of women surrounding Dash and took his arm. "Sorry if you've been mauled. We don't get a lotta guys up here."

He smiled and she noticed most of the women had their heads cocked to the side, practically drooling. "You have a very nice staff. It's a pleasure to meet all of you."

"C'mon, I'll have you dusted for prints and then give you the quick tour." She led him back to her office through the disappointed looks from the staff. Gretch was waiting with big eyes. "Dash, this is Gretch, my assistant. Gretch, this is Dash."

He took her hand and Keira could see Gretch swallow hard as she looked up at a man at least a foot taller. "Gretch, it's a pleasure."

Gretch managed a soft, "Uh-huh."

Keira bit her lip, trying not to laugh. She'd never seen her assistant at a loss for words around a man, even at photo shoots when she was with those shirtless gods who posed for book covers. "Anyway, this is my office, and through that door is what we refer to as my editing cave."

Dash nodded as he looked at all the framed book covers that lined the walls. "You edited all of these?"

"Yeah. Gretch helped on most of them. Every one is a best-seller."

"Wow. Impressive. You're obviously very good at what you do."

"That's why they pay me the big bucks."

Keira's line rang and Gretch took the call, still staring at Dash. "Keira Madison's office, this is Gretch... oh, hi Bella, she's right here." She put the call on hold. "It's Bella."

Keira gave Dash an apologetic look. "I'm sorry but I absolutely have to take this call. Gretch can give you the tour and by the time you get back I'll be ready to go."

Gretch looped her arm around Dash's elbow. "Be more than happy to, boss."

"And this is where the magic of book covers happens, our art department. Oh, and our boss is here today." Gretch opened the glass door and led Dash inside. "This is our publisher, Jill Howland, and our art director, Cassie Knowles. Guys, Dash Riley."

Jill's eyes widened as she looked up at Dash and shook his hand. Cassie, the pert, thirty-something brunette artist looked away from the huge monitor on her desk and turned to them. She slid her glasses to the tip of her nose and checked out Dash. "Well, hello there. Are you the new model?"

Jill leaned toward Gretch and whispered. "Damn, I sure hope so."

Dash blushed a bit. "No, I'm just visiting."

"Friend of Keira's," said Gretch. "Giving him the quick tour of our operation. Cassie, I assumed you wouldn't mind showing him what you do."

"I certainly don't mind at all."

Dash moved around behind the artist and looked over her shoulder. "So, you're creating a book cover?"

"Trying to," said Cassie, turning back to her work. "Though the untrained eye may think I'm wasting time looking at porn." The screen was filled on one side with a dozen photos of shirtless hunks and on the other with a bunch of heart-shaped graphics and a color palette. "I've got the girl for this one but every guy I Photoshop in with her doesn't look right. They don't have what I call 'artistic chemistry.'"

126

Jill moved next to Dash and looked over the other shoulder. "Cassie prefers them to look like a couple."

"Right," said the artist, who clicked on a folder that brought up several past book covers. "See, these people go together."

Dash nodded. "You're right, I see what you mean. They look like couples."

"I like to get the models squared away and then work with the concept that Keira has given me for this particular book. But so far, none of the male models or stock photos I've used seem right. They all look like androids compared to the girl. She has a very unique quality that I've really not seen before. Innocent but sexy, if that makes any sense. I need a guy who doesn't necessarily have everything on display, if you get my drift. I still need someone incredibly good looking, but someone whose personality shines through his face." The artist clicked back to the screen featuring the models.

Dash studied the photos. "I thought the shirtless guys were required to sell romance novels."

Jill nodded. "Very often they are, but this is a very special book known as a 'sweet romance.'"

"That means there are no sex scenes in it," said Gretch. "Not my taste, but they do sell a lot. Though this particular book that she's working on is fantastic."

"Anyway," said the artist, "Keira knows it will be a best- seller. And she's never wrong when it comes to book covers. That's why they call her Cover Girl. Anyway, we need a unique quality that goes beyond the basic pecs and six-pack." She turned and looked up at Dash. "You ever do any modeling?"

He chuckled a bit. "Back in college for a men's suit catalog. Ancient history."

The artist turned to Gretch. "You know, he might be just the type… maybe I've been looking for the wrong kind of guy. I know he doesn't really resemble the male love interest in the book, but he's got that twinkle in his eyes like the girl and that does convey

127

the personality of the character—"

Dash shook his head and put up his hand. "Whoa, hold on. I, uh, already have a day job."

Cassie grabbed a camera and stood up. "Humor me, will ya? Let me see how you look with our heroine. C'mon, it won't hurt. You don't have to be an actual model, I just want to see if your type is what I need to be looking for. You've got that look which says you're up to something."

"Probably because I am."

"Good to know," said Gretch.

Cassie held up the camera. "So can I take your picture?"

Jill gently took his forearm. "C'mon, Dash, be a sport."

Dash shrugged. "Fine. Knock yourself out."

"Smile, and then don't smile." The artist pointed her camera and took a few shots of Dash. "Thank you. As they say on Broadway, we'll let you know."

"Sure. By the way, who's the woman you've already picked for the cover?"

The artist turned back to the computer and clicked her mouse, the screen filling with one of Lauren's photos.

Dash's jaw slowly dropped as his eyes bugged out.

Chapter 13

Alex and Juliette headed to lunch near Times Square, going over another phone call that would be coming from Keira.

"So," said Juliette, "she's gonna ask me to change the physical characteristics of Lexi to approach those of Miss Texas. And you want me to agree, argue, be a difficult diva, what?"

"Don't just cave in immediately, but be receptive to it. Tell her you understand that the cover is critical to the success of the book and that you defer to her judgment."

"Got it. What else?"

"She's not wild about the foreshadowing in chapter six. Thinks it gives away too much."

"Is that where Lexi meets the guy who's wrong for her?"

"Yeah. She wants to edit most of it out."

"Do you have a problem with that?"

"I do, but she knows a helluva lot more about the genre and I trust her."

"Very good, you're admitting women are smarter. You'll make someone a great wife."

"Smartass."

"Okay, Alex, what else?"

He went over the high points as they walked. "I think that about covers it."

"Fine. Meanwhile, in light of the woman taking the lead and kissing you, where are you on the romantic front?"

"You mean with Keira?"

"Sorry, I forgot you have more than one woman taking charge romantically. Yeah, Keira."

"What happened the other night was different than with Lauren… that was the usual making out at the end of a date. Keira was freaked out over the shooting, very emotional. I'm not sure if her kissing me was the result of what happened or something else. With her, I don't know, it was like she saw me in a different light all of a sudden."

"Probably because you may have saved her life."

"Still not sure how she feels. It was only one kiss. But a damn good one."

"So she's in the lead over Miss Texas?"

He was about to answer as they reached a corner in Times Square. What Alex saw stopped him dead in his tracks. "Oh. My. God."

"What?"

He pointed up at a video billboard.

Juliette looked up and saw it. "Well, I guess you just got another variable thrown into the equation. This is one hell of a love triangle."

Alex stared at the huge television screen filled with Lauren in a bikini, looking even more sultry than the stuff he'd already seen. Long hair swept over one shoulder, smoky eyes, nearly spilling out of her top, mouth slightly open as she looked at the sunblock in front of it, the bottle of which was an obvious phallic shape. The video looped to the beginning after ten seconds.

Juliette shook her head. "If your jaw hangs open any longer you'll be get recruited by Wal-Mart as a mouth-breathing cashier."

The traffic cop in the middle of the intersection pointed at them and the rest of the crowd waiting to cross the street. "C'mon, c'mon! Let's go! We're walkin' here!" he yelled, using the classic

Dustin Hoffman line as he stood in the middle of total gridlock. Alex and Juliette crossed the street as the officer tried to direct traffic and relieve the congestion. But too many male drivers were leaning out the window staring at the video. Alex was still locked in on Lauren's advertisement as he passed the cop and walked right into the fender of a car. "Jeez, watch where you're going, buddy," said the cop, who shook his head. "Just what I need, pedestrians running into cars."

They zig-zagged through the traffic jam and reached the other side of the street, where the corner was clogged with men looking up at the billboard.

"Wonder who the lucky bastard is hittin' that?" said a hard hat.

"She can rub sunblock on me any time," said another.

"Rather rub it on her," said a third.

Juliette squeezed Alex's elbow. "I think the entire city is all of a sudden envious of you."

"Uh-huh."

"So, you were saying about Keira?"

"Huh?"

Keira headed right for Gretch's desk after lunch and cocked her head toward her office. "Okay, I want your opinion."

Gretch followed her in and shut the door. "How was lunch?"

"Had a terrific pastrami sandwich."

"Hello! I wasn't asking about the food."

"Oh. Dash was great company, as usual."

"No afternoon delight?"

"Of course not. And now I'm gonna have that stupid song stuck in my head for the rest of the day. So what'd you think of him?"

"First impression or the total package?"

"Whatever. Though I assume with you they're the same."

Gretch sat down and crossed her legs. "Well, you're right, the guy is incredibly good looking. And, damn, he's really tall but I'm sure he's worth the climb. I'd like to rappel down him. I mean, he had half the staff walking into walls and the other half needing drool buckets. I'm not sure if I've ever seen a more handsome man and he blows away the models we use on book covers. If we're comparing purely on physical appearance between him and Alexander, it's no contest. I mean, Alexander's cute but Dash is off-the-charts smokin' hot. I'd do him in a New York minute."

"You'd do the guy at the hot dog cart in a New York minute."

"Who, Javier?" She shrugged. "Yeah, I guess you're right. He's doable."

"What about your bullshit detector?"

"It didn't go off. I mean, he seems like a decent guy, polite, opens doors for the women, actually listens when you're talking. Then again he might have been on his best behavior to make a good first impression on the staff."

"Nah, Dash is always like that."

"So far. Remember, you haven't known him that long. You're still in the dating honeymoon period. Down the road he could morph into a reclining chair that belches and orders you to bring him a beer, then uses his pot belly as a TV tray."

"True. Though I can't imagine Dash ever having an ounce of fat."

"Anyway, it's hard to give you my complete opinion since I haven't spent as much time around him as I have with Alexander, who I like a lot and think is a good match for you. But…"

Keira sat up straight, eyes wide. "But… what?"

"Look, Keira, guys who are that attractive know it and also realize they can have any woman they want."

"So you're wondering why he wants someone like me."

"I didn't say that. And, by the way, any guy would be an idiot not to want you."

"Thanks. But I don't stop traffic like he does."

"I'm just saying guys who look like that often feel like they have the upper hand in the relationship because they know they can get another woman in a heartbeat. Which is why you need to be yourself with him. Don't be on your best behavior. Don't walk on eggshells worrying you might lose him. Kick ass and take names. Take no prisoners and take no shit. If he still sticks around after you show him you're his equal, then he might be a keeper."

"Might?"

"The other guy may have saved your life. Pretty hard to top something like that. If he'd take a bullet for you after knowing you for such a short time, imagine what he'd do as your husband."

"So what do I do?'

"Keep burnin' your candle at both ends, sweetie. But now that I've seen Dash, I want first dibs if you end up with Alexander."

"I figured as much. So I assume you're rooting for me to end up with Alexander so you can have Dash."

"I'm not rooting for either guy, but given the choice of leftovers, again, it's no contest."

"Though you may remember he likes to take things slow."

"Keira, I know how to make men hit the accelerator. By the way, if you ever get to that stage where you draw a line down the middle of the pad and compare them, there is one sure-fire way to break the tie."

"What's that?"

"The point is moot since I know you're not the type to do it."

"What????"

"Find out who's better in bed. If you're gonna spend a lifetime with someone, you need to know."

"I can't sleep with two men at the same time."

"Yeah, I know. Which adds to your problem."

Lauren grabbed Alex's hand as she practically bounced up and down on her couch, locked in on the TV. "One more minute. I'm so glad I can watch my first commercial for the first time with the man who made it possible."

"Well, I think your talent made it possible."

"Yeah, but without you calling Roger, I wouldn't have gotten my foot in the door."

"I'm glad it worked out for you, Lauren. Have you seen the spot yet?"

"Nope, it'll be the first time for both of us. Meanwhile, I've got my face in Times Square and a bunch of magazines that came out today!"

Not just your face, young lady. "Yeah, I happened to be there and saw the video billboard. You looked great."

"Thanks, you're sweet." The prime-time show faded to black and she sat up straight. "Oooh, here it comes."

The video faded up showing a scorching sun with waves of heat rising off the sand. Then a shot of Lauren spreading out a beach towel and ever so slowly lifting her cover-up over her head, revealing the red bikini and incredibly toned abs as she stretched. She sat on the towel and the video went to slow motion as she rubbed the sunblock over her legs, stomach, and cleavage. It was all Alex could do to keep his jaw in place. Then Lauren turned over and struggled to put the stuff on the middle of her back as a shirtless hunk walked up and said, "You look hot, Miss." She looked up, handed him the bottle and said, "Do me, please?"

Alex swallowed hard.

The hunk kneeled down, took the bottle and began applying the sunblock to her back. Lauren looked straight into the camera. "You can still sizzle without burning." The logo for the sunblock flew across the screen as Lauren turned over, sat up, and shook out her hair as the camera panned down her glistening body. Then it faded to black.

Lauren started to clap. "My first commercial!" She turned to him. "Did you like it?"

He was still staring at the TV in shock. "It was terrific."

Her phone rang. She looked at it and her face tightened. "Uh-oh."

"What?"

"I knew this was coming. It's my mother."

"Calling to congratulate you?"

134

"Just the opposite." She answered the phone. He watched her smile slowly fade and could hear a woman yelling at the other end of the call for a solid minute. Lauren rolled her eyes. "Well, I'm sorry you feel that way. But I'm an actress now and I've got a modeling job for a book cover coming up and I'm not going to give up my dream— hello?" Lauren shook her head and tossed the phone on the coffee table. "She hung up. And she's not pleased with me. What a surprise."

"What was the problem?"

"She said I was almost naked and that the magazine ad was very suggestive and she won't be able to show her face in church ever again and she'll be a pariah in the neighborhood. Then she called me a tramp and hung up. You don't think I look like a tramp, do you Alex?"

Tramp? No. Seductress? Spot on. "Of course not. That's ridiculous."

"I mean, for goodness sake, it's just a bikini. I'll admit it's pretty skimpy, but seriously, it's not like I posed nude. Which I would never, ever do, by the way. And she said the magazine ad was dirty."

Dirty? Nah. Suggestive as hell, you betcha. "I wouldn't worry about it, Lauren. My parents weren't wild about me going into television news either. You have to stay true to yourself. You have a dream, so follow it. And I'd say you're off to a good start. Don't give your mother the power to ruin your celebration."

"Thank you but… aaauuugh!" She threw up her hands. "She drives me crazy. My family pretty much disowned me anyway for moving up here. Said New York was a den of sin, that everyone was evil and I was going straight to hell."

"I assume you have discovered that it is not Babylon, though there is a town by that name on Long Island."

"True. But hey, I'm glad you could be here to watch my maiden voyage on national television." She patted his hand. "I know I can count on you to be supportive."

"I'm real happy for you, Lauren. I'm sure it will lead to bigger and better things. Your face is definitely out there now." *Among other obvious assets.*

Her eyes widened. "Well, since this was my first television gig I wanted your opinion on something. Be right back."

Lauren got up, headed to the bedroom and closed the door. Alex grabbed his cell and checked his email, finding a note from Roger alerting him to the fact the commercial was running tonight. He scrolled through the rest for a few minutes until her voice broke his train of thought. "Alex, you ready?"

"Ready for what?"

She opened the door and walked into the room wearing the same red bikini she'd worn in the commercial, then struck a pose in front of him, hands on hips. "They say the camera adds ten pounds. So what do you think?"

Chapter 14

Juliette put two fingers from each hand on her forehead and closed her eyes like a clairvoyant. "I am sending you my thoughts. Open your mind. See if you can guess what I'm going to say next."

Alex plopped down onto the couch. "Let me get this straight."

She opened her eyes and smiled. "I knew you were psychic!"

"Go ahead, say it."

"Soooo… let me get this straight. The woman whose face and incredible body heretofore only known by you is now plastered all over a Times Square billboard along with hundreds of city buses and subway platforms, the woman who made a commercial for skin care look like late-night cable, the woman who is going to be the face of your upcoming novel, actually parades herself in front of you in a string bikini that looks like it's about to give way… and she doesn't do to you what she looks like she's about to do to that bottle of sunblock?"

"I'm pretty sure she wanted to. Actually, I'm glad we didn't go that far."

"Ah, that speaks volumes. You're still hung up on the redhead."

"Why do you say that?"

"Because I know you, and I know you're monogamous when it comes to dating and if you did anything sexual with Sizzle Girl you wouldn't be able to go out with Keira. You're a one-woman guy, and that's part of the reason I love you. And since you just said you're glad the bikini babe didn't drain you of all bodily fluids, that tells me you want to keep your options open with the redhead."

He slowly nodded. "Yeah, guess so. Anything sexual is the point of no return."

"Let me ask you this… if she leads you to the bedroom the next time you see her, will you be able to resist?"

"Probably not. After last night… well, if she tries that again on the next date I think I'll be pretty much powerless against her. She's like some fantasy come to life."

"Next question. Do you think she was trying to seduce you?"

"Not sure since I kinda put the brakes on."

"Final question. If Keira were not in the picture—"

"I still wouldn't be home."

"You answered that too quickly. Thinking with the wrong head can get you in trouble, young man. Still think she's the proverbial girl next door?"

"That might be a stretch. Let's call her a nice girl that enjoys being naughty who may have grown up in a different neighborhood."

"Yeah. And I think you might possibly be getting played by a world-class seductress."

"Cut her some slack, Juliette. She grew up in a different world than we did."

"Cut her some slack? She straddles you in that bikini and makes out with you and you come home looking like you need to seek medical attention after four hours, like the guys in those erectile dysfunction commercials. What the hell do you call it if not a seduction? You already admitted she's got the upper hand with you."

"Women from the South are different, I guess. Besides, you haven't met her yet, so please reserve judgment."

She shook her head, threw up her hands, and exhaled. "Obviously you have rose-colored glasses when it comes to Sizzle Girl. You're falling for her, aren't you?"

"I'm not sure, but I do like her a lot."

"Alex, please be careful with this one. Because right now she's got you wrapped around her little finger and she could snap your heart like a twig."

"I'll try."

"I hope so. You're too important to me and I don't want to see you make a bad decision." Juliette sat down next to him, wrapped one arm around his shoulders and pulled him close. "By the way, was it true about the camera adding ten pounds in her case?"

He shook his head. "No. She actually looked better in person, if that's even possible."

"Uh-oh. Poor Keira."

"What do you mean, poor Keira?"

"She's cute, but she doesn't stand a chance against a top-heavy bikini model who sexually waterboards you."

"Hard as this may be for you to believe, things are still neck and neck between Lauren and Keira."

"Really? One kiss versus what was basically a lap dance from a girl with the body of a centerfold? That woman on the billboard is now every man's fantasy, and she wants *you*."

"I know, it doesn't make sense, there's just something about Keira. I mean, Lauren's terrific, I enjoy being with her, she's uh, very affectionate, there's a huge physical attraction—"

"That last part is what worries me. No red-blooded man could possibly think clearly with her on his lap."

"But Keira has that X factor. I can't put my finger on it, but I'll figure it out. And my God, that one kiss… I've never felt a connection like that before."

Juliette patted him on the hand. "Wow, you're not just comparing women based on looks. You know, there may be hope for your gender after all."

Keira wished she could simply deal with the author directly.

Because Alexander sat there, making things more difficult,

seemingly fighting her every suggestion while the actual author seemed receptive. It was time to eliminate the middle man, if at all possible. At least from the editing process anyway.

She stared at the cell phone, which sat on the high round table in the editing cave. Sadly it didn't have a photo of the author, just the name. "Moving on to chapter ten. I really have a problem with that first kiss between Lexi and Jamison."

"Okay," said the author, her voice filled with gravel from the potato chips. "What's the problem and what do you suggest?"

"While this is a sweet romance we need to spice things up a bit at this point in the book, tease the reader a little, just the way a woman would tease a man. Their first kiss shouldn't be her giving him a peck on the cheek. She needs to convey the notion she's interested in a romantic relationship, not being just a friend."

Alexander looked up at her. "Really? I think their relationship is moving along at a decent pace. They don't need to sleep together yet."

Keira shook her head. "I'm not saying that. Look, we've carried the reader along for nine chapters, we need to get the ball rolling on the romance, show the possible sparks between the two. Let them feel the electricity between Lexi and Jamison."

The author chimed in. "Okay, I see where you're—"

Alexander interrupted. "I still don't see a problem here."

Keira turned to him. "You're a single guy, put yourself in Jamison's place. You seriously think he's going to be satisfied and want another date after he takes her out for a romantic dinner and carriage ride through Central Park and all he gets is a kiss on the cheek? I don't know any man who would hang around after that. She needs to let him know she's really interested, has to send some signals."

"But we get to that in chapter fifteen."

"Way too long a wait. The reader wants some action at this point. And so do I."

"I disagree."

Keira looked to the speaker phone hoping for a lifeline from the author and heard nothing. She got up and started to pace. "Look, Alexander, you can't string along the reader forever when it comes to romance novels. While we get the 'happily ever after' payoff at the end, we have to make the journey interesting and enjoyable. The reader wants them to be together; we have to show it's possible. You can't stall forever."

"They do it on TV shows all the time. You ever watch *Castle*? You had to wait years for them to kiss."

"This isn't a television series, and this book is different, like every book. Besides, in *Castle* we knew there were sparks between the two main characters from the get-go, and that kept the viewers interested and wanting them to get together. We need the same strategy here. At this point in the book we know Lexi is a take-charge kind of gal, and for her to act this way doesn't make sense. I'm not saying she needs to give the guy a lap dance, but we need sparks at this point. Her date with Jamison needs to end with some romance, not with a kiss you'd get from your sister."

Still nothing from the speaker phone.

He folded his arms. "Okay, well how do you think she should act that *would* make sense?"

She'd had enough of his stubborn attitude. "This is how the scene should play out." Keira moved around the table and stood next to him, then swiveled his chair around so he was facing her and looking up. She put her hands on the arms of his chair. "After the carriage ride he walks her home. It's chilly and he notices her shoulders are hunched up. She's obviously cold, so he does the chivalrous thing, takes off his jacket and wraps it around her. She really appreciates the old-fashioned gesture and takes his hand. They reach the front of her building. Lexi gets up on the step so she's looking down at him, taking the position of control. She would slowly grab his necktie." Keira reached out and took hold of Alexander's red silk tie, slowly twisting it once in her hand. "She's now leading him, pulling him close, running her fingers through his hair. Their lips are inches apart." Keira played with his hair as she gave the tie a gentle tug, pulling him near enough to catch a whiff of his Polo cologne, her favorite. The scent made her lose track and go off on a tangent. "By the way, you're wearing Polo, right?"

He nodded, mouth slightly open, staring up at her.

"Thought so." She took his head in her other hand and slid her fingers through his thick hair, stealing his breath. Her pulse spiked as her voice softened to a more sultry tone, dripping with lust. "Then she'd pause as she looked into his eyes. Not a shy, demure look but a strong one that lets him know she's in charge at this particular moment, that she's a woman who sees something she wants and takes it. And the reader knows she wants to take him, not right now but definitely in the future. Then she gives him her best shot." She locked eyes with Alexander, looking down at him, her take-no-prisoners persona in control. Suddenly the world around them disappeared. She pulled his necktie until their lips met, and gave him one incredibly long kiss. The electricity shot off the charts, running through her entire body. She felt his hands touch her waist and slide up the small of her back. She relaxed her grip on his tie, let go of his hair, and leaned back as she licked her lips, keeping her eyes connected with his. "Like that. She's in control. And unless he's dead, he just got the message that she's very interested in something more and that she will take him whenever she wants to. On her timetable. Got it?"

Alexander looked up at her, eyes wide, mouth hanging open, his hands still on her waist. "You've, uh, got a… very valid point."

She stood up straight and smiled as she traced his jawline with one long red fingernail. "Thank you. Now *that's* a first-kiss scene."

Then the realization of where she was and what she had done hit her.

"Oh my God…" Her hands flew to her mouth.

He furrowed his brow. "What?"

"Alexander, I'm… I don't know what came over me. I shouldn't have done that. I got caught up in trying to make a point—"

"Point taken. Point taken very well. I agree wholeheartedly."
He shot her a devilish grin. "Feel free to make any other points
you have in mind."

She shook her head as she backed up. "No, no. This is not like
me… I mean, geez, we're at the office, this is so—"

"It's late. There's no one else here, Keira. We're alone. And you
should see what happens after hours in television newsrooms."

"This is not how I usually work with my authors."

"I should hope not, since they're all women." He got up and
moved toward her, then took her shoulders. "Look, if you're going
to apologize every time you kiss me, perhaps it might be better
if it were my idea." She tried to back away. He followed until she
was against the wall, but she didn't stop him. She let herself go.
He took her head in his hands and kissed her, totally in control.
Her hands had a mind of their own as they slowly slid up his
chest, taking inventory of the muscles under his shirt until they
ended up around his neck, fingers locked. Their lips parted and
he leaned back. "There. Now you don't need to apologize. And
I'm sure as hell not going to. Got it?"

"Point taken, Alexander. Point taken very well." She leaned
forward. "My turn."

Juliette sat transfixed at what she was hearing over the phone and
finally hit the mute button, not wanting to interrupt what was
happening. She leaned back and slowly munched on a potato chip
as she listened to what was transpiring at the office.

"Forgive me, dear roommate, for eavesdropping. But this is too
damn good. It's just like a romance novel!"

He was kissing her again when realization number two hit her.
"Mmmmm!" Keira let go of him and waved her hands.

He broke the embrace and backed up. "For goodness sake,
Keira, what now?"

She pointed at the speaker and whispered. "Your cousin's still on the phone."

His eyes grew wide. "Oh, shit!"

They both walked back to their chairs and Keira leaned toward the speaker. "Alex, you still there?"

"Oh yeah." She heard a chuckle.

"Did you, uh, hear anything?"

"Highly entertaining. And I didn't have to pay three bucks a minute to listen. Now I wish this was a Skype call."

Her face flushed and she saw Alexander begin to blush. "I'm so sorry. That was highly unprofessional of me. This has never happened before."

"No apology necessary, Keira. My cousin is a cute guy, so I certainly understand why you can't keep your hands off him."

Keira buried her head in her hands. "Dear God."

She heard the author laugh. "Oh, lighten up, Keira. Besides, what I heard sounded a hell of a lot better than what I wrote. I certainly agree with you on editing the scene with the first kiss. I'll write it up just the way I heard it."

"Listen, I think that's a perfect stopping point for today. We'll talk soon, okay?"

"Sure, Keira. Now you two don't stay up too late... *editing*." Another chuckle.

The call ended and she leaned back in her chair, then turned to Alexander. "We need to talk."

He smiled at her. "Yeah, I guess we do."

"I need to put all my cards on the table and be totally honest with you. I really like you, Alexander."

"I kinda picked that up. I really like you too."

"Unfortunately I'm physically attracted to you."

His face scrunched up. "Not sure why *unfortunately* is attached to that sentence."

"Because, if we're going to get this book done, you can't be kissing me."

"Uh, in case you've already forgotten, you started it. Twice."

"I know, but you kept going. You didn't have to kiss me back."

"What the hell did you expect me to do?" He shook his head. "Keira, when a beautiful woman kisses me, I'm not gonna run away."

She tried unsuccessfully to hold back a smile. "I appreciate the compliment, but I'm not beautiful."

"Every mirror in New York would strongly disagree."

"You're sweet. Look, there's something else you need to know. I've been dating someone. Nothing serious, but I do see other people. So if that's a problem—"

"It's not. We're adults. I don't own you and you don't own me. And since we're doing the cards-on-the-table thing, I'll be honest with you as well. I'm also seeing someone, but it's nothing serious. And you should know that while I can date more than one person at a time, I can only be serious with one at a time." He leaned forward and gave her a soulful look. "You understand what I'm saying?"

"Yeah, me too. I'm the same way."

"And by the way, I'm also very attracted to you as well, Keira, which I do not consider unfortunate. So what's the problem?"

"The quality of this book."

"I thought you loved the book."

"I do. I'm talking about making it the best book it can be. And I can't do my best work on *Ring Girl* if my decisions are going to be clouded by any physical relationship we might have. I need to remain objective."

"So what are you saying? We can't date?"

"We can hang out as friends, but we can't do anything physical. At least not until the editing of the book is done."

"Excuse me?"

"I think that will work best for me. We still get to know each other but hold off on the physical stuff."

"So basically you're turning our relationship back into the

original scene with Lexi and Jamison in chapter ten. I take you out for a romantic dinner and carriage ride through Central Park and you give me a kiss on the cheek."

"Basically. But without the kiss."

"Is pre-marital hand-holding off the table?"

"Be serious, Alexander."

"I'm trying to be, but you're not making a lot of sense. This whole thing sounds like giving up love for Lent. Or that we're a couple of teenagers waiting to turn sixteen. If two people are attracted to each other, it's natural for them to kiss."

She got up, moved to the bookshelf and pulled a paperback from the stacks. "I want you to read something."

"What, forty different ways to take cold showers after kissing a hot redhead? Celibacy for dummies?"

She turned and handed him the book. "No. Romance novel written by my best friend. It's about a couple that holds off on the physical stuff till the very end but they really get to know each other very well along the way. Then it's happily ever after."

"So they kiss by the end?"

"Yes. Among other things."

He looked at the book, turned it over and shrugged. "Fine, I'll read it."

"Thank you."

"But I have one problem with this whole scenario. How can I compare you to anyone else I'm dating? And how can you do the same? Sounds like apples and oranges."

"Often times love happens when friendship catches fire. Our relationship will be pure."

"If I wanted pure, I would have become a priest."

She locked eyes with him but didn't say anything else.

He exhaled, not looking happy. "I guess I have no say in this matter."

"Nope."

"So you're taking control."

"I am a take-charge kinda gal. Just like Lexi in the book."

"Well, whatever. You're worth it."

"Thank you. I have a strong suspicion you are as well."

"But I do have one complaint, Keira."

"What's that?"

"I didn't get to finish my last kiss. You interrupted it. One for the road?"

"Well, I guess not seeing your last kiss all the way through wouldn't be fair." She smiled, leaned forward, took his head in her hands, and gave him a passionate kiss. She broke the embrace and leaned back. "That should hold you till we're done editing."

"Uh, that was supposed to be *my* kiss."

She shrugged and smiled. "Sorry. Like I said, I'm a take- charge girl."

"Damn, Keira. We gotta get cracking on this book."

She started to chuckle.

"What now, Keira?"

"I was just thinking, if you were the actual author of this book, it would be a hell of a scandal. Imagine the cover of a New York tabloid. *Editor sleeps with author after giving him six-figure advance.*"

"What are you doing home?" Juliette looked up from her book as Alex walked in and tossed his satchel on the couch.

"Uh, I live here."

Juliette got up and followed him as he headed into the kitchen. "Well, what happened after you hung up? I didn't expect you to be back tonight after Keira's semi-erotic play-by-play of chapter ten. C'mon, c'mon, I want details." She was wide-eyed and excited, bouncing up and down on her toes.

"Nothing happened. That's the problem."

"Seriously? What I heard sounded like one of those phone sex calls. I figured she hung up so abruptly so she could get back to attacking you."

147

"Unfortunately, what you heard is all that happened."

"I don't understand."

Alex recapped all the details as he pulled a plate and a glass from the cabinet.

Juliette put her hands on her hips and shook her head. "I'm not even going to say it this time."

Alex sliced off a piece of Juliette's chocolate rum cake, poured a glass of milk, carried both to the kitchen table and sat. "I know. It's just another piece of this bizarre puzzle I've created."

"So the deal is that you can date Keira but you cannot touch her."

"That's about it."

"How exactly is this going to clear up your feelings about her? Or her feelings for you?"

"Beats the hell out of me."

"I don't understand this woman. She's obviously attracted to you and yet she does something like this."

"Between the two of them I'm going to explode. Please scrape me off the wall when I'm gone." He shoved a piece of cake into his mouth, savoring the rich chocolate, and talked through it. "I get her point. She's really committed to her work and the book… which is why I can't argue with her. I mean, if us having a romantic relationship is going to have a negative effect on the novel…"

"So what are you gonna do?"

"I have no choice."

"In other words, you're still interested and willing to wait?"

"Again, no choice."

"Damn, I gotta hand it to ya. Most guys would leave skid marks." Juliette moved behind him and started to rub his shoulders. He relaxed as she pushed her thumbs into his tight muscles. "I'm sorry this is so frustrating for you. But I'm not sure how you'll be able to compare two women when one wants to hold hands while the other treats you like a carnival ride."

His cell rang and he saw Lauren was calling. "Speaking of the latter…"

"Maybe she'll talk dirty to you."

"Stop it." He answered the call. "Hi, Lauren."

"Hi, Alex. I apologize for calling so late—"

"Oh, I just got home, no problem. What's up?"

"Well, I'm sorry but this is unavoidable. I'm going to have to take a rain check on our date Saturday."

"Is everything okay?"

"Alex, you are not going to believe this, but I'm on a five am flight to Hollywood tomorrow morning because my agent got me a screen test for a major motion picture!"

"Wow, Lauren, that's terrific!"

"I know, this is all happening so fast, and all because I met you!"

"Well, your talent is obvious. I'm just glad people are noticing. How long are you going to be out there?"

"Three or four days. He's got me lined up to meet a bunch of producers and then my audition is Monday. Anyway, I'll call you as soon as I know anything. And again, I'm sorry to cancel on you for this weekend."

"Don't be ridiculous, this is a great opportunity for you. I'll see you when you get back. Break a leg, Lauren."

"Thanks, Alex. Talk soon. Bye."

"Have a safe trip. Bye." He ended the call, tossed the phone on the table and buried his head in his hands. "I don't believe this."

Juliette placed one hand on his shoulder. "So what's up with bachelorette number two?"

"Got an audition in Hollywood."

"Not surprised. She's the latest It Girl. So why are you glum?"

"She had to cancel our date for this weekend."

"Huh. Well, I guess you can take your 'look but don't touch' girl to a matinee. Maybe your hands will brush in the bucket of popcorn."

"How exciting."

"Well, so much for you getting attacked this weekend," said Juliette. "I'll go run you a tub of cold water and throw some ice in it. Not sure a shower will do it at this point."

Chapter 15

"You kissed him in the editing cave? Wow, Keira, this is like the publishing version of the mile-high club." Gretch took a seat and studied her face. "Alas, for some bizarre reason my boss does not look thrilled. Spill."

Keira shook her head. "It wasn't a make-out session. I was merely trying to illustrate how the first kiss in chapter ten should go and I got carried away actually showing him."

"Damn, that's clever. Acting out a love scene. I gotta try that with an erotic novel."

"I wasn't being clever. Like I said, I got carried away. And he kissed me back."

"Oh, the horror! You poor thing!"

"Anyway, it was during our conference call and the author heard it over the phone—"

Gretch's eyes grew wide as she slapped the desk with her palms. "Get! Out!"

"Yeah, talk about embarrassing. And apparently she really got a kick out of the call and liked my interpretation of what should happen in chapter ten. Anyway after we end the call with the author I figure it's time to be totally upfront with Alexander and set the ground rules going forward."

Gretch put up her hands. "Whoa, wait a minute... you start

kissing a guy at the office and then you sit down and set ground rules? Oh, I can't wait to hear what these are."

"I can't think clearly around him, Gretch. He distracts me. So until the book is done, it's hands off."

"What the hell does that mean?"

"Nothing physical. It would cloud my judgment."

"I would think a night in the sack with him might clear your head."

"Just the opposite. The book has to come first, Gretch. And if I'm romantically involved with Alexander I won't be able to be objective about the novel."

"Sounds like kissing the guy *helped* the editing process. The hell with objectivity, perhaps you should jump ahead to chapter twenty."

"Funny. Oh, and I told him I was seeing someone else. Turns out he's doing the same. But neither one of us is in a serious relationship. Apparently he's of the same mindset as I am when it comes to monogamy."

"So, wait… you're not going to date Alexander till the book is done?"

"Oh, we can still date. We just can't do anything physical."

"So, let me get this straight. You're still gonna date both Dash and Alexander."

"Correct."

"And while you can be a bad girl with Dash your relationship with Alexander will be like two kids in the fifth grade."

"Strange way of putting it, but yeah."

"How the hell are you gonna compare the two guys?"

"Like I told Alexander, our relationship will be pure."

"It will also be boring. And for him, probably very frustrating. This is not a good thing to do to a guy you like, especially after you've already stuck your tongue down his throat. You can't go backwards with guys, they see that as you wanting to be the dreaded 'just friends'. I'm not sure you can keep him interested until the book is done."

"It works for me, Gretch. And when the book is finished, the gloves come off, so to speak."

"I would imagine after all the built-up frustration, that's not all that will come off."

"Hey, you were the one to tell me to take charge, so I took charge."

"I didn't mean to take charge like Sister Mary Celibate." She waved her hands. "Hold on. Back up a bit. You said Alexander was also seeing someone."

"Yeah."

"And I'm going to assume that, being a guy, he's not taking this other woman out and ending the date with a handshake."

She shrugged. "I don't know, but it's fair to assume."

"You're gonna lose him, Keira."

"I don't think so. He's different. He'll wait a few months."

"No, he won't. He'll lose interest. He may be different than most guys but he still has needs. This isn't someone going off to war and the other person waiting, Keira. Men are wired different and if he's getting his jollies from another woman, you're gonna be left in the dust. He's just going to consider you a friend. And guess what... since you'll be playing tonsil hockey with possibly the best-looking man I've ever seen, you'll be doing the same."

"I don't think so."

"This is insane. It cannot possibly work, Keira."

"It has to work. I simply can't risk a bestseller because I'm infatuated with a guy."

"Just infatuated?"

She blushed a bit. "Fine. More than that."

"What was Alexander's reaction to said ground rules?"

"He was not happy."

"Wow, what a shock. Tell you what, I'll be happy to keep him warm till the book is done."

"You'd corrupt him, Gretch."

"Yeah, but I'd have him well trained. He could do all sorts of things to you that you never thought of and then thank you for the privilege."

"I'm sure."

"Well, Dash is certainly the winner in more ways than one."

"How's that?"

"He not only gets to go out on normal dates with you, but you'll be getting all worked up when you're out with Alexander and then you'll attack Dash. He won't know what hit him."

"I can act normally around Dash."

"Bullshit. I've seen him, remember? Even *I* can't act normally around him."

Gretch buzzed Keira from the outer office. "Keira, oh, Keira…"

Her assistant's playful tone told her something was up. "What?"

"Alexander on line one. Dash on line two."

"Both at the same time? Shit."

"This oughta be good. I'm coming in to watch."

Keira paused a moment as she looked at the two flashing lights on her phone. Gretch walked in, took a seat, placed her elbows on the desk, rested her chin on her palms and smiled at her. "What?"

"Admit it, you can't decide which call to take first, can you?"

Keira looked down and shook her head.

"Aha! Romantic vapor lock." She cocked her head at the phone. "Put it on speaker."

"No!"

"Well, pick one, you're not a cable TV company where you can leave people on hold all damn day."

Keira reached toward the phone but stopped, her hand hovering over the two lights.

"Oh, for God's sake!" said Gretch, who reached over the desk and punched a button.

"Keira Madison…"

"Hey, it's Dash. Catch you at a bad time?"

"No, this is fine. Can I put you on hold for just a moment? Gretch needs something." She pointed at Gretch and snapped her fingers.

Gretch yelled, "Keira, I have to get your signature on this *right now*!"

"Sure, I've got time," said Dash.

"Thanks." Keira put Dash on hold and punched the other button. "Keira Madison…"

"Hey, it's the guy you can't kiss for a few months. You might remember me. We met in the stacks, romance section."

She couldn't help but smile. "Hi, Alexander. How you doin'?"

"You got a minute? I promise not to talk dirty."

"Very funny, but can you hold a sec? Gretch needs something." She pointed at her assistant.

Gretch yelled, "Hey, Keira, I need your notes for the art department!"

"Sure," said Alexander.

Keira's pulse quickened, her armpits grew damp. She put him on hold and picked up Dash's call. "Hey, I'm back."

"Listen, I gotta take a trip this weekend about a campaign gig for next year after I'm done with Senator Bradley. I hate to do this to you, but I have to cancel for Saturday. Rain check?"

"Sure, Dash, I understand."

"Thank you. Normally I'd postpone the meeting but this could be a huge client. I'll make it up to you. I'll holler at you when I'm on my way back."

"Okay, then, talk soon. Bye."

"Bye."

The line went dark and Keira picked up Alexander's call. "I'm back."

"If you're busy I can call later."

"No, no, all the fires are put out. What's up?"

"I was wondering… in light of the new ground rules… if you'd like to have lunch on Saturday and catch a matinee. I promise to have you home by four."

She laughed. "Four, huh?"

"Well, maybe four-thirty if the theater runs a ton of previews."

"Oooh, I dunno, four-thirty is kinda pushing my curfew…"

"It's not a school night, Keira."

"Well, okay."

"Terrific, I'll pick you up at eleven. Don't dress sexy otherwise I won't be able to help myself."

She laughed again. "I'll wear a burlap sack. See you then." She ended the call and looked up to see Gretch smiling at her. "What?"

"It's just fun to watch my boss sweat in her attempt to juggle two men. Damn, I should have made popcorn for this. So what's the deal?"

"Dash has to go out of town and canceled for the weekend and Alexander is taking me out for lunch and an afternoon movie."

"You cheap bimbo. One guy cancels and you've got another on the line in ten seconds. But, bottom line, Dash won't be around after you work up your appetite with Alexander."

"Apparently not."

"How sad for you. But there's something you need to consider about spending the afternoon with him."

"What's that?"

"Alexander may have a second date for Saturday *night*, so *you* may be the one getting *him* prepped. Shoe's on the other foot, sister. How's the fit?"

The realization hit her and she shook her head. "I don't wanna think about this anymore. Can we get back to editing?"

"Sure, but this is more fun."

Keira heard his laugh as she stepped off the elevator into the lobby. Alexander was chatting with the doorman, both of them smiling. He was definitely dressed down; khakis, docksiders and a blue button-down long-sleeved oxford. Unfortunately, the casual preppie look was yet another turn on, as he somehow looked more appealing in this outfit than in a suit. He looked over and spotted her. "Hey, right on time."

"If I wanted to be back by four, I had to be prompt."

"Right, curfew." He gestured toward the door. "We'd better get rolling or your dad will send out a search party. I hope you told him I don't have a motorcycle or any tattoos."

"Funny. Let's rock."

He glanced at her outfit as he held the door: skinny jeans, stacked-heel boots, and a royal-blue top. "I forgot to ask if compliments are off the table in light of the new rules."

"Absolutely not. Why?"

"You look nice, that's all."

"Thanks. So do you."

"I'd say you look hot, but, ya know, it might get something started."

She shot him a smile. "Well, good thing you didn't say it. You wouldn't want to go rogue on the first day of the new rules." She stepped out onto the street and he led her to a minivan with a network news logo. "Uh, *this* is your car?"

"Of course not. Like most New Yorkers I don't own one. But I still do some stuff for the network researching stories and teaching interns, so the boss lets me borrow a car from time to time."

"So where are we going?"

"Jersey. A little out-of-the-way restaurant I'm sure you've never been to." He opened the door for her and she got inside. Her eyes widened at all the electronics that practically covered the dashboard. A police scanner, computer tablet, two-way radio, and a few other electronic items she didn't recognize. Tapes, pens, and notepads littered the front seat. Media parking passes hung from the sun visors. Alexander got behind the wheel. "Sorry for the mess, but reporters are sloppy. It's not a limo, but it'll get you there." He turned to face her. "Now, before we get going you need to be mirandized."

"I need to be what?"

"Mirandized, news version. You know how cops read people their rights when they arrest them? I need to tell you the rules of riding in a news car."

"There are rules?"

"Yes. You have the right to be in this vehicle. Since the car is marked with the network logo, anything you do or say is seen as a reflection on the network. Therefore, you do not have the right to throw litter out the window or give someone the finger while riding in it."

"Flip the bird?" She pointed to herself. "*Moi*?"

He didn't respond but cocked his head to the side.

"Fine, I admit I can get emotional in traffic. I'll sit with my hands folded."

"The other thing is that since you are now in a news unit, you will be called by your last name, and will refer to me in the same manner. This is what we do in the business. Got it, Madison?"

She saluted him. "Copy that, Bauer."

"Good. You're now an official member of the media."

"You honestly do that to everyone?"

"Yep. Especially the interns and rookies. Took a new kid out once and he flipped the bird at someone, and that someone turned out to be an advertiser who called the network president. Since then we actually have to mirandize people. You don't want to have the general public think media people are a bunch of jerks. Though it's not exactly a stretch."

"I'll be a good girl." She turned around and looked at all the gear in the back seat. "Damn, this thing is a like a rolling newsroom."

He cranked the car and pulled out into traffic. "Basically. These days you can pretty much shoot and edit a story without going back to the station. One of the reasons I got out of the business."

"But you're not totally out. You just said you did research."

"True, but it's on an occasional basis."

"So, you researching anything interesting right now?"

He nodded. "Yeah, typical political cover-up."

"Anyone I would know?"

"Senator Bradley."

She sat up straight. *Dash's client.* "You, uh, find anything interesting?"

"Not yet, but I will. Every politician has skeletons in the closet. Normally I wouldn't tell you what I'm working on but all the networks have someone digging on this particular story. Just a matter of who finds the smoking gun first."

"And said smoking gun would be?"

"That's the part I *can't* tell you, Madison."

"I thought you left because you were sick of the bias in the news business."

"I am, but in this case the new boss is objective and I'm helping Juliette on the story. She's as unbiased as they come. Last of a dying breed."

"So you still like news?"

"In some ways, and it will always be in my blood, but that's not why I left a full-time job. All this technology made doing stories in the field easy, but it killed the newsroom camaraderie that was so important to me. When you never get back to the newsroom, you miss all the relationships. And that's what made a career in TV news so special. Being on camera had nothing to do with it. It was all about telling great stories with a bunch of creative people."

"Yeah, I know what you mean. I hate those days when I work from home. The girls at the office add so much to my day. Especially Gretch."

"She's a character."

"More than that. She watches out for me."

"You don't look like you'd need someone to do that."

"You'd be amazed."

Her face beamed as he led her up the steps to the old-fashioned silver diner facing the Jersey shore. "I had no idea this was here."

"Well-kept secret. Food is great as well, and I did pick up on your affinity for diners."

He opened the door and she breathed in the deep-fried air of the restaurant, which mixed with the sounds of fifties music. The waitresses were dressed in poodle skirts and high school letter sweaters. The place was time-warped back to a simpler era and brought a huge smile. "Wow, what a cool place."

"One of my favorites. Did a story out here years ago and have been coming here ever since. You'd be amazed at the off-the-beaten-path places you discover as a reporter."

He led her to a booth and she slid in on the red bench seat, noting the old-fashioned juke box selector on the table. "I love these things."

"It works, just like the one at that place we had breakfast." He reached into his pocket, pulled out some change and dropped a bunch of quarters in front of the selector. He flipped through the choices, put a quarter in the slot and punched a couple of buttons.

"Wha'ja pick?"

"An appropriate song."

A few seconds later the voice of Frankie Valli filled the restaurant. She smiled and nodded as she recognized the tune. "My Eyes Adored You. Cute."

He shrugged. "Hey, it's the ultimate 'look but don't touch the girl' song. I figured it was appropriate considering your ground rules."

"You gonna carry my books later?"

"Ah, you know the lyrics."

"I love the music from that era." She started flipping through the selector. "Listen, Alexander—"

"What's my name?"

"Oh, sorry. Bauer, I know this whole situation must seem really strange to you, and I appreciate—"

"Forget it, Madison. Let's just have a nice day, okay? Enjoy each other's company. No pressure. I want you to always be relaxed around me. You're in charge, remember? I won't do anything you

160

don't want me to do."

Right now I want you to take me. Her shoulders relaxed and she melted into the seat. "You're something else. I don't know too many guys who would do this."

"I don't know too many women who would do this either."

"Oh, stop it." She picked up a menu. "So what's good here?"

"Everything, but I suggest the patty melt. And they make these giant killer chocolate malts for two that we can share. You know, fifties' style. One glass, two straws. Unless you think I have cooties."

"Never crossed my mind." She bit her lip and raised her eyebrows. And, you know, we have shared more than a malt in my office." She snapped the menu shut. "Sounds good to me."

The waitress cleared their empty plates and replaced them with dessert, a huge chocolate malt. "You want two glasses?"

"We'll share," said Keira.

The waitress put a straw in front of each of them and headed back to the kitchen.

Keira licked her lips. "Looks delicious." She stared at the malt, which had a huge amount of whipped cream on top. Suddenly something hit her in the forehead. She looked down at the table to see a straw wrapper, then looked up to see him smiling at her with the straw in his mouth. She folded her arms and gave him a stern look like a teacher. "Did you do that, young man?"

He shrugged. "Not me. Probably some kid shooting straw wrappers."

"Uh-huh." She peeled the top of the wrapper off her straw. "Bet I can hit the cash register from here."

"Bet you can't."

She put the unwrapped end of the straw in her mouth, pointed it toward the checkout counter, waited for him to turn his head, then shot the wrapper at him, hitting him in the cheek.

"Hey!"

"Damn kids."

She carried the popcorn while he held the sodas as they walked down the aisle on the right side of the historic theater. She admired the ornate gold carvings that framed the giant silver screen, the bright-red seats. "Gorgeous place. I didn't know any single-screen theaters were left. You find this on one of your stories too?"

"Yep. It's on the national registry of historic places. More than a hundred years old. They only show movies on the weekends. I also know where there's an actual drive-in. Maybe, y'know, when we're old enough and allowed to go out at night."

"I think that's doable. Don't think there's enough room in the news car for us to get in trouble."

"True. And it would reflect poorly on the network." He stopped about halfway down and turned to her. "How about here?"

She turned and looked at the screen. "Couple more rows."

They moved closer to the screen and he gestured toward the seats. "After you."

"I can't sit on your left."

"Why not?"

"Because I'm left handed and I've noted you're a righty. If I sit on your left and we have the bucket of popcorn in the middle, I'll be reaching across my body and so will you. If I sit on your right it will be easier for both of us to reach the popcorn and less of a chance we'll drop any."

He slowly nodded. "You've obviously given this a lot of thought."

"Listen, Bauer, I'm obsessed with food and when you're a southpaw this stuff is important. Consider it the theater equivalent of your mother's 'walk on the sidewalk' rule."

"Okay." He slid into the row first and she took a seat on his right, then propped the bucket of popcorn on the armrest between them.

"See how convenient this is?"

"So what do you do if you're at the movies with a left- handed guy?"

"I put the bucket in my lap and let him reach."

"Somehow, Madison, that doesn't surprise me."

Keira was relaxed and happy as they headed out of the theater parking lot. "Good movie. And a great theater. Damn, that screen was massive."

"Yeah, I love coming here when I can, especially when there's a blockbuster showing. The place may be a hundred years old but they've got a state-of-the-art projection and sound system, and the acoustics are fantastic."

"So how many of these 'best-kept secrets' do you know from your reporting days?"

"Dozens. Honestly, I toyed with writing a travel book on unique places in the northeast."

"Then they wouldn't be our secrets."

"Oh, they're *our* secrets now?"

"Since you shared them, they were yours but are now mine as well. Hence, they are ours."

"I'm beginning to see a pattern in your logic."

"There isn't one, Bauer. Part of my charm. The only common denominator is that I like to be in charge."

"Yeah, I kinda picked that up."

"And ya know, this last name thing makes me feel *more* in charge. Got it, Bauer?"

"Yes ma'am."

"One more time, don't call me ma'am. I'm not old."

"Got it, Madison. Listen, there's one more unique place on the way home, by the way, but it's already past four-thirty."

She shrugged. "I'm not in a hurry. What is it?"

"Old-fashioned penny candy store just off the parkway."

Her eyes lit up. "Seriously?"

"Yeah, but the candy is no longer a penny. They've got those licorice allsorts you can't find anymore. Get 'em shipped over from Great Britain." He looked over at her. "You wanna go?"

"I'd love to." *Hmmm, time to find out if the other woman is in the picture for tonight.* "Unless, you know, you have plans for tonight and need to get back right away."

"Nope, free as a bird. What time do I need to get *you* home?"

Well, damn, he just did the same thing to me. This guy is too damn smart. What the hell, he's being honest with you. Be honest with him. "I don't have plans either. Besides, I can always go for a sugar fix."

Keira popped a piece of licorice in her mouth, savoring the sugary sweetness as they headed home. "Love the round ones with the coconut. My grandmother used to have these at Christmas. I'd forgotten how good they are."

"Glad you like 'em. My favorite too." He looked over and reached into her bag, grabbed a piece and popped it in his mouth.

"Hey! You've got your own bag. Stay away from mine."

"Tribute. You know, you literally were the proverbial kid in the candy store back there."

"While I'm obsessed with food, sugar is at the top of the pyramid." She held up a piece of licorice, licking her lips as she studied it. The round black disc in the middle surrounded by the pink coconut. "Damn, I wish you could buy just these. I could live on them."

"That can probably be arranged." He glanced over at her. "Honestly, I don't know where you put it. After demolishing that huge bucket of popcorn and getting a refill."

"It was free. I wanted you to know you got your money's worth."

"That's not why you got it. You ate the whole thing."

"I've always been thin and have a high metabolism. But I'm solid muscle so I burn it off. I dread the day when my metabolism slows down and I become a couch potato in sweatpants eating bon bons. But until then, if you wanna keep me happy, feed me sugar and junk food."

"Are there any sweets you *don't* like?"

"Twinkies. Can't stand to even look at 'em. I was thrilled when they stopped making them so I wouldn't have to see them in stores next to the TastyKakes, but then they brought the damn things back. Ironically they're featured in my all-time favorite movie."

"Which is?"

"*Die Hard.*"

"Really? I don't know a whole lot of women who have an action flick as a favorite. Especially considering your line of work."

"Hey, after reading about romance all day I'm not in the mood for anything warm and fuzzy. I need to see stuff blow up and the good guys win. And Bruce Willis is so snarky. But I still cringe every time I see the Twinkies in the movie."

He furrowed his brow as he kept an eye on the traffic. "Where are the Twinkies in the movie? I don't remember them being part of the plot."

"The cop on the outside, Al, loves 'em. He's buying them in a convenience store when he gets the call, remember?"

"Okay, sure. But now that I remember it, I think he was buying those snowball things."

She shook her head. "Nope, Twinkies. Trust me, I've watched that movie a dozen times."

"Still think it's snowballs. But I haven't seen *Die Hard* in a while."

"Wanna bet? I've got a copy at home. I can show you as soon as we get back."

He gave her a look. "Fine. What's the bet?"

"If I'm wrong, you get a kiss."

He nodded. "Which tells me you are convinced that you're right."

"I am."

"So what do *you* get if *I'm* wrong? Since I am now reasonably sure that I am."

"You take me to that drive-in sometime."

He started to laugh. "You're not a very good gambler, Madison. Sounds like a win-win situation for me."

Alex glanced at the clock as the credits rolled on *Die Hard 2*. It was now ten o'clock and they had watched two movies. "Nothing beats the original, but it's still a good one."

Keira drained her wine glass, her eyes drooping a bit. "You game for another?"

"You sure? You look a little tired."

"Nah, I'm fine. Wine just relaxes me." She poured herself another glass and topped his off.

"I realize this is a marathon, but I don't think I can get through all five. How about we skip to number four. I like that better than the third one."

"I'll fire it up."

He slumped back into the overstuffed leather couch as Keira got up and swapped out the DVDs. *I agreed to bring her back by four and now she's not letting me go home. So much for her ground rules.* She turned and shot him a soft smile as the machine whirred into action, then moved back to the couch, grabbing her wine glass off the coffee table.

"You need anything, Bauer?"

"I'm good."

"Comfortable?"

"Yeah. Very. It's a good couch."

"I wasn't referring to the couch." She sipped her wine and slid closer to him, then grabbed his hand, lifted his arm and wrapped it around her waist as she lay her head on his chest, stealing his breath and sending a bolt of electricity through his body. "*Now* I'm comfortable. Boy, that's some good wine."

He breathed in her strawberry shampoo as the movie started, but it was hard to pay attention with her soft red tangles brushing against his face, even with Bruce Willis going through terrorists like Kleenex.

For someone who came up with the rules, she sure was getting close to breaking them.

Two hours later he stretched out his legs as the movie ended. "I think that's the second best one in the series."

No reaction.

"Madison?"

Still nothing.

He craned his neck around to see her face and found her fast asleep, jaw slightly open. "Hey, Madison…"

She didn't stir. The wine had obviously put her down for the count. He shook her a bit. She didn't move. The woman was dead to the world.

"Well, off to never-never land. C'mon, Sleeping Beauty, let's get you to bed." He sat up straight, slid one arm under her legs, the other supporting her back, and easily lifted her, then carried her down the hallway in search of a bedroom. She stirred a bit, instinctively wrapped her arms around his neck and rested her head on his chest, but didn't wake up. An open door revealed a four-poster antique bed. Alexander carried her in, put her down on the bed, gently slipped off her boots and placed them next to the night stand. He pulled the covers up to her chin. "Good night, fair princess." He kissed his fingers and pressed them to her forehead. Keira rolled onto her side and grabbed the pillow, still asleep, looking like a smiling angel as moonlight spilled onto her face. He was about to leave when he saw a pad and pencil on the night stand. He wrote her a note and propped it up against the lamp, then headed back through the apartment and left, slowly locking the door behind him so as not to disturb her.

He headed for the elevator thinking it was the most fun he'd ever had on a date, and he didn't even get kissed.

It was all he could do to keep himself from going back and getting into bed with her.

Chapter 16

The sunlight spilled through the bedroom window onto her face, making Keira crack open one eye. The clock read nine-thirty, her head felt like it weighed twenty pounds. "Ughhh. Too much wine. Revenge of the grape." She held her forehead with one hand while she threw back the covers with the other, swung her legs out of bed and was about to get up when she saw the notepad propped up against the lamp.

Madison,
You won.
This coupon is good for one trip to the drive-in.
  -Bauer

"Awwww." She stood up and started to head to the bathroom when she realized she was still in her clothes from the day before, then spotted her boots next to the night stand and realized he'd taken them off. "Damn, what a gentleman."

And damn, he could have gotten into bed with me.

She started to replay the events of the previous day, thinking how Alexander had really gone out of his way to make the day enjoyable. She remembered putting the third movie in the DVD player and then wrapping herself with his arm. She had been seriously buzzed and he could have easily made a move, which she probably would not have been able to resist.

And yet he didn't. Instead, he tucked her in.

A great idea popped into her head, but she had to get moving.

She'd swung by her office and gotten the address from the publishing contract. With a grocery bag in each hand filled with the makings of a terrific Sunday brunch, she headed to his apartment wearing a huge smile. It would be a nice surprise and a way to reciprocate for what he had done. And, as a bonus, she'd get to meet the actual author of *Ring Girl*. Her heart rate kicked up a notch as she reached the door. She heard classical music playing and gently knocked.

"Hang on a minute," said a female voice.

Finally! Gonna meet the author!

"You forget your key again—" the door opened and what Keira saw was not anything close to a morbidly obese woman.

Instead she found herself looking at Alexander's stunning blonde friend wrapped in a very short red bathrobe while drying her hair with a towel. "Oh, hi. Juliette, right?"

The blonde's eyes went wide. "Yeah. And you're Keira. The editor."

"I, uh, thought I'd surprise Alexander with brunch since he took me out for such a nice day yesterday." *And obviously he topped it off with a hot babe after I warmed him up.*

"Oh, he's not here but he'll be right back. Come on in." Keira walked in and Juliette shut the door behind her. "The, uh, water was out at my place and Alexander let me come over and take a shower."

"Uh-*huh*." Her heart sank as the red flag went up like a rocket. Juliette was obviously the other woman he was dating. She looked around the apartment, which was spotless and definitely had a woman's touch. *What the hell, I'm here, may as well meet the author.* "Is his cousin here?"

Her face tightened. "No. He had to take her somewhere. But he should be back any minute. Let me give him a call and tell him you're here."

Keira detected a bit of worry in Juliette's face as the woman picked up her cell phone. *She's trying to cover up something.*

She heard the door open and turned to see Alexander walk in holding the morning papers. "They were out of bagels—" He stopped dead in his tracks as he spotted Keira, eyes filled with surprise. "Hey, Keira, I, uh, didn't know you were coming by."

"Thought I'd surprise you with brunch. A little thank you for yesterday."

He turned to Juliette.

The blonde moved forward and took the papers. "Did you get your cousin dropped off okay?"

"Huh?"

"Your *cousin. Alex.* I assume you dropped her at her mom's without any incident?"

"Oh. Yeah."

Something's definitely not right.

"Great. I know that getting her out of the house and visiting her mother will do her some good. Oh, and thanks for letting me use your shower. My super says the water in my apartment should be back on in a few hours. I'll get dressed and get outta here so you two go ahead with your brunch."

Keira put the bags down on the dining-room table. *Maybe I can press her for more information.* "You're welcome to join us, Juliette. I brought plenty of food." *Because I was expecting a four-hundred-pound woman and instead found a size four.*

"I've actually got a brunch date of my own, but thank you for the offer. Well, let me get dressed and get going or I'll be late." Juliette turned and headed down the hall.

Alexander started to pull the food out of the bags and set things up on the table.

Keira reached out and gently took his arm. *I have to know.*

170

There's no point in going any farther in this relationship if he's nailing some other woman. "I'm sorry to show up unannounced like this. I didn't know you had someone here and if I need to leave—"

He turned and took her shoulders. "I know what you're probably thinking, but there's nothing between me and Juliette. When I told you we're platonic friends I was being honest. I'm sure it looks like there's something going on with her in a bathrobe on a Sunday morning, but there's not. She's not the other person I'm seeing. And remember, I told you I can't be serious with more than one person at a time. When I got home I went to bed by myself."

She looked into his eyes and hoped he was being truthful. "Sorry, guess I was feeling a bit… well, forget it. I don't own you, even if there was something going on. When I saw her the way she was dressed, I just assumed…"

"Juliette is my best friend, and she's over here a lot. She's like a sister to me. But that's as far as it goes, okay?"

"Yeah." She looked down at the floor.

"Hey, c'mere."

She looked up to see him with his arms spread wide. She moved forward and he wrapped his arms around her. She hugged him hard, surprised at how much she needed to do so. He leaned back, sliding his hands down to the small of her back and locking his fingers. "We okay? 'Cause I'm not letting you go till we are."

She offered a soft smile. "Yeah, we're fine."

"You sure?"

"Yeah."

"Good. Ha! Got a free hug! Take that, rules!" She chuckled as he continued to set up the table. "This is really nice of you. But you didn't have to do this."

"And you didn't have to take me out for such a great day yesterday. By the way, I apologize for falling asleep. It wasn't you, it was the wine. I really can't hold my liquor."

"Not a problem. But also good to know for future reference."

She felt herself blush. "And, uh, thanks for helping me stagger

171

down to my bedroom."

"I didn't."

"Well, I woke up in bed. How'd I get there?"

"You were dead to the world. I had to carry you."

"Seriously?"

"Fortunately you don't weigh anything." His face flushed a bit as well. "I always try to provide turn-down service. Though in your case I should have left some licorice with the coconut on the pillow. Now, if we're done with the serious talk I'm gonna take a wild stab and assume you're hungry."

He smiled at her, his look draining whatever anxiety she had left out of her body.

But she did realize she had been feeling something she didn't expect.

Jealousy.

"Damn, that was close."

Juliette walked in as Alex was reading the Sunday *New York Post*. "Yeah, no kidding."

"From now on I'll look through the peephole to see who's at the door. I thought it was you. I'm sorry, Alex, she caught me off guard and I had no idea she was coming by."

"Hell, I didn't know either. I didn't even know she knew where I lived. But nice recovery by you coming up with the excuse."

Juliette shook her head. "Not much of an excuse. I don't think she bought it."

"Really? She seemed okay after you left."

"The woman's not stupid, and I saw the look on her face. The whole thing sounds pretty lame. If the tables were turned, you showed up at her place and the door was answered by a dripping wet man in a towel, what would you think?"

"You've got a point." He looked at the clock. "Thanks for taking off. Where did you go for three hours?"

"Called a friend and actually met for brunch, then went to a

172

museum. Really, no big deal."

"Yeah, it was. I'm sorry I've put you in this position, Juliette."

"Well, you owe me big time. But meanwhile, here's the bigger problem… what happens if she shows up again some morning and I'm here? Alex, I think it might be time to come clean about everything. I mean, from what you're telling me you've got a nice relationship going with Keira and the longer we drag this on the worse it will be when she does find out. You remember what we say in the news business about politicians and lies."

"I know. The cover-up is worse than the lie."

"And this particular cover-up seems to have a mind of its own."

He nodded.

"So? Waddaya gonna do?"

"Lemme talk to Bella."

Juliette sat down, reached across the table and took his hands. "This is no longer just about your book, Alex. You've got two women you like and if this thing blows up in your face, which it has a good chance of doing, you could lose both of them. And from the way you talk about them, I'm thinking one of them is right for you."

"Yeah, but which one?"

"Sorry, don't have a crystal ball. But soul mates don't grow on trees. Neither do nice girls."

Gretch leaned back and sipped her coffee. "You're not actually buying her bullshit story, are you?"

Keira folded her hands in her lap and looked up at the ceiling of her office. "I dunno. I want to."

"Seriously? The woman was taking a shower at his place because the *water was out* in her apartment? And I suppose the dog ate her homework."

She looked back at Gretch. "It's possible, though the way they both reacted tells me there's more to the story."

"How did they react?"

"She looked panicked when she answered the door because she was expecting him. And when he got back he looked the same. But Gretch, when he says Juliette is simply a platonic friend, I'm inclined to believe him. He doesn't strike me as a liar."

"Huh. Well, remember what I told you after my first impression."

"What?"

"That he's not an open book. Meanwhile, what about the author, did you finally meet her?"

"Apparently I just missed her. Alexander had taken her to see her mother."

"Too bad. But back to the hot girl in the bathrobe. How did you feel?"

"What do you mean?"

"Initial reaction when you saw her. You'd just had a great day with the guy who didn't take advantage of you while you were buzzed and then the next morning you show up all excited to see him and are greeted by a dripping-wet babe. What was the first thing that went through your mind."

"Honestly?"

"No, lie to me. Of course I want you to be honest."

"Fine. I was a little hurt. Jealous even. I almost felt betrayed that he was nice to me all day and then may have spent the night with her. Even though now I'm reasonably sure he didn't."

"And you were thinking that you maybe should have dragged him into your own bed the night before when you had the chance."

Keira held out her wrists as if she were waiting to be handcuffed. "*Mea culpa.*"

"Basically your so-called 'look but don't touch' ground rules are going down in flames."

"I dunno. Maybe. Probably. It seemed like a good idea at the time. Now I'm not so sure. He gave me a hug and I felt fireworks."

"Just from a hug?"

"Just from a hug. I didn't want him to let go."

"When you got cozy with him on the couch, what did he do?"

"Nothing. Just held me."

"Didn't try anything?"

"Nope. He was following the rules."

"Even though you weren't by torturing the guy. Do you wish he'd made a move?"

"Kinda sorta."

"C'mon, out with it."

"Fine. I wish he'd tried something. I wanted to be kissed. Gretch, I'm just more confused than ever. Easy to say it's okay to see other people, but when you actually *see* him with another woman… even if she's not the one… I guess it hurts. More than I expected. And Juliette's so damn beautiful. You should have seen her right out of the shower without makeup. The woman is flawless, like a china doll."

Gretch locked eyes with her, giving her a soulful look, and softened her tone. "Did it ever occur to you that two men see *you* as flawless?"

"Yeah, right."

"You really don't understand your own appeal, do you?"

She shrugged. "I've never thought I was anything special. But enlighten me. Why are these two terrific men after me?"

"Wow, you got about an hour? Let me see… you're incredibly smart, very talented, an independent woman. You can be a gunslinger one minute while you negotiate million-dollar deals with agents who play hardball and the next you're a little girl if someone gives you a box of chocolate-covered nuts. You're fun, have a great personality, everyone who knows you likes you, you've got that gorgeous red hair, eyes the color of the Caribbean, you're cute as hell. You can light up a room and command it at the same time. You're a decent human being who has been like a big sister to me… do I need to go on?"

"No. But thank you."

"Meanwhile, where does this leave you and Dash?"

"Don't know that either. But there's a new twist in this love polygon."

"And said twist would be?"

"Alexander does some freelance work for the network, researching. Anyway, he's currently looking into some dirt on Senator Bradley."

"What does a politician have to do with this?"

"That's who Dash works for."

"Shit, you gotta be kidding me!"

"But wait, there's more... he's doing this research for Juliette."

"So, if I'm reading this right, Alexander, Juliette and Dash could actually cross paths?"

"I don't even wanna think about it."

"Damn, Keira, this is the convergence from hell. Do you think Dash would work for someone who's dirty?"

"He doesn't seem like the type, but it is politics."

"Could you trust him if Bradley is dirty?"

"Don't know. Depends on if he *knows* the guy's dirty. Maybe there's really nothing for Alexander to dig up."

"We can only hope. Do you trust Alexander?"

"Actually, I still do. He was so cute on Saturday, Gretch. We got in the news car and he made it a rule we had to call each other by our last names, like reporters do. I love when he calls me Madison."

Gretch rolled her eyes. "Wow, what a turn-on."

"Trust me, it was cute. But back to my original worry... I still think there's another explanation as to why Juliette was in his apartment, because, as you previously stated, the whole 'water being out' thing *does* sound like a bullshit story. I mean, why else would she be there if she hadn't slept there?"

Suddenly Gretch's eyes grew wide. "Oh, my God! I think I just figured it out!"

Keira sat up straight. "What, they're married?"

"No. Juliette is not his girlfriend."

She nodded. "Yeah, he already told me that."

"And there's someone else who lives in his apartment."

"Right, his cousin. What about it?"

"What if Juliette is the *author's* girlfriend?"

Keira's jaw slowly dropped. "You think that's even remotely possible?"

"Look, Keira, that would make sense. It might explain the bullshit story, their panicked reactions. It might be why the author doesn't want to come out in public. Maybe she's afraid of coming out of the closet and by becoming a public figure her personal life would be under scrutiny. Or maybe Juliette is the one who doesn't want to come out since she's a well-known reporter. Or they both want to keep their lives private."

"You think that could be it?"

"Hell, it makes a lot more sense than the water in her apartment being out. Look, if she's staying the night and not sleeping with Alexander, and you believe that part, there's only one other person for her to sleep with."

"A stunner like that with a morbidly obese woman?"

Gretch shrugged. "Heart wants what the heart wants. Look, he's coming in today so just bring it up. I bet I'm right."

Alex nodded as he looked over Keira's editing notes. "I think these are fine. And I like the new version of chapter ten." He shot her a smile.

"A bit of literary deja vu."

"Especially since what I read was what you acted out. I'm sure it wasn't exactly hard to write something that actually happened." His pulse quickened as the memory flashed through his mind.

Her face flushed a bit. "Yeah, that part was easy."

"Seriously, the scene works very well. Much better than the original. I will try to defer to your judgment in the future and not be so difficult."

"Thanks. I think we're getting on the same page."

"And in the case of chapter ten, you and I literally *are* on the same page."

"I think we ought to get off the subject of chapter ten before we get into trouble. For me it's like page twenty-seven of *The Godfather*."

"Huh? What's on page twenty-seven?"

"Sonny Corleone nails a bridesmaid against the wall in very graphic detail. The scene made it into the movie."

"And you know this little tidbit of information... how?"

"I'm a romance editor. I had to, you know, study the craft."

"*The Godfather* isn't exactly a romance novel."

She bit her lower lip as her eyebrows did a little jump, giving her a naughty look. "It was research."

"Uh-huh."

"Alexander, speaking of being on the same page... about my showing up unannounced at your place—"

"I told you, no big deal."

"Not that, but... about Juliette."

Oh shit. She's not buying the story and thinks I slept with her. "You have to believe me. There's nothing romantic between us."

"I do believe you. But I think you were protecting your friend from the truth."

Okay, where's she going with this? "I don't understand."

"Look, if she spent the night at your place, with someone other than you who happens to live there, I understand. I get it. I mean, personal privacy and all that. And I understand why she and your cousin might not want people to know... you know..."

She thinks Juliette is a lesbian! And has a relationship with my cousin!

Hmmm... this could be a way out.

Don't say anything.

She studied his face. "Soooo?"

"Yeah?"

"Am I, you know, on the right track?"

"I, uh, really shouldn't say anything."

She nodded and smiled. "Sure, I understand. Trust me, I guard my privacy fiercely as well."

Juliette stood over him, hands on hips. "So now I'm a lesbian?"

He shrugged. "I, uh... uh... "

"You, uh... uh... what?"

"I didn't actually confirm it."

"But you didn't deny it either."

"No."

"What exactly did you say when she asked if I was in a sexual relationship with your cousin who doesn't exist?"

"I didn't say anything. I figured I'd let her believe whatever she wants, because she obviously didn't buy the story about the water being out and you dropping by for a shower."

"Not surprised at that one."

"Me neither."

"So, to recap the situation for those of you scoring at home, which *you* are not doing, by the way, or on the road either... you just spent a terrific day with the redhead, who you're not allowed to get physical with though she wrapped you around her like a blanket Saturday night, only to have her face drop like a rock when she saw your roommate just out of the shower looking like she was doing the walk of shame, while at the same time you're in a physical relationship with a drop-dead gorgeous bikini model preparing to be the face of your novel who tortures you to the point you need an ice bath, all of this while you are maintaining the ruse that the author of said novel is your morbidly obese agoraphobic cousin who is in a same-sex relationship with your roommate, who must now pretend to be a non-existent lesbian author when on the phone."

"I think you've just about nailed it."

"Alex, this has really gotten out of hand. I thought it was bad yesterday but now the smelly brown stuff is *this close* to hitting the spinning blade. And the fan is set on high."

Chapter 17

MEET AMERICA'S SIZZLE GIRL

By Jan Smithson

Her arrival on a video billboard caused massive gridlock in Times Square. Since then you can't avoid her smoldering gaze and incredibly toned bikini bod, as her ad for Sizzle sunblock seems to be everywhere, from television to subway platforms.

And it's beginning to look as if Lauren Hale, now known as the Sizzle Girl, is going to have more than fifteen minutes of fame. The Texas transplant was waiting tables at an upscale Manhattan restaurant last month; now she's in demand by everyone and her agent is having no trouble filling her schedule. In fact, she's booked solid for the foreseeable future.

"It's all happened so fast, and by pure chance meetings," said Hale, her soft Southern drawl filling the air as she stretches out on a couch in her tiny apartment. The woman who has definitely added sizzle to the sunblock industry looks like anything but the bikini-ed babe in the ads; with a baggy New York Giants sweatshirt and jeans, upswept hair, glasses, and little makeup, she looks like the proverbial girl next door. Put her side by side with the billboard and you'd never guess it was the same person. Which is just fine with her. "I haven't been recognized once. Then again, I don't go out in public wearing a string bikini with a top that's two sizes too small and more makeup than I normally use in a year." Incredibly, the woman who is stopping traffic in Manhattan could barely get arrested as an actress in Texas because she looked too sweet and innocent. "Yeah, I guess that ship has sailed. I used to be stuck with all the Snow White parts. Now I think it will be just the opposite." She credits her newfound success to acting classes in Manhattan and serendipity. "I met a nice guy in a drug store and mentioned I was a struggling actress, so he called a friend who produces commercials, I went for an audition, and all of a sudden I'm the Sizzle Girl. Then a romance novel editor ends up at one of my tables in the restaurant, out to dinner with the same guy no less, and she hires me to pose for a book cover. If that's not enough, after the commercial hit the air I get a call from my agent and next thing you know I'm on a flight to Hollywood to try out for a role in a major motion picture. My guardian angel is certainly aligning the stars in a big way."

After an audition in Tinseltown, Hale is waiting to find out if she'll get the role in a new romantic comedy filled with A-listers. "They had me read for two parts; the main heroine and her best friend. The script is really fun and I'd be thrilled with either role. I'm supposed to know one way or the other pretty soon. Meanwhile, my agent got me two more national commercials. One for shampoo and the other for a fitness chain."

And while her acting resume might get longer, it's the Times Square billboard that caught the attention of a sports magazine editor. Hale has already been signed to model in next year's swimsuit issue. "Funny, it's the first time I ever wore a bikini. I'm kind of modest and have always stuck to one-piece suits. But I'm not complaining. Frankly I'm shocked at the reaction because I don't think I'm anything special."

Millions of guys would disagree. As for the question every single man wants answered, well guys, you'll have to keep wondering.

If Sizzle Girl has a Sizzle Guy, she's not telling. "My private life is private, and will always be that way, so I really won't discuss anyone I'm dating. I will say that I am really impressed with the men in New York. They're professional, they dress so well and they're real gentlemen." Her eyes twinkle a bit. "Do I date? Yeah, but that's all you're getting."

Hale said she plans to make New York her permanent residence even if Hollywood comes calling. "This is home for me now, this is where my luck changed. I love the people here and the pulse of the city. New Yorkers are very driven but still manage to be polite and they have such big hearts whenever there's someone who needs help. I do miss driving a car but I love the fact that I can go out at two in the morning and get something to eat."

As for Sizzle sunblock, her ad is not a one-time deal as a sequel is in the works. "They've got me lined up to do a commercial for the Super Bowl. So the red bikini will be back. I've asked for one that actually fits, but I don't think that's happening."

And she's got her head on straight. "I still fill in at the restaurant when I'm free and they're shorthanded. Let's face it, this could all end abruptly and I could be in those *whatever became of* magazines ten years from now."

Juliette put the newspaper down and looked up at Alex. "Well, this either complicates things or simplifies them."

He furrowed his brow. "That doesn't make sense."

"Okay, look. If she gets the movie role she'll be out of town for God knows how long. Outta sight, outta mind. On the other hand, absence makes the heart grow fonder."

"I've never been a fan of long-distance relationships."

"I don't know a single person who has made it work. And knowing you, I can say it wouldn't."

"Her career is taking off like a rocket whether or not she gets this part. She told me her agent has her booked solid for months and she's already got a couple of parts in shows that are produced here."

She pointed to the paper. "Anyway, from reading that it doesn't sound like fame will go to her head and she'll dump you for a movie star."

"But you never know. Fame does funny things to people, as we've both seen at the network."

"Very true. So what's the plan?"

"Seeing her on Saturday."

"And Keira?"

"Taking her out on Friday."

"I wish you were doing the reverse."

"Why?"

"Cause Keira's gonna get you all worked up and Lauren will reap the rewards. Or provide relief, depending on your point of view. If you went out with Lauren first, you'd get all your physical needs out of your system by the time you picked up Keira."

"Don't think so. The redhead does things to me. Even if I can't touch her."

"I guess absence of physical contact makes the heart grow fonder as well. Or other body parts."

"Juliette, I cannot stop thinking about kissing her in the office."

"It will be hard for you to forget now that it's in the book. Soooo… how many times have you read that particular chapter?"

He blushed. "Way too many."

"Bella, I've got a problem."

Bella Farentino heard the worry in Keira's voice over the phone. "Something about the book?"

"No, not at all. The book is coming along fine, I'm almost halfway through the editing process and we've hired the woman for the cover."

"So, your problem would be?"

"Alexander."

"What, you don't like working with him?"

"No, it has nothing to do with work. I, you know, really like him."

"I thought we established that a while back, Keira. And that he likes you."

"Well, there are a couple of other factors involved. I'm also seeing someone else and so is he."

Bella's eyebrows went up. "Keira Madison? Dating two men at the same time? Hang on, let me turn on the Weather Channel to find out when hell froze over."

"No, it's true. And I like both of them."

"Nice problem to have, honey. So what's the deal with Alexander?"

"We sorta… had a moment in the office a few days ago."

"Like, an argument moment or a romantic moment?"

"Romantic. Anyway, I realized I couldn't be physical with him until this book was done because I couldn't be objective. His kiss does things to me."

"That's what kisses are for, honey. A kiss is a man's signature. And you want a guy with good handwriting."

"I know. We had a great day Saturday, he was a perfect gentleman, didn't make a move, and then Sunday I showed up at his apartment with brunch and this gorgeous blonde friend, who he claims is platonic, answered the door just out of the shower in a bathrobe."

"Whoa, back up. Why didn't he make a move? I thought you had a moment in the office." Bella's eyes widened as she listened to the tale of the crazy ground rules, the lame excuse, Gretch's theory on the blonde, Keira's interest in another guy, who was apparently the most gorgeous man she'd ever seen.

"So, Keira, let me get this straight. You're all over the fantasy guy and won't touch Alexander?"

"Correct."

"Which one do you like better?"

"I don't know. They're about even."

"And you want me to find out if Alexander's hot friend is a lesbian?"

"If you wouldn't mind."

"You want me to find out who the other woman is that he's dating, if that's the case?"

"No. I just need to know if he's sleeping with the blonde. If he is, I'm out."

"Got it, I'll see what I can do." A gentle tap on the door made her look up. She saw Alex standing there. "Listen, Keira, I've got a meeting with one of my agents. I'll talk with you soon, okay?"

"Sure, Bella. Thanks. Bye."

"Bye." She hung up and shook her head at Alex. "Honey, you got some 'splainin' to do."

His eyes grew wide as he put his palms up. "What?"

She pointed at the phone. "That was Keira. Apparently she showed up at your place and found, in her words, a smoking-hot babe in your apartment drippin' wet and barely dressed."

He nodded and sat down. "My roommate, Juliette. The woman who has been pretending to be the author on the phone."

"Well, she's wanting me to find out if the blonde is a lesbian and was in a bathrobe because she spent the night with your faux cousin. Good God, Alex, this is getting out of hand. I'm sorry, I didn't think this plan would go so far off the rails."

"So do we tell her the truth?"

"I know Keira, and I know she'll be pissed off. But I can always take one for the team and tell her the whole thing was my idea. How much do you like her?"

"A lot. An awful lot."

She folded her hands on her desk. "Meanwhile, I understand you have someone else on your dance card. Who's the other woman that you're actually dating?"

He blushed a bit. "You know the girl on the Times Square billboard? The Sizzle Girl?"

Her jaw slowly dropped. "The brunette in the bikini? Holy shit! Are you—"

"No. I haven't slept with her. I can't do that and date someone else."

"I'm impressed."

"But Sizzle Girl is, shall we say, very affectionate."

"And you still haven't slept with her? Damn, Alex, I don't know many men who could turn down a woman like that. Which girl do you like better?"

"It's sorta even."

"And the deal is you can't touch Keira?"

"Right."

"But you can get your paws all over billboard girl."

"Right. Her name's Lauren. And generally her paws are all over me."

"I would think that would leave Keira at a significant disadvantage, especially considering the girl on the billboard looks like she could nurse a small village."

"Actually, no. And here's something that makes it worse. Keira met her and hired her to be the cover model of my book."

Bella's jaw dropped. "Are you friggin' kidding me?"

"I know. I took Keira to dinner and Lauren was the waitress. This was all before the billboard and the TV commercial hit. Anyway, she's going to be the face of my book."

"Brilliant decision on Keira's part, great for your book, but it does complicate matters more." Bella exhaled, leaned back and looked at the ceiling.

"I saw the look on Keira's face when she dropped by, and she acted a bit hurt. I think she's intimidated by Juliette."

"Why, is she a bitch?"

"No, she's stunning. When Keira called her a smoking-hot babe, she wasn't kidding." Alex pulled out his cell phone, tapped a few keys and turned it toward Bella. "That's her."

"Wow. She's gorgeous. I can see why Keira might be a bit jealous. Well, we'll figure something out. But you do impress me, Alex."

"How's that?"

"You get to canoodle with every man's fantasy and yet you're hung up on a plain Jane you can't touch. That speaks to your character."

"You're assuming I think Keira is plain. In some ways she's more attractive than the girl on the billboard."

"And what ways would those be?"

"Can't put my finger on it, Bella."

"I can. You've got something in common with Keira."

"What's that?"

"You both think alike when it comes to what's attractive."

Chapter 18

Gretch had read Keira the riot act about taking control of the situation with both men by turning up the heat, physically. Shopping and a makeover. The salon had done wonders with Keira's hair, her makeup was flawless and the new teal halter dress fit perfectly. She'd picked up some sky-high heels that would put her at a reasonable height for her towering date. She had to admit, she had never looked this good. And Gretch was right, it was empowering. Keira looked in the mirror and declared herself ready for her date with Dash. Besides, he'd be there to pick her up at any moment.

And then the phone rang.

She looked at the Caller ID and saw his name.

Oh, shit.

"Hi, Dash."

"Keira, sorry to do this to you, but we're in major damage control at the campaign. Things really hit the fan. I'm afraid I'm not going to be able to make it tonight."

"What happened?"

"It's easier if you just turn on the news."

"Which channel?"

"Six. Look, I sincerely apologize—"

"Don't worry about it, go put out your fire."

"I'm afraid this is a four-alarm blaze, but I'll give it a shot.

Thanks for being so understanding."

"No problem, Dash. Give me a call when things calm down. Bye."

She shook her head and tossed her phone on the counter, yelled "sonofabitch!" then headed for the television in the living room. She turned it on and the picture cleared, showing the distraught face of New York's senior senator, who was hurriedly racing to his car trailed by a news crew. The red banner across the top of the screen read "Exclusive". Keira turned up the sound. The reporter's voice filled the room.

"...the documents and photos we acquired just hours ago clearly show the misappropriation of funds by the Senator, who used campaign contributions to pay for his weekend trysts at a thousand-dollar-a-night hotel with his mistress, a woman thirty-five years younger. This is a huge blow to his career, as Bradley had been seen as a safe bet for re-election."

Damn, that voice sounds familiar. Then Keira's jaw dropped as she saw the face that went with it.

Juliette.

Holy shit, Alexander must have found the smoking gun.

She watched as Juliette's report included photos pulled from social media of the sixty-year-old Senator in a romantic clinch with a young woman in a seriously short skirt and revealing top. Followed by a shot of Bradley hugging his wife after his last election win. The story ended with a live shot of Juliette standing in front of the Senator's campaign headquarters.

Where Dash was no doubt pulling his hair out.

"No way to spin this one," she said, as the phone rang again.

Alexander.

"Hey, Bauer."

"Hi, I know this is short notice, but I was wondering if you were free to celebrate with me."

"What are we celebrating?"

189

"In case you haven't seen the news, I helped take down a crooked US senator."

"I just saw Juliette's story. And your smoking gun. How did you get this stuff?"

"Let's just say the young generation tends to over-share everything. So, you wanna split a bottle of champagne?"

"Sure, why not. Where do you wanna go—" The buzzer from the doorman interrupted her. "Hang on, someone's here to see me."

"Yeah, I'm in the lobby."

Keira heard the elevator bell ring and knew he would arrive any moment.

She'd be celebrating with one boyfriend, who had put the other boyfriend on the unemployment line.

He knocked, she opened the door and his jaw dropped. "Whoa."

She studied his face. "Whoa, what?"

"Damn, Madison, you look amazing."

"Well, you said you were in the lobby so I threw something together."

"Oh, gimme a break. You were obviously going out. We can do this another time. I'm sorry, I didn't mean to show up unannounced."

"Hey, I did it to you. Besides, my plans got canceled at the last minute so my dance card is free."

"Huh. Lucky for me."

"Well, you gonna stand in the hallway all night staring at me, or are we going to attack that champagne?"

"Much as I wouldn't mind staring at you, the champagne will get warm."

So will I.

Keira threw back the last sip of champagne, which, considering it was on an empty stomach, went right to her head. She needed food, and soon. "You had dinner yet?"

"No. What are you in the mood for? My treat."

"How about we order in some Chinese?"

"Seriously?"

"What, you don't like Chinese?"

"No, I love it, but it'd be a waste."

"By now you should know I'll clean my plate, Bauer."

"Not that, I meant it would be a waste not to take a beautiful woman in a spectacular dress out to dinner."

"You're too sweet to me."

"Hey, I've already had a great day and feel on top of the world, what could be better than having a girl like you on my arm out in public."

"Oh, so I'm just arm candy to you now?"

"You did say sugar was at the top of the pyramid."

Dinner was fabulous. She finished the last bite of cheesecake, tossed her napkin on the table, leaned back and patted her stomach. "Excellent choice for dinner. I've never been here."

"Glad you liked it. Though it's not one of those 'best-kept secrets.'"

"Obviously, the place was packed when we got here. I'm impressed that you got a table without waiting."

"Friends in high places."

"So, did they name this restaurant after the street from the Monopoly game?"

"Park Place? Actually, they did. The owner wanted a name that conveyed wealth and everyone knows it's an expensive property on the board."

"Interesting. Though you don't need that property to win the game."

"What, Park Place? Hell, you get that one and Boardwalk, and it's game over."

"That is a common fallacy in Monopoly strategy."

He furrowed his brow. "Really? Those two get the most rent

on the board."

"It's about quantity, not quality if you wanna win the game. I always buy up the cheap stuff on the first row. Mediterranean. Baltic. Slumlord strategy. Low rents but they're steady. I buy up the whole block, put up hotels, and you're bound to land on one every time around. You pass Go, collect your two hundred bucks, and turn it right over to me."

"Still think you'd be better off with Park Place and Boardwalk."

"Wanna bet?"

"What, on a game of Monopoly?"

She shrugged. "Why not? I got the game at home. If you're so sure you can win with the high-rent district, prove it. Tell you what, I won't even buy those if I land on them. Put up all the hotels you want."

"You're serious?"

"Bring it. Put your Monopoly money where your mouth is, Bauer. Unless, of course, you're afraid to lose."

"Fine. What's the bet?"

"Same as before. You win, you get a kiss. You lose, you take me to another best-kept secret."

"Alas, fair damsel, you're still not a good gambler. Another win-win wager. I accept the challenge."

"Sonofabitch!" He shook his head as he landed on Baltic, counted the play money and gave it to her. "Busted again." He threw up his hands. "I give up."

She grabbed the money and smiled. "Ha! That's three more best-kept secrets you owe me."

"So now I'm up to four, including the drive-in."

"Yep." She leaned back and yawned, covering her mouth. "Oh, excuse me."

He looked at his watch. "Wow, it's one-thirty."

"Time flies when you're a rich, successful slumlord with a whole street of fleabag hotels."

"Go ahead, rub it in. Well, it's late and I assume you have to work tomorrow morning, so I'd better get going."

"Yeah, I've got a meeting at nine." They both got up and she walked him to the door. "I had a really nice time, Bauer."

"Yeah, me too."

"Glad you showed up out of the blue."

"Glad I could show you off in public."

"Oh, so I'm worth showing off?"

"Why do you continue to question my compliments?"

"As previously mentioned, it's part of my charm."

"Well, as for showing you off, obviously you didn't notice the looks you were getting. Does wonders for the male ego." He turned and faced her, giving her a soulful look as he put his hands lightly on her waist. Keira got a lump in her throat as they locked eyes. She had never, ever wanted to kiss a man as much as she did right now. "Don't suppose there might be a consolation prize? Y'know, on our bet?"

She cocked her head and looked up. "Hmmm… well, you've already got four upcoming dates with me."

"Oh, so instead of us 'hanging out as friends' we're actually calling them 'dates' now?

"I suppose we can make that distinction. And arc four of them not enough of a consolation?"

"I had something more immediate in mind."

I was supposed to be Dash's date tonight and instead I desperately want his competition while the other guy probably just lost his job.

I can't do this.

Yet.

She moved forward and hugged him hard, noting that with her new heels she was a shade taller than him. She rested her head on his shoulder. "Look, Bauer, I think we both know that if we start kissing I won't be able to stop."

"I can be the strong one. I promise to stop at one."

"Yeah, right. Doesn't work for kissing or potato chips."

He held her, gently stroking her hair for a minute. Then he pulled back and smiled. "Okay, Madison. I'll settle for the four dates. But…"

"But… what?"

"If we start, I have a feeling I won't be able to stop."

Gretch stuck her head in Keira's office a few minutes before noon. "Someone here to see you."

Keira looked up and saw Dash standing next to her assistant, droopy-eyed and looking fried. "Hey, come on in."

"Sorry to drop by unexpected," he said, as Gretch left the office and closed the door. "But I was hoping you were free for lunch. I need a friend right now."

Annnddd… cue the Catholic guilt.

"Absolutely." Keira got up and gave him a hug. "Dash, I'm so sorry for what happened."

"Hey, not your fault. Political scandals go with the territory."

She moved back behind her desk as he took a seat. "Did you see it coming?"

He shrugged. "I knew Bradley had a roving eye, but most of them do. However, I didn't think he'd actually cheat on his wife, who is an absolute saint. Well, she *was*, anyway. She's not doing the 'stand by your man' routine. Already hired a divorce lawyer and is gonna clean him out."

"Don't blame her. So, what are you gonna do now? Can you hook on with another campaign?"

"Probably not. Too close to the election. Though I really need to find something. The feds froze the campaign account so I can't get paid, and they owed me a lot. Plus I was due a huge bonus if we won, which was in the bag. I doubt I'll ever see a penny. They'll probably return everything to the donors."

"Yikes." She took a quick glance at her watch and knew she wanted to catch the cover artist before heading out. "Hey, take a walk with me. Wanna drop by the art department and then I'll take you to lunch. My treat."

"Well, hello again." The artist smiled and sat up straight as Dash followed Keira into the art department.

"You two know each other?"

Dash nodded. "We met during the tour when Gretch took me around."

Keira then turned back to the artist. "So, let's see our prospective Mister Rights for *Ring Girl*."

The artist tapped a few keys on the computer and the sample covers filled the screen. "I'm not sure we've got what you're looking for, Keira. None of the models seemed to have the right look to go along with Lauren. But you be the judge. Maybe you'll see something I don't."

Keira looked over her shoulder as the covers filled the screen one by one. "Nope. Uh-uh. No. No way. Not even close. Dammit, they're all the wrong. I'll know him when I see him. We're gonna have to keep looking."

"Maybe not," said the artist, who cocked her head at Dash. "I took a photo of your friend just for the hell of it because he's the type you're looking for, and I took the liberty of Photoshopping him in. He wasn't posing, but... well, see what you think. Jill already gave it a thumbs-up."

A mocked-up cover of Lauren and Dash filled the screen. Keira's eyes went wide. "Oh my." She turned to Dash and waved him over. "Come look at this."

Dash moved behind the artist and chuckled. "That might be one for the scrapbook."

"Scrapbook, hell," said Keira. "You're perfect for this novel. And you look great with Lauren. Imagine what we can do with a real photo session and you two in the same room."

"Seriously?"

"I'm not kidding, Dash. You both have that gleam in your eyes, that certain something. There's a sort of devilish chemistry."

"How can I have chemistry with someone I've never met?"

"Trust me, I'm an expert in chemistry, and I'm not talking about the kind you took in high school. And you've got it with Lauren."

"Keira's never wrong," said the artist. "That's why we call her Cover Girl."

His face tightened. "I dunno. I only did that modeling thing years ago to pay my tuition."

Keira put her hand on his shoulder. "Well, I can't give you that much, but it will pay the light bill until you find another campaign. C'mon, you said you're always behind the scenes and it's not like anyone in politics will ever see this and make the connection."

"You really want me to pose for a book cover?"

"It'll be fun. And your face will be on a best-seller. It'll take one day, tops. A session with a makeup artist, a few different outfits, and boom, you're done and you get a nice check. C'mon, Dash, I need the perfect guy for this cover and you're it. And if there's a sequel, we'll probably use you again."

He shook his head and smiled. "Oh, what the hell, I guess I can use the cash."

"Great, thank you so much."

The artist gently touched her forearm. "Oh, Keira, one more thing you forgot. Remember, I don't have a photo of the author for the back cover. So I need to know what you want to do with that space."

"I didn't forget. I've got the perfect solution. Something that's never been done."

The waiter took their order and headed to the kitchen. Dash still looked lost in thought. "Cheer up, Dash, you just had a little freelance modeling job fall in your lap. And you're helping me out."

He forced a smile. "Sorry. I really do appreciate you doing this for me."

"Hey, you're the one doing me a favor. Besides, you'll be back in politics for the next cycle."

"True. Thankfully I'm not implicated in any sort of cover-up. Damn, what a mess. Didja catch the headline on the front page of *The Post*?"

"Yeah. Speaking of said cover-up, can I ask you something?"

"Sure."

"In light of what just happened with the Senator, I was wondering how you manage to work with people who aren't exactly, you know, ethical. I mean, Dash, you're a good guy and politics is a dirty business. It seems a lot of those people end up on the police blotter or in divorce court."

"Well, I thought about that when I was younger and wore rose-colored glasses, thinking people really ran for office because they wanted to change the world. But I came to realize that most politicians are a bunch of narcissistic sleazeballs."

"So how do you reconcile working for them?"

"You have to look at it this way... you put character aside and choose the clients who can do the most good."

"Really? Character doesn't mean anything to you?"

"Look, Kennedy was a horrible adulterer but a great president. Carter was faithful and one of our worst presidents. When you want to help someone get elected, you back the person who can change things for the better. That candidate is not always the best human being. Or even a decent one."

"So in your mind it's kind of the 'ends justify the means' thing."

"Pretty much."

"Huh. Interesting way of looking at it."

And an interesting method of looking the other way.

Gretch's eyes went wide. "Do you realize what you've just done?"

"Yeah, I found Mister Right to pose with Lauren. It's gonna make a great cover."

"And... what else?"

She shrugged. "Dash's face will help sell books."

"Still missing the obvious."

She put up her hands. "Fine, I'll take *Keira is clueless for a thousand*."

"The answer is... you're going to put one of the guys you're dating, one of the guys you like a lot, who is possibly the best-looking man we've ever seen, in close contact with the most desirable woman in America who will be wearing a very revealing outfit."

Oh.

"Didn't think that one through, did you, boss?"

Nope, sure didn't.

"Well," said Gretch, "guess you may as well throw the biggest temptation we can find at him. If he can resist her, you've got yourself a keeper. I guess you'll know in a week."

Chapter 19

Lauren beamed as Alex walked into the photographer's studio. "I'm so glad you came!" She started to get up out of the chair but the makeup artist put one hand on her shoulder and stopped her. "Oh, sorry, can't hug you. It'll ruin my makeup."

"Not a problem. I'll take a rain check."

"Well, it's gonna be a big hug because… wait for it… I got the part!"

"In the movie?"

"Yep, I'm gonna play Jordana Starr's best friend! Can you believe it?"

"Lauren, I'm so happy for you."

"Thank you. Once again, all because I met you. Anyway, I'll tell you all about it after we finish taking pictures."

"Sure, Lauren. Can't wait to hear all the details."

"And thanks again for coming. I feel more comfortable with you here. Especially in these outfits."

He couldn't see what she was wearing under the smock.

But he had a good idea it would be something revealing.

The sight of a shirtless Dash being misted by the photographer's assistant stopped Keira and Gretch in their tracks as they entered the studio. Jill Howland was already there, staring.

Gretch's jaw dropped as she grabbed Keira's arm. "Tell me again why you had a chance with that and didn't take advantage."

"Damn."

"I thought you already saw him with his shirt off."

"I caught a glimpse when we first met, but... damn." Keira absentmindedly licked her lips as she stared at his glistening torso.

Gretch was still gawking. "I'm giving you my notice. I want to be a photographer's intern in charge of misting. Check that, I want to *be* the mist."

Keira turned to Jill. "I think this is the first time I've seen you at a photo shoot. Not exactly on a publisher's to-do list."

"I, uh, was a little concerned about you using an inexperienced model."

"Oh, give me a break."

"Fine, I wanted an up-close-and-personal look. Anyway, I unfortunately have to head back to the office."

"We'll hold the fort."

"I'm sure. Send me the shots when they're done." Jill turned and headed for the door, then glanced back to get one last look before leaving.

Keira looked back at Dash. "We're gonna sell a shitload of books."

"No kidding. We could just sell the cover without the manuscript. You still sure you want to expose him to Lauren?"

"Huh?"

"Roll in your tongue, boss."

Dash looked up and smiled at them. "Hey guys, didn't know you were coming."

Keira and Gretch started walking toward him. "Well, we thought you might be a little nervous so thought we'd drop by."

Gretch leaned up and whispered in her ear. "Liar."

"Thanks, guys, I appreciate it."

"All done," said the photographer's assistant, a young buxom blonde who looked longingly at him. "If I can do *anything* to make you more comfortable, don't hesitate to ask."

"Honey, take a number," whispered Gretch.

Dash smiled at the assistant. "Thanks."

The girl turned around, her neck craned around like an owl facing him, and walked right into a tripod.

Keira and Gretch stopped in front of his chair. His ripped physique looked even more impressive up close. "Have you met our heroine yet?"

He shook his head. "No, but the photographer said she's not an experienced model either, so we're in the same boat. By the way, great timing on this job. If you'd scheduled it for next week I wouldn't have been able to do it. I just got hired for a campaign in Los Angeles."

"The big one for next year?"

"No, for the home stretch of a current campaign, though I did get the gig for next year as well. This is just for two months. Someone on their staff recently quit so they needed a replacement quick. I'll be leaving in a few days. Tell you about it when we're done."

"Who will you be working for?"

He looked down and brushed off his trousers. "You, uh, probably never heard of him. Mayor of LA."

"What's his name?"

"Uh, Marvin Voper."

Gretch wrinkled her nose. "Ewwww. You're working for *him*?"

Keira turned to her assistant. "You know who that is?"

Dash touched Keira on the forearm. "So, you said there would be other photos today?"

Hmmm. Changing the subject. Gotta find out more about this. "Yeah. We're doing the cover here and then something different for the back cover since there won't be an author photo. We're going to get some shots of you and Lauren out and about town, looking like you're out on a date."

"And I get to wear a shirt in those?"

"Yes, Dash, you do. Along with a suit and tie. But what you've got above the waist is gonna sell a lot of books."

A door opened across the room. Keira watched Dash's eyes widen and jaw hang open as Lauren entered the room.

And then Keira's own eyes bugged out and her pulse shot up when she saw Alexander following her. "Hey, Bauer, what are you doing here?"

"Oh, Lauren invited me. Didn't know you'd be here."

Uh-oh. Alexander and Dash in the same room.

And Dash is locked in on Lauren like a heat-seeking missile.

Gretch talked under her breath. "And the hits just keep on comin'."

Alexander's jaw hung open when he saw Dash. "*That's* the guy who's supposed to be Jamison? I didn't write— I mean, I didn't picture him that way. He's not a Greek god in the book."

"True," said Keira, "but he looks good with Lauren in a test mock-up. And it will help sell a lot of copies."

"Have you used him before?"

"No. He's not really a model. Just, uh, someone I know."

Keira studied his face, which looked as though the confidence was being drained out of it, as if someone had pulled a plug. Dash moved toward them and stuck out his hand toward Alexander. "Hi, Dash Riley."

Alexander shook his hand as he looked up at the chiseled hunk of beefcake who towered over him. "Alexander Bauer."

"He's the author's cousin, working on the book with us," said Keira.

"Ah," said Dash.

The photographer walked toward them. "Okay, let's get set up."

Dash smiled at Keira. "Well, here goes. Wish me luck." He leaned down and kissed her on the lips.

She saw Alexander's eyes widen in her peripheral vision.

By the time she turned to look at him he was biting his lower lip and looking at the floor as he headed back to a chair.

That's the other guy Keira is dating.

I've got no shot.

Alex forced himself to smile for Lauren as she got in position for the photo shoot. She smiled back as she moved next to Dash.

She had never looked more seductive. Her outfit seemed to show off her incredible assets more than the bikini. A tight crop top so pushed out by her boobs that the bottom hung down about two inches in front of her toned abs. A black leather knee-length skirt and stilettos. Eyes done up like an Egyptian princess. A red wig the color of Keira's hair.

He wasn't the only one who noticed. Dash looked as though he wanted to devour Lauren, even though Keira was a few feet away.

Hell, he's big enough, it probably takes two women to satisfy him. And he's good looking enough so they'll be happy to share.

The photographer started giving directions to the models. "Lauren, move next to him and lay your head on his shoulder. Dash, wrap one arm around her waist." The two moved into place as the photographer turned on an electric fan, which made Lauren's hair blow back from her face. He looked through the viewfinder and started snapping photos. "Lauren, slide your pinky under his waistband. Take your time. And keep looking at each other." She blushed a bit, then slowly ran her finger under his belt, stealing Dash's breath. His eyes grew wide as he stared down at her. "Okay, now Lauren, lean up like you're going to kiss him. Slightly part your lips. But Dash, don't bend down. Keep staring at her."

Alex shook his head as the irony hit him.

The guy on the cover of the book I wrote is going to steal both the women I'm dating.

Gretch put her hand on Keira's shoulder and pointed at Alexander. "You're gonna need some damage control over there. The guy looks like someone ran over his dog."

Keira took a quick look. "I told him I was dating someone else."

"Not too many *someone elses* look like Dash. Trust me, boss, unless you do something to pump up Alexander, you can stick a fork in any possible relationship."

Then Keira looked back at the photo shoot and Lauren's effect on Dash.

And Dash's obviously undivided attention.

"Boss? What about Alexander?"

Keira was still locked in on Lauren. "You think they're real?"

"I don't know, but I believe she's the poster child for the phrase *My eyes are up here*."

"They've really got some chemistry."

The photographer moved out from behind the camera. "Okay, guys, one more pose. Dash, if you could pick Lauren up. Cradle her like a bride. Lauren, I want you to wrap your arms around his neck." Dash leaned down and easily scooped Lauren into his arms. She locked her fingers behind his neck. "Great, guys. Now look at each other." He moved back behind the camera and squeezed off a few more shots. "Terrific. Looking good." He paused and leaned out from the camera. "Okay, if you two wouldn't mind, can I get a kiss?"

Dash looked at Lauren. "You okay with that?"

She nodded. "Sure. Actors do it all the time."

The photographer moved back behind the camera and the sound of the auto-winder filled the room as Lauren leaned up, took Dash's face in her hands and gave him what looked to be a long, passionate kiss.

Keira felt her blood pressure spike. "Okay, that's enough," she said under her breath. "You can stop now."

But they kept kissing as Lauren ran her hands across his massive shoulders, then through his hair.

The photographer kept shooting for what seemed like an eternity, then stopped. "Okay, guys, that was terrific. Looked very real."

But they didn't stop kissing. Dash pulled her closer. Lauren's eyes widened and she started to push his shoulders, obviously trying to get him to stop. Finally their lips parted but Dash didn't put

Lauren down. He kept staring at her like there was no one else in the room. Then he whispered something to her loud enough for them to hear. Keira's eyes widened as her blood boiled.

Gretch reached over and patted Keira's hand. "Hey."

She kept watching Dash and Lauren as her jaw clenched. "What?"

Gretch grabbed her chin and turned her head so that they were facing each other. "You're Keira Madison. You've got the world by the tail. And you know romance. You know where this plot is going and how this story ends. So get your ass in gear and take charge of this situation like the heroine in this book. You *know* what you have to do to get your Jamison."

Keira slowly nodded, got up and headed toward one of the men.

"Hey."

Alex turned away from Dash and Lauren to find Keira standing next to him. "Hey. The, uh, cover should be good. I guess they're going out now to shoot some stuff around town."

"Yeah. Let's go to dinner."

"Huh?"

"Dinner. You know, that meal after work we all eat every day?"

"You want to go to dinner *now*?"

"No, next week. It's five o'clock, this girl is hungry and she wants you to feed her."

He shrugged. "I dunno, Keira, I'm not in the mood to go out tonight. I'll be better company another day."

She grabbed his arm and pulled him out of the chair. "Listen, Bauer, I've got four dates coming from you and I'm cashing one of them in right now. And you're good company anytime."

"Look, I—"

"You're not welshing on a bet, are you? I kicked your ass in Monopoly fair and square. You're taking me out. End of story."

"You don't have to—"

"Stop talking, get out your phone and make us a reservation so

I don't miss my evening feeding. C'mon." She clapped her hands twice. "Chop chop."

He locked eyes with her, his filled with hurt.

"Bauer, listen to me. I *want*… to have *dinner*… with *you*. Do I make myself clear?"

Damage control wasn't working. Keira watched Alexander pick at his stuffed mushrooms as he remained quiet. "Your appetizer okay?"

"Yeah, it's fine."

"Mine's delicious. Another great choice. You seem to know all the great places to eat around town."

"Yeah, I'm good for something."

"You're good for a lot of things, Bauer. Listen, I wanted to tell you—"

"Hey, look who's here!"

Dash's voice interrupted her. She looked up to find him and Lauren standing next to their table.

Oh.

Shit.

"Oh, I didn't know you were shooting the back-cover photos here."

"Yeah," said Dash, now decked out in a dark gray three- piece suit. "Took some pictures in the front near the fountain. We're all done."

"It went very well," said the photographer. "I think you'll be pleased."

"Can't thank you enough for the opportunity," said Lauren, turning heads in a tight emerald green dress.

"I think you're a great choice," said Keira, who then turned to look down at her dinner. "You too, Dash."

A waiter arrived at the table. "Will you two be joining them for dinner? Otherwise it will be an hour wait."

Oh.

Shit.

She had no choice.

And then Alexander surprised her.

What the hell, may as well find out if Keira's serious about this guy. If I'm wasting my time with her, I need to know now.

Alex stood up and held out a chair for Lauren. "Please, join us."

She smiled and took the seat next to him. "Why thank you, kind sir."

Dash grabbed the chair next to Keira, who suddenly looked like she had itching powder in her clothes. Her shoulders hunched up while her eyes went wide.

Alex sat and adjusted his chair. "So how'd it go?"

"Great," said Dash. "We went to Central Park, took some shots in a hansom cab, then Rockefeller Center near the skating rink, then here. Hope everything comes out okay."

Alex kept his eyes on Keira. "I'm sure it will. You two look great together."

She didn't say anything. Just sat there with her hands in her lap.

Lauren picked up a menu. "So, Keira, when is the book coming out? I can't wait to see the cover and read it."

"In a few months. I can email you the cover and an advance copy of the manuscript before that."

"Great. I'm so glad I got to do this before I leave."

Keira furrowed her brow. "Where are you going?"

"You forgot already? Hollywood!"

"Oh, right."

"I'll be gone for about three months. I leave in a few days, so the timing was perfect for this shoot. I've got so much to do before I go, then I have to find a place to live, get the lay of the land."

Alex patted her hand. "She's about to be a big star."

"All thanks to you."

Alex turned to Dash. "What about you, Dash? More modeling jobs?"

He shook his head. "Nah, I work in politics. Hadn't done any modeling since college. Keira twisted my arm to get me to do this."

Oh, really.

Dash leaned over and wrapped one arm around Keira's shoulders. "But hey, she's a great gal, it was the least I could do."

Keira's face tightened.

Lauren snapped her menu shut and turned to Alex. "Would you be a dear and order the salmon for me? I need to freshen up and get some of this makeup off. I'm sure it looks good for the camera but I feel like a streetwalker." She got up, moved around the table, and grabbed Keira's hand. "C'mon, Keira, I need a little help."

Keira's eyes filled with fear as she got up to head to the ladies' room with Lauren, leaving the two men she was dating alone to talk.

Chapter 20

"What do you mean, you think you lost them *both*?"

Juliette wheeled her suitcase against the wall and sat next to Alex on the couch. "It's a long story," he said, "but basically I think I've gone from two girlfriends to none." Juliette listened intently as he recapped the events of the previous day.

"Just because you know who the other guy is doesn't mean you've lost Keira."

Alex grabbed his tablet, opened the email containing some of the photos from the photographer, and turned it so Juliette could see. "This is the guy."

Her eyes bugged out. "Whoa. Good God! She hired Thor for your book cover? He doesn't look anything like the Jamison in your novel."

"Nope. Sure doesn't."

She was still staring at the photo. "So that's your competition."

"Yeah, but I'd say it's no contest. There's no way she'd choose me over him. The guy's about six-five and looks like he could break me in half."

"Well, you're not about to get in a duel over her."

"Keira's got it bad for him. You should have seen her when the guy picked up Lauren and started kissing her during the photo shoot. She looked really jealous."

"Hell, I'd be jealous of Sizzle Girl. Damn, that woman has a body."

"It was like I wasn't even there, Juliette."

Juliette grabbed the tablet, turned it face down on the table, then took his hands. "And meanwhile, Sizzle Girl is headed out of town for three months."

"Yep. So she's basically gone as well."

"Let me ask you this… were you jealous when Thor was kissing Sizzle Girl?"

"She was acting."

"Still, you felt nothing?"

He shrugged. "Not really."

"Next question. Which upsets you more, her leaving or knowing who Keira is dating?"

"What difference does it make?"

"Put it this way… who would you miss more if they're both out of the picture?"

"Keira."

"I think you just figured out which one is the girl for you. You really want the redhead, don't you?"

"Lauren's terrific, but I have a real special chemistry with Keira."

"Then fight for her, Alex."

"I can't beat a guy like that."

"I don't mean physically. Be strong, show her it doesn't matter that she's dating a guy who looks like a comic book superhero. I know it probably hurt to see him kiss her and made you feel inadequate to some degree, but you can't let that show. Besides, you're the best man I know. If she chooses you, she's a smart girl. If she goes for the purely superficial, she wasn't right for you anyway. You need to know if she's your Lexi. You wrote your dream girl in your book; it's time to find out if she actually exists."

"What do you mean you think you lost them *both*?"

Keira placed a cup of coffee in front of Gretch and sat behind her desk. "Dash is off to California and obviously smitten with Lauren."

"Ah, yes. I was wondering when the photo shoot would rear its ugly head."

"Can you believe what he asked her right in front of me? If she wanted to move in with him while she was working on her movie? And you could tell it wasn't an invitation for her to use a spare room."

"I know. But Lauren politely declined. Gotta love her."

"Yeah, she's something else."

"So Dash has a roving eye for the new rack in town. What a surprise. Did you happen to notice that when the photographer finished shooting them kissing Dash wouldn't stop and Lauren was trying to push him away?"

She frowned. "I noticed."

"Pretty rude to do that in front of a girl you're dating, don't ya think? Looks like a big red flag to me. Anyway, he's outta town, so why do you think you lost Alexander? You two did eventually go out to dinner, right?"

"And here's where the plot thickens. Dash and Lauren wound up at the same restaurant shooting some photos for the back cover and ended up having dinner with us. I mean, after hitting on Lauren he sits next to me and puts his arm around me. Gretch, I've never been more uncomfortable in my life. Then Lauren asks me to go to the ladies' room, which leaves the two guys I'm dating at the same table. God knows what they talked about."

"You don't really think they compared notes, do you? I mean, look at this logically… Alexander obviously knows Dash is the other guy you're dating, but Dash has no idea you're seeing Alexander. And no way Alexander would bring up the subject."

"True."

"So was Alexander still wearing his lost-puppy dog look at dinner?"

"For a while, until Dash and Lauren showed up. Then, get this, *he's* the one who invites them to join us."

Gretch nodded. "Makes sense."

"How does that make sense? Why in the world would he want Dash around?"

"He wanted to see more of your relationship, how you act around Dash, and vice versa. Find out if he still has a shot with you."

"Of course he has a shot. And a damn good one."

"Keira, you could find the most self-confident guy in the world and he'd get taken down a notch seeing a guy built like Superman with his shirt off kissing you on the lips."

She shook her head. "Yeah, that didn't exactly help matters."

"Oh, almost forgot… and this might help you sort things out. The politician that Dash is going to work for? Marvin Voper? Big-time womanizer. Known as Voper the Groper."

"Really?"

"Makes Bill Clinton look like an altar boy. Anyway, if it were me, I'd be wondering how a guy I was dating could reconcile working for a total sleazebag who treats women like dirt and has had several sexual harassment suits filed against him. That's another big red flag, sweetie."

"Uh-huh."

Gretch pulled out a legal pad and drew a line down the middle. "It is obvious you're not getting the fact that Dash has more red flags than a Russian parade. Time for some old-school stuff. We have to compare the two."

"Seriously?"

"Humor me. Dash versus Alexander."

"I don't wanna do this, Gretch. It's like being in high school."

"Trust me, it will put things in perspective to get them down on paper. Works every time."

Keira waved one hand. "Fine."

"Good. Let's start with the initial attraction. Physical attributes. Dash first."

"Obviously he's off-the-charts gorgeous. And he's huge."

"Hung like a stallion, eh?"

"You know damn well I haven't slept with him!"

"You don't have to sleep with a guy to know—"

"Stop it!"

"Just bustin' your chops, boss."

"Very funny. You may write that Dash is a very tall, very large man with a perfect face and body. Even in my highest heels I get a stiff neck looking up at him. Once I had my shoes off and he had to pick me up to kiss me."

"I'll bet that was fun."

Keira blushed at the memory. "It was not unpleasant."

"I can imagine. So as far as physical appearances go, you think he's perfect."

"You've seen him, Gretch. Anything wrong with him?"

"Nope, not a single physical flaw I can detect. And that's why you can't see the red flags. You're thinking with the wrong head, like a man. Now let's compare him to bachelor number two."

"You saw them together. Dash looks like he's twice the size of Alexander."

"I didn't mean that. I meant how do you see Alexander, physically?"

"He's almost like two different guys. He looks good in a suit, very businesslike. He's not classically handsome but has that boyish thing going. When he's dressed casual, with that tousled hair he's beyond cute. Got those great eyes and a warm smile. And I don't get a stiff neck since I'm a little taller than him in heels."

"Does that bother you?"

"I mean, I wish he were a few inches taller, but no. It's not important."

"How about him? Ever ask you to wear flats?"

"He's never said anything about it."

"Good. He's confident. And he turns you on? Physically?"

"Oh yeah."

Gretch wrote on the pad. "Now, tell me what you guys do on dates."

"With Dash, it's been dinner and back to his place to make out."

"You poor thing."

Keira paused a moment to collect her thoughts. "Come to think of it, we've never done anything else."

"Hmmm. No movies, Broadway shows, concerts, Mets games?"

She shook her head. "Nope. Dinner and making out every time."

"And Alexander?"

"We always do something interesting and fun. He's exactly like Jamison in the book. Full of surprises."

"Okay, careers?"

"Dash works for politicians and Alexander teaches ethics at a college."

"Kind of *no contest* there. Who's the better kisser?"

"No contest again. Alexander."

"Hmmm, surprise answer. Okay, I know you like smart guys, so who's more intelligent?"

"I'd say they're even."

"Who's more fun to talk to?"

"Dash is very interesting, has some fascinating stories about politics. Alexander is great at conversation as well. But he does make me laugh every time we're together."

"So he's a smartass like yourself?"

"A smartass like *you*, is more like it."

"Final question: how does each one look at you?"

"How do you mean?"

"You know, that look which goes right into your soul. Does either man give you that?"

"Alexander does."

"I coulda guessed. From the look on Alexander's face, he's got it bad for you. You could almost see his heart break when Dash kissed you."

"Yeah, I know. I felt bad for him."

"Oh, one more bonus item…" She wrote on the pad. "Alexander would have taken a bullet for you."

Keira nodded. "That's hard to ignore. And really hard to forget."

"You shouldn't *ever* forget it." Gretch put the pad on the desk, turned it around and slid it toward Keira. "Oh, and a last question. I guess I don't have to write this down. Do you think Alexander would have asked another woman to move in with him right in front of you?"

She shook her head. "Of course not."

"But Dash did."

"Yeah." Her answer was barely audible.

"So, does this clear things up a bit for you, boss?"

"You're lobbying for Alexander, aren't you?"

"I know who's right for you, and, deep down, so do you. Besides, he's the one you have the most fun with, right?"

"Yeah. But I enjoy Dash's company as well. And, you know, his physical attributes are hard to ignore."

"His roving eye is hard to overlook as well. Do you trust him?"

"I don't know."

"Excuse me? I couldn't hear you."

She exhaled and shook her head. "No."

Gretch sipped her coffee and stood up. "A purely physical relationship would work for me, but I know you, boss. You're not a 'friends with benefits' girl and you have to be able to trust the guy you're with. And when you're both old and gray, you'll want someone to play Monopoly with who will make you laugh until your false teeth fall out."

"You're right, but there's still one obstacle."

"What's that?"

"Alexander is dating someone else, too. And I don't know who it is. When Dash kissed me it might have chased him into her arms. And another thing… Alexander doesn't know Dash is headed out of town for a few months. He'll think we're still dating and give up on me."

Gretch folded her arms. "Well, then, put on your boxing gloves and fight for him. That is, if you really think he's your Jamison."

"I think he might be."

"So do I. But before you start, are you willing to admit Dash is wrong for you? And stop justifying his actions because he's gorgeous?"

"I guess."

"You *guess* or you *know*? Keira, you shouldn't even need to look at the pad to figure out who's the better man. Because you already knew it when we left the studio."

"Fine, I won't see Dash anymore. You're right, Gretch. But cut me some slack. I've never had a guy that good looking interested in me. It pumped up my ego, okay? A girl can overlook stuff when a guy looks like Dash."

"That's how a girl can get in trouble."

"I know. Look, it made me feel good knowing he wanted to date me when he could have anyone."

"How does Alexander make you feel?"

She smiled and her eyes took on a dreamy look. "Happy. Beautiful. Special. Safe. Comfortable. I get excited when I know I'm going to see him. And I miss him when he's not around. I hate saying good night. I'd rather say good morning the next day."

"Finally, the light bulb turns on. In the meantime, I think it's high time you said *hasta la vista* to that ridiculous hands-off rule you have. If you're gonna win this battle, you need everything you've got. Time to bring your 'A game', sister. Pucker up."

"You're right again. And we've only got one more chapter to edit anyway."

"Great." Gretch pointed to the phone. "Now call him up and ask him out for the weekend before the mystery woman sinks her claws into him for good. Tell him the book will be done and you want to celebrate. He'll know what that means. The ball's in your court."

"Yeah. Gretch, how old are you?"

"Twenty-eight, why?"

216

"For the last few minutes you sounded a lot older than me. Wiser, too."

"Keira, I may play the role of party girl now, but trust me, when it comes time for me to walk down the aisle, I'm gonna do it with a guy like Alexander."

Lauren greeted Alex with a big hug as he entered her apartment. "This will be the last time you see this place, 'cause when I get back I'll have enough money to rent something bigger than a closet."

"When you get back you'll be a star."

"Eh, we'll see. Fame is a very fickle mistress. I might just be the flavor of the month."

"I seriously doubt it."

"You and my agent. Though he does have me booked for several months of work along with the movie. Anyway, come sit with me, we need to talk before we head to dinner."

Uh-oh. She's dumping me. Hollywood has already gone to her head.

They walked to the couch and sat. Lauren faced him and took his hands. "Alex, you're one of the nicest men I've ever met."

"Uh-oh. Here comes the 'but'. Or 'you'll make some girl a wonderful husband'."

She shook her head. "No. There's no 'but'. Though you will make a wonderful husband. Alex, I'm not saying goodbye to you at all. But I think we need to be totally honest about our feelings. I appreciate the fact that you've been straight with me from day one, telling me you were dating someone else."

"Well, sure."

"That someone else is Keira, isn't it."

He furrowed his brow. "How in the world did you know?"

"The way you looked after Dash kissed her. And the way you didn't look the same way after Dash kissed me."

"Not sure I understand."

"You look at her differently than you look at me. You were

217

jealous when someone kissed her and not jealous when the same guy kissed me. You were jealous when we joined you for dinner and he sat next to her. Alex, I can tell Keira is something special to you."

"So are you, Lauren."

"As you are to me. Look, we have a great time together, I'm physically attracted to you and I think you feel the same way. But it's pretty obvious after watching you two the other day that she has your heart. And you have hers."

"I'm not so sure about that. There's the little matter of Dash. A guy like that, well… you've been around him. He's perfect."

Lauren shook her head. "Pffft. Perfect, my ass. He's all wrong for her. Geez, Alex, he hit on me in the studio and she was a few feet away, asked me to move in with him in California. And I know she heard him. What a sleaze. And if you think I'm interested in Dash, no way. When Dash and I kissed, I was doing an acting kiss and he was sticking his tongue down my throat. It was all I could do to finish the photo shoot and I was so glad you asked us to join you guys for dinner so I could sit next to you. Trust me, a girl like Keira would never end up with a guy like Dash. You may think he's perfect in a physical sense, but you're ten times the man he is."

"But, as for you and me… bottom line… you don't want to see me anymore?"

"That's not what I'm saying at all. Look, Alex, I'd love to end up with you, but there's someone in the way named Keira. So here's the deal. I'm going to be gone for three months. During that time I don't want you to wait for me. I want you to find out if she's your soul mate. If she is, I'll be happy for you. If not, we can pick up where we left off when I get back and next time you see me I *will* haul your ass in bed."

"You really want me to do this?"

"Alex, I tried like hell to seduce you. I literally threw myself at you in a bikini and I could tell you resisted because there was someone else on your mind and you weren't sure about me. Or her. So be sure, Alex. If she's your perfect match, you owe it to yourself to find out. And you owe it to me. I want you, I seriously want you, but not if your heart is pining for someone else."

"You're an amazing woman, Lauren."

"Actually, I'm an idiot for doing this and will probably kick myself down the road for losing a great guy like you, but I have to know. If you're going to be mine, I want you one hundred percent. I'm not the kind of woman who can deal with the ghosts of old girlfriends or a bunch of 'what ifs'. When it comes to soul mates, you need to be absolutely sure."

"Okay, but you need to know something else. I'm not exactly the man you think I am. I haven't been entirely honest with Keira."

"She doesn't know you're dating someone else?"

"No, she knows that. She, uh, doesn't know I'm the actual author of the book."

Lauren shook her head. "Not sure I understand."

He told her the whole story, half expecting her to throw him out of the apartment. Instead, she simply listened and nodded. "Still think I'm an honest guy?"

"Alex, I really don't think it's a big deal. It's not like you've been cheating on her or something serious like that. Besides, it was your agent's idea and you just took her advice. And you're gonna tell her after the book comes out."

"I know, but this whole thing has taken on a life of its own."

"I wouldn't worry about it. Keira seems like a sensible girl. She'll probably be pleasantly surprised. And what girl wouldn't want a guy who writes romance?"

Chapter 21

Central Park was surprisingly quiet as the horse pulled the hansom cab, the only sounds the clip-clop of its hooves, the full moon shining bright on a cloudless night. Between the wine and Keira's revelation at dinner that Dash was out of the picture, Alex felt perfectly relaxed. Keira slid closer, grabbed his left arm, lifted it, and put it around her shoulders, then leaned her head on his chest. Her floral perfume blended with the crisp night air. "You chilly?"

She took a sip from her wine glass. "Until I get more antifreeze in me, keep me warm, big boy."

"My pleasure." He stole a look at her legs as she stretched out. "That's a beautiful dress, by the way."

"Thank you. Just bought it. Gretch picked it out. She thought you'd like it. Personally I think it's too short."

"No such thing."

She looked up at him and shook her head. "Typical man. You'd probably be happy if I showed up in hot pants."

"What can I say? You've got great legs, Madison."

"Thanks, Bauer." She reached over and patted him on the knee. "I am so glad the book is done."

"You and me both." He pulled her a little closer, ran his hand up and down her arm. She looked up at him and gave him a soft smile, then leaned back.

Keira was feeling no pain. Too much wine again. But she didn't care as they slowly walked toward her apartment, her plan firmly in place. After Dash's behavior at the photo shoot he had been given an exit visa, and she'd made sure to tell Alexander. Gretch and her legal pad of comparisons were right; it was clear Alexander was the better man anyway. Too sweet, too decent, too much fun, too damn cute, a perfect gentleman whose electric kisses were still playing on a loop in her memory. Besides, the guy risked his life for her. He was the rare man who respected her as an equal but instinctively played the traditional role of protector when the bullets flew. Dash may have had the body that would sell a million books, and it would have fulfilled a fantasy to take a ride on that train, but Alexander was possibly her soul mate. Plus, she needed to move fast and take the lead over whatever mystery woman he was dating. She had one shot and she had to make it count. With a block to go she reached out and took his hand, entwining her fingers with his. He looked over and gave her a soulful look as he squeezed her hand. "You know, Bauer, it occurs to me that you have set up this evening just like Jamison and Lexi's date in the book. Romantic dinner and a horse-drawn carriage ride through Central Park. A slow walk home on a moonlit night. You giving me your jacket because I'm cold."

"Yeah, I guess we are following the script."

"Yep, it's chapter ten in real life." She pulled his jacket tight around her shoulders as they reached the steps of her building.

"Are we talking the first draft of chapter ten or the revised version?"

She scrunched up her face and looked to the sky. "I'm thinking we completely blow it up. Major re-write. We need to really get inside the head of our heroine. Hmmm… what would Lexi do?" She tapped her finger on her chin.

"A peck on the cheek?"

"Nah, that never works in a romance novel and I already killed that with my red pen. Something that gives the reader hope that the two will get together. Something else, something more… daring."

"How daring are we talking here?"

"Well, not page twenty-seven of *The Godfather*. Lexi wouldn't be wild about getting nailed against the wall. And, you know, possibly having a doorknob pressed into your back doesn't sound terribly comfortable."

"And she's not that kind of girl. She has class."

"Very true."

"She also realizes she's got an old-fashioned gentleman. He gave her his jacket because she was cold and now he's got his shoulders hunched up, so she figures he's either chilly, nervous, or both."

"I'd say she's very perceptive."

"About which one?"

"She doesn't know. Anyway, back to that daring plot point."

"Ah, yes. I mean, she can't just send the guy home after a great date in which he did the chivalrous thing with the jacket. But she's already sent him a signal that she's in the mood by snuggling with him in the carriage and taking his hand on the way home. The reader has more than likely picked that up."

"So in this re-write, what's going through Jamison's mind?"

She turned to face him, took both his hands. "Why don't you play editor? What do *you* think is running through his mind? What would the average guy be thinking at this point?"

"It doesn't matter because he's not the average guy."

"True. He's very special."

"However, we've already established that he's a typical man from the short dress comment and having his arm around her during the carriage ride definitely got his motor running. He got the message and doesn't want the date to end. He's had a great time and she looks stunning. His ego is soaring from being out with such a beautiful woman. He's really smitten with her and wants her to invite him up for coffee."

"Oh, he's *smitten*, is he?"

"Definitely. He's pretty much powerless against her right now

222

and unfortunately she knows it. And he knows that she knows. The ball is definitely in her court."

"But *he's* the man. Why doesn't *he* take charge?"

"Well, they've been going slow and he doesn't want to seem too forward. She's like this precious gem and he doesn't want to take the chance of losing her by making a move too soon. But, remember, she's the star of the book and the readers like that she's strong and independent. They're more interested in what *she's* going to do next. Because at this point the reader has gone through ten chapters and wants things to get moving."

"Ah, you remembered that from our editing session."

"Among other things. Never knew editing could be so much fun."

"Neither did I. Beats the hell out of spellcheck. Anyway, back to our story. You don't want to tease the reader forever. And as you know, Lexi is a take-charge kind of girl. So in your rewrite you'd have her take charge, correct?"

He nodded. "I think Jamison would really appreciate it."

"She wouldn't scare him away if she made the first move?"

"No way. He really wants her to take control."

"I see. So here's the deal. She's not going to 'invite' him in."

His face dropped. "She's not?"

"No. The key word being 'invite'. You think she got her hair done and bought a new dress and matching heels to send him home early? Pffft. Besides, she's had a few drinks and her inhibitions are down. But she's still in total control of the situation. She's going to take his arm, tell him she's got some great wine chilling and lead him up the steps. He really doesn't have any say in the matter." She took one arm and they started up the stairs.

"And of course he's going to let her lead."

"Damn straight. You did say he's powerless against her."

"I did. She's his Kryptonite."

Alex leaned back on the couch as Keira brought two glasses of wine and handed one to him, then sat down and turned to face him. She raised her glass. "To Jamison, a wonderful hero."

He clinked her glass. "To Lexi, the perfect heroine." They both took a sip. "Wow, great wine."

"Thought you'd like it. So, back to the story. Jamison really thinks she's perfect?"

"Pretty much."

"Lexi wouldn't get it. She's not the best-looking girl on the planet."

"She doesn't have to be because she's perfect for *him*. And in the eye of this particular beholder, she *is* the best-looking girl on the planet."

"Ah, I see. Good to know."

"So is he perfect for her?"

She reached out, took his glass, and set both glasses on the coffee table.

"Aren't we going to finish our wine?"

"Don't you want an answer to your question?"

"The reader sure does."

"Well, there has to be a bit of suspense here. Lexi has to 'find out' if he's perfect for her. She has to be absolutely convinced, even though she's pretty sure. Normally they would sip wine for an hour or so, but that doesn't happen in this particular rewrite because she can't stand to wait any longer. She has to know the answer to your question. At this point Lexi has had enough small talk for the evening. And the wine was an excuse to get him up to her apartment."

"But wouldn't Jamison have come up for a cup of coffee? Sounds like a hole in the plot."

"Wine is more romantic and sends him a signal. Coffee is too casual. Coffee says 'friends'. Wine says 'lovers'."

He nodded. "Makes sense. So, since she put the wine aside and can't stand to wait any longer, what's next?"

Keira tucked her legs underneath her and kneeled facing him, then started to run her fingers through his hair. "Well, Lexi can't hold back anymore. She's been attracted to him since the day they met. She loves how he can be a hopeless romantic and take her on a carriage ride one day and then play board games with her on another while being a perfect gentleman and keeping his hands to himself. He's the rare combination of sexy and fun. Oh, and brave, very brave. A guy who would protect his woman at all costs, even though he respects her as an equal. He's old-fashioned in that way. He possibly saved her life earlier in the story."

"He doesn't think that was a big deal."

"She does. A very big deal. He would have taken a bullet for her. Not many guys would do that."

"So, is *she* smitten?"

Keira looked up at the ceiling and smiled. "She plays her cards close to the vest and has kept him guessing, but at this point she's ready to make her move." Keira swung one leg out as she leaned up, turned, and sat on his lap, straddling him. His pulse rate rocketed. "So she climbs on top of him and slowly loosens his tie, because it's going to be in the way."

They locked eyes as she removed his tie. "In the way of what?"

"Of her taking off his shirt. Which she is going to do very slowly, working one button at a time, though she really wants to simply rip it off, sliding her hands inside his shirt and lightly running them over his chest, savoring the touch of his toned muscles. Then she places one hand over his heart and discovers it is beating very fast. As is hers. But since he's a gentleman he doesn't dare put his hand on her chest. So she does it for him."

Alex swallowed hard as he looked up at her. She took his hand and placed it on her chest, her heart going as fast as his own. She ran one hand behind his head and through his hair while the other remained over his heart. "And, uh, what's Jamison doing at this point?"

"Oh, the poor guy is ready to explode. And, as previously mentioned, he's powerless, but he's getting the message loud and clear. So he puts his hands on her waist, leans back, and enjoys the torture."

Alex put his hands on her sides, slid them to the small of her back and gently pulled her closer as she continued to unbutton the shirt. "And when she runs out of buttons, he kisses her, right?"

"Nope."

"No?"

"She kisses him. She's in total control, remember?"

Keira reached out, took his head in both hands and kissed him softly. Their lips parted. "I like this rewrite."

"Me too." She got up and extended her hand. "That's the end of the chapter."

He furrowed his brow. "That's the end? She's gonna stop *there*?"

"Remember the rule; end every chapter with a little cliffhanger. The plot has to drive the reader forward. So Lexi holds out her hand and the reader *has* to turn the page to find out what happens next. Will she lead him to the door or the bedroom? And if it's the latter, what will she do to him? Inquiring minds wanna know."

"So hurry up and turn the damn page."

Chapter 22

He reached for her hand as he got up, but she pointed at the coffee table. "Bring the wine." He picked up the glasses. Keira hooked one finger under his belt and led him toward the bedroom.

His eyes widened. "I take it Lexi is not showing him the door."

Keira headed down the hallway, smiling as he trailed behind her. "Very perceptive." They turned into her bedroom, already brightly lit. She let go of the belt, took the two glasses of wine and set them on the nightstand, then took his shoulders and turned him so they were facing each other. "Next, she needs to get his shirt off. Since, you know, she hasn't seen what he's got above the waist." She leaned forward and kissed him while she pulled off his shirt and tie. "That was easy."

"Nice distraction."

"Now Lexi takes a quick inventory of Jamison with his shirt off."

"Is she pleased or disappointed?"

Keira licked her lips as she gave him the once-over. "Oh, she's very much pleased. You might say she's pleasantly surprised at the buffed shoulders and the fact that he doesn't seem to have an ounce of fat on him. She smiles, pats him on the ass and tells him to light a few candles and get in bed while she goes off to the bathroom to change."

"And what is she changing into?"

"Ah, he doesn't know, which is part of the anticipation that is driving him wild. He'll have to wait." She turned and headed into the bathroom, then closed the door.

Alex quickly lit two candles near the bed, practically ripped off his clothes and climbed under the covers, propping himself up on one elbow so he could keep an eye on the bathroom. "So, you putting on a pair of those angel wings in there?"

"Not practical. Wouldn't fit through the door. And tonight Lexi is no angel."

"Bikini and heels?"

"This ain't a beauty pageant, Bauer."

"Catholic-schoolgirl outfit?"

"While I could probably still fit into mine, no. And you have a dirty mind, young man."

"Slinky nightgown?"

"Not something from a lingerie store or costume shop. So stop asking and be patient."

"We're not dragging this into another chapter, are we?"

"No. But shut the hell up and let me change. Work on the rewrite. Jamison needs a great line when Lexi makes her big reveal. One that tells the reader he's blown away."

"I'm on it."

"Maybe *she's* the one who's gonna be *on it*."

"Clever, but that line might be a little too cheesy."

"You've got a point."

Alex piled up two pillows and leaned back on the four- poster bed, taking a look around her bedroom: a small oak desk with a laptop in the corner; deep-red curtains framing a large window. A large Monet print dominated the wall opposite the bed while a small flat-screen television sat atop the dresser. He heard the door creak open and whipped his head in that direction. He saw her hand reach out through the crack.

"Lexi is about to make her entrance," she said. "But it's too bright in the room. She has to set the mood." He saw her hand turn the switch and the lights dimmed. Then the door opened wide.

His jaw dropped. "Whoa."

"As an editor you'd need something more clever than that."

She was wearing his shirt, necktie, a pair of stiletto heels and nothing else. Keira had her hair up and wore a pair of horn-rimmed glasses. "That looks a helluva lot better on you than me."

"Excellent line! So he's pleased with her little seduction outfit."

"Beats the hell out of angel wings. And I do like the business look with the hair and glasses."

"Well, she is the boss. Both in the boardroom and the bedroom."

"No complaints here. I hate glass ceilings. Mirrors are okay up there, though."

She smiled as she reached the bed. He rose up and extended his hands toward her, but she pushed him back and climbed on top of him, straddling him as she sat on his stomach. She leaned forward and gave him a soft kiss, then sat up straight and slowly undid the necktie. She took off the glasses and tossed them aside, then reached behind her head, pulled out a clip and shook out her hair, letting it hang down so that it lightly brushed his chest. Fireworks shot through his body. The flickering candlelight made her red tangles shimmer like they were on fire. "At this point Lexi has him right where she wants him."

"I think that's pretty obvious. So, she likes being on top?"

"As previously mentioned, she's in control. She begins to unbutton the shirt, then pauses and asks him a question."

"And that question would be…"

"Do you think you can handle me?" She shot him a seductive smile as she removed the shirt and tossed it aside. He didn't say anything as she sat up straight, hands on hips, giving him a good look at her. "Well? Am I too much for you?"

"He's speechless because she's hotter than he ever imagined. Smoking hot. But at this point he pretty much knows he's the one about to be handled."

"He's very perceptive."

"He's also ready for this scene to get moving." Alex smiled and reached for her, but she grabbed his wrists, leaned toward him and pinned them behind his head against the mattress. He tried to rise up but she pushed him back down and kissed him.

When their lips parted she looked right into his soul. "Relax and let me take you."

His eyes flickered open as the sun sent fingers of light into the bedroom. Alex saw Keira was still asleep, her head on his shoulder, her body practically on top of his, an arm across his chest, while one long leg was entwined around his. His arm was curled around her slim waist. He savored the touch of her incredibly soft skin, breathed the scent of the strawberry shampoo from her hair. He thought about getting up but it would wake her, and being tangled in bed with a sweet redhead was much more appealing.

About twenty minutes later she stirred and her eyes cracked open. She looked up and saw him smiling at her. "You just wake up?"

"Nah. Been up about twenty minutes."

"And you were just laying here looking at me?"

"The sun was hitting your hair just right. Made you look like an angel. Didn't want to move."

She gave him a big smile. "You never run out of compliments. You're always so sweet to me."

"You're incredible, Madison."

"You're quite the perfect partner yourself, Bauer."

"Guess I found my Lexi."

"And I found my Jamison."

"I had no idea that you, uh—"

"Could be aggressive?"

"Well, yeah."

"Neither did I. Guess a girl just needs the right guy to let her hair down. Kryptonite works both ways, you know."

"So I take it from that statement that *you* are also powerless against *me*?"

"I'll never tell." She looked at the clock. "Damn, we slept past ten."

"It's Saturday. Who cares?"

"True."

"You hungry?"

"By now you should know that's a stupid question. I'm always hungry."

"Sorry, I forgot. What are you in the mood for?"

"Hmmm… let me think." She looked down at his waist. "Well, how about that. Looks like you've recovered nicely."

"Pretty easy when you wake up with a beautiful woman wrapped around you like a snake."

She blushed a bit. "Well, you did seem to like me on top, so I figured I may as well spend the night there." She leaned up and rolled on top of him, grabbing his wrists and pinning them behind his head like the night before. "So relax, and I'll show you what I'm in the mood for. Breakfast of champions."

"Well, look what the cat dragged in."

Alex blushed as he entered the apartment and Juliette got up from the couch to greet him. "Hi."

"*Hi*? That's all you have for me? You do the walk of shame at one in the afternoon and all I get is a *hi*?"

"You know I don't kiss and tell."

"Yeah, but the look on your face and the fact you're wearing yesterday's shirt that smells of woman's perfume and has a long copper hair on the shoulder tells me you finally got the redhead."

"More like the redhead got me. Damn, Juliette, the woman is insatiable. She pretty much drained me of all bodily fluids."

"You complaining?"

"Hell, no! The sex was incredible. Keira *knows* stuff."

"Stuff?"

"Let's call them 'bedroom skill sets.'"

"Well, she does run the romance division. I'm sure she picked up a lot of interesting techniques from the books she's read. Especially if she's edited some erotic ones."

"But I never expected her to take charge in the bedroom."

"Every man's dream. By the way, what happened to book- cover Thor?"

"She didn't elaborate, but she said he wasn't right for her and she wasn't going to see him anymore. Plus she said she liked another guy better anyway."

"The other guy being you."

He nodded. "Yeah, I sorta picked that up."

"See, I knew she was smart and not superficial. And you'll be reminded that you defeated a Greek god every time you look at your book cover." Juliette moved forward and gave him a hug. "I'm really happy for you, Alex. Sounds like you hit the jackpot and Lauren was right about Keira being your soul mate."

He nodded. "She's definitely my Lexi. But there's the little matter of our great deception. I still have that big hurdle to get over."

"Look, Keira was smart enough to ditch the other guy for you, she's not going to let the author thing get in the way."

"I dunno, Juliette. I still worry about that."

"So when are you gonna break the news?"

"Bella wants to do it about a month after the release since Keira has really been pushing hard to get the author out of the house on a book tour. Bella's theory is that the by the time the book has been out a while it will make for a great story and women will realize that men can write romance, since they've been reading it."

"Well, I'm sure it will be fine. So what's next?"

"I'm gonna change clothes and then take her to another of those best-kept secrets of the tri-state area. She really likes those. I just hope she can deal with the *ultimate* best-kept secret."

"Well, if she can't, you do have a backup plan."

He furrowed his brow. "What backup plan?"

232

"Hot girl named Lauren. You forgot her already?"

"No, of course not."

"Well, remember what she told you. If things don't work out between you and Keira, she'll be around. Considering what she did for you, I'd say she'd be a pretty good catch."

"True."

"So does that make you relax at all about the big secret?"

"Not really."

"Well, whatever happens you're gonna end up with a great woman."

"I know. But I want to end up with Keira."

Keira practically floated across the floor as she headed for her office, head held high, wearing a huge smile, her hair bouncing with each step. Gretch spotted her and raised one eyebrow. "Well, someone looks awfully happy for a Monday morning. Let me guess... it isn't because the Giants won yesterday."

"Had a great weekend." She headed into her office as her assistant followed.

Gretch grabbed a chair. "Okay, details."

Keira sat behind her desk and looked up at the ceiling. "Just a great weekend."

"Oh, please. Considering the hands-off rule expired and the 'cat that ate the canary' grin on your face, I know you did more than hold hands. And you probably swallowed more than the canary."

She blushed. "You know I don't like to kiss and tell."

"Bullshit. You've been kissing and telling since you met him. And, dammit, you owe me after I got you all gussied up Friday afternoon. I deserve to live vicariously through you on this one."

"You of all people don't need to live vicariously through anyone."

"Whatever. Details. Now. Spill."

She looked back at Gretch. "Fine. Your strategy was spot on."

"I already knew that. I want to know about the results of said strategy. How did he respond to the hair, the dress, the

233

take- no-prisoners attitude away from the office?"

She shrugged, playfully bit the tip of her tongue while her eyebrows did a little jump. "Gretch, I can't believe it, but… I took him."

Gretch raised one eyebrow. "Excuse me?"

"Like you said, sometimes shy guys want to be led. So… I led."

"He didn't make the first move?"

"Nope. He was still a little apprehensive and even said as much. So I took charge, dragged his ass to the bedroom, got on top and basically had my way with him."

"Damn, stop the presses: Keira goes dominatrix on a guy. So how did he respond?"

"Very well, considering my neighbor called 911 after he got a bit loud."

"Holy shit! The cops showed up?"

She began to blush. "Yeah. Kind of embarrassing when I answered the door in my robe and had to explain that no one was being tortured. Though I had pretty much done exactly that to the guy. Alexander was red as a beet. The cops laughed their asses off."

"Obviously he enjoyed himself."

"We both did, Gretch. I've never felt a connection like I had with him that night."

"So, I'm assuming the other mystery woman is out of the picture?"

"She is now."

"Good for you. I'm really happy for you, Keira. He's a great guy."

"Yeah, he's my Jamison."

"So, already got this coming weekend planned?"

"He's gotta teach at a journalism seminar Saturday all day and won't be back till late, so I thought it would be the perfect time to deliver the author roses personally."

"You're not gonna send them like you usually do before the release?"

She shook her head. "Nope. It's time I actually met this woman. I'm going to call her up and if she's home I'm going to be outside her building with the flowers. Alexander won't be around to run interference, so I'm pulling an end run. Besides, I need to take a face-to-face shot at getting her out to book signings. She can't be a voice on a phone if we're gonna sell a million of her books."

Chapter 23

Odds were good the author would be at home. And with Alexander off in Connecticut all day, she'd be the one to answer the door.

It was time to pry the recluse out of her cave; morbid obesity and fear of public places be damned. Readers wanted to meet authors, it was that simple. And book signings were huge. Keira *had* to get Alex Bauer out in public, even if she had to hold her hand at every bookstore. She's hire a hypnotist if she had to.

She held a dozen roses in one arm as she stood in front of the Bauer residence. She dialed the author's number on her cell.

The unfamiliar ring of the burner phone Alex had given her startled Juliette. Keira was the only person with the number.

Then, panic set in.

Alex hadn't told her a call was coming and wasn't here to prompt her on what to say. The book was done, what could she possibly want? There were no more editing changes to discuss. She took a deep breath and answered. "Hello?"

"Hi, Alex, it's Keira, how you doin' today?"

"Just fine, Keira. Very excited about the release coming up."

"Well, you should be. Your life is about to change in a very big way."

"Yeah, I guess so. Listen, I really appreciate what you've done to the book. You've made it so much better. I can certainly see why you're in charge of the romance division."

"Thank you, that's very kind of you to say."

Change the subject. "And I'm not the only member of this family impressed with you. I'm not sure if I've ever seen my cousin so happy, and I know it's because of you."

"He makes me very happy too."

"I'm so glad. From what I hear you guys get along great. So is there anything I can do for you?"

"Well, actually, I have a tradition with authors just before the release day."

A knock on the door distracted Juliette and she headed for it. "Hang on a minute, Keira. Someone's at the—"

Her jaw dropped as she opened the door and saw Keira standing there, on the phone, holding a bouquet of flowers.

"—door."

Keira's face tightened as she saw Juliette standing there, holding a phone, obviously shocked to see her. "Juliette?"

"Keira, I uh—"

"That was you on the phone." Keira talked into her cell and heard her own voice on Juliette's speaker.

Juliette slowly nodded and stepped aside. "Please, come in. Let me explain."

"Yeah, I guess you need to because I'm totally confused." Keira walked in as Juliette shut the door behind her.

Juliette gestured toward the couch. "Please, have a seat."

"Something tells me I need to be standing up for this. Where's Alex?"

"In New Haven, at the journalism conference."

"Not Alexander. Where is his cousin the author? And why were you talking to me on the phone as if you were her? What's going on?"

Juliette bit her lower lip. "Keira, Alex *is* the author."

"Yeah, I know that. Where is she?"

She shook her head. "No, you don't understand. There *is* no cousin Alex. She doesn't exist."

Keira's furrowed her brow. "Now I'm really confused. Are you trying to cover for her because you're—"

"Keira, there is no *woman* named Alex who lives here. The man you know as Alexander is the author of the book. *He* is Alex Bauer."

"What? You're not making any sense."

Juliette exhaled. "Please sit, it's a long story."

"No, I'd rather not. But continue."

"Sure. Alexander is Alex. And vice versa. He wrote the book."

"Oh, come on! He wrote *Ring Girl*?"

"Yes. It started out as a short story he wrote in college but he fleshed it out into a novel."

"You really expect me to believe a man wrote this book? How could a guy possibly get inside the head of a woman like that?"

"If you knew him as well as I do it is not surprising. Plus, he spent his career in an industry dominated by women, he was raised by a single mom, and I'm his best friend. He submitted it to Bella and she was shocked when she met him. She couldn't believe a man could write such an emotional romance. Bella felt that if she told editors the book was written by a guy they'd have a pre-conceived notion about it and not be as interested, and that some editors wouldn't even consider it. She was doing her job as an agent. She told him she was selling his literary voice, not his gender."

Keira's jaw slowly dropped as she tried to process it all. "Alexander... Alex... really wrote the book?"

"He did." She raised her right hand. "Swear to God, he wrote it. I watched him do it."

"Why didn't he tell me after I bought it and the deal was done?"

"Bella felt that if you and your staff knew the truth the story would leak and hurt sales. They planned to tell you after the release since you said it was sure to be a bestseller. Bella thought it would be an amazing story after the book caught on and the big reveal would spur sales even more when women found out they'd been reading an incredibly emotional romance written by a guy. And the fact that he's a cute guy wouldn't hurt either."

"This is unbelievable."

"I know, but it's true."

"You all lied to me."

"Keira, please try to understand—"

"Hang on a minute." Keira put up her hand. "So you live here?"

"I do."

"And that time I dropped by, with you out of the shower, you also lied to me then."

"I didn't know what else to do, Keira. I knew it looked bad after you two had such a great time the night before so I had to come up with an excuse. I didn't want you to think I was sleeping with him and hurt your relationship."

"And then he led me to believe you were in a same-sex relationship with his cousin."

"According to him, you came up with that explanation."

"But he didn't deny it."

"I know this all sounds bad, Keira."

"Sounds *bad*? How many lies are we dealing with here? The cousin doesn't exist, Alexander is really Alex, you're not a lesbian, and you guys live together. For all I know, you two are actually married."

Juliette shook her head. "Look, Alex and I have worked together and been roommates for years. But it's strictly platonic, like brother and sister. We really are best friends and you have nothing to worry about."

"So you're not the other woman he dates."

"No, and the 'other woman' you're referring to is out of the picture. You're probably not going to believe this either, but she actually picked up on the fact that Alex was hung up on someone else, and she told him to find out if you were his soul mate. If not, she'd be waiting."

"You expect me to believe a story like that?"

"It's true. Keira, Alex can't be in a sexual relationship with more than one person. He's not wired like most guys. He never would have spent the night with you if he was seeing someone else. He's as monogamous as it gets."

"Right now I'm worried about what other secrets he's kept from me."

"There's nothing else, Keira. Alex is the most decent human being you'll ever meet. Trust me—"

"*Trust you*? Seriously?"

"He's been agonizing over this since the deal… and falling for you only made it worse. He felt terrible keeping the secret from you."

"There's a difference between a secret and a lie."

"He was going to tell you."

The words grew thick in her throat. "Was falling for me part of the plan?" Her voice cracked. "Is that also a lie?"

Juliette locked eyes with her. "No, Keira. What he feels for you is as real as it gets. I've known him a long time and I've never seen him fall head over heels for anyone like this. You and only you have his heart. He's crazy about you. You have to believe me. More important, you have to believe him."

"I don't know what to believe right now. Or who to believe." She felt her eyes well up a bit as her anger rose. "Here." She tossed the roses to Juliette. "Give them to the author, whoever the hell that person actually is." She turned and headed for the door.

"Keira, wait—"

"I've heard enough, Juliette." She opened the door, left the apartment, and slammed the door behind her.

Then she burst into tears.

Alex looked at his watch as the train zipped by the corporate part of Connecticut. The conference had wrapped up ahead of time, he'd caught an earlier train and he'd be back in time to do something fun with Keira. He was going to show up at her place, surprise her. His cell buzzed, telling him he had a text.

What he saw made his heart drop.

Keira knows everything. Not happy. Call me ASAP
-Juliette

He hit the call return button and drummed his fingers on the armrest as he waited for Juliette to pick up. "C'mon, c'mon…"

"Alex, thank God you got my message."

"What the hell happened?"

"Alex, I'm so sorry. Keira showed up out of the blue when I was on the phone with her." Juliette recapped the story.

Alex broke out in a cold sweat as he rubbed his temples. "Dammit, I knew this would happen. Should I call her now or go straight to her place? I'll be home in an hour and a half."

"Maybe neither. She's pretty steamed and at this point she's not in the mood to believe anything you tell her. Might want to give her a while to cool off."

"Seriously? I think I need some serious damage control right away."

"Sometimes women need to be left alone, Alex, and this is probably one of those times. But I do know who you need to call right now."

"Who?"

"Bella. She might be the only one to get you out of this mess."

"Yeah, I'll call her right away. Be home soon."

"Try not to worry, Alex. Everything will turn out okay. Keira's a smart girl and deep down she knows you're a great guy. She won't want to lose you."

"I'm more worried about losing *her*. I *can't* lose her, Juliette. I just can't."

"She's smart, Alex. It might take a while, but you guys will be okay."

"Hope you're right. Bye."

"Love ya, roomie. Bye."

He hung up the phone and started to call Bella, then decided to ignore Juliette's advice. He had to start picking up the pieces.

Right.

Now.

He dialed Keira instead. The call went straight to voice mail.

Damn. She won't speak to me.

He decided not to leave a message.

Alex trembled and felt his eyes well up.

On the eve of his greatest professional accomplishment, he was about to lose his true love.

Suddenly, being the author of a bestseller didn't mean a damn thing.

Gretch locked the door to her apartment and smiled at her hunky date. "Okay, Jeff, let's rock."

The tall, twenty-something sandy-haired man smiled as he escorted her down the stairs. "This must be a good show. Tickets were really hard to get."

"Yeah, a few people at the office saw it and loved it." She heard footsteps heading in their direction along with a few sniffles. *Great, gotta walk by someone with a cold.* Then she stopped when she saw who was walking up the stairs.

Keira.

Looking like someone had run over her dog. Red eyes, mascara running, quivering lips. "Good God, Keira, are you okay?"

Keira bit her lower lip and shook her head as her eyes welled up.

Gretch took her arms. "What happened?"

"Long story." Her voice broke. "Alexander…"

"What? What happened to Alexander? Is he okay?"

"He lied to me."

"Oh geez." Gretch put her arms around Keira and gave her a strong hug, then started leading her up the stairs. "C'mon, sweetie.

Let's get you inside."

Her date looked at his watch. "Uh, we're gonna be late. And these are two-hundred-dollar tickets."

Gretch whipped her head around at the guy. "Can't you see my friend needs me? That she's in pain?"

"Well, we can only spare about five minutes, so make it quick."

"Why don't *you* make it quick and get lawst, buddy."

"C'mon, Gretch—"

"If you don't have the heart to help a friend in need, you're not good enough to take me out."

"You're serious?"

Gretch opened the door to her apartment and pushed Keira inside. "Goodbye, Jeff. Take your tickets and shove 'em." She walked inside and slammed the door, then turned to Keira. She'd never seen her boss look this way. The woman was a shuddering mess. She led her to the couch, they both sat down and Gretch took her hands.

"Gretch, I'm so sorry I ruined your date."

"Obviously he was a jerk, so screw 'im. And you're more important to me anyway. Now what happened with Alexander? You said he lied to you? About what?"

"Everything." Keira told her the entire story. Gretch listened intently, holding her hands tight the entire time. When Keira was done Gretch extended her arms. "C'mere." Keira leaned forward and rested her head on Gretch's shoulder, hugging her hard. Gretch gently stroked her hair. "It'll be okay, Keira."

"No, it won't," she said through sobs. "I can't trust him."

Gretch pulled back and wiped the tears from Keira's face. "It's not that bad, sweetie. We'll work it out. Meanwhile, you're staying here tonight."

Alex was greeted with a hug from Juliette the minute he walked into their apartment. "Thanks, I needed that."

She pulled back and studied his face as she kept her arms

wrapped around his waist. "You're a wreck."

He nodded. "I'm scared to death of losing her, Juliette. I'm sorry, I couldn't wait. I tried calling her. Went right to voice mail. She won't even speak to me."

She reached up and brushed his hair. "She will, give her some space. Keira's got a lot to process right now but I have a feeling she'll come around. You get hold of Bella?"

"Left her a message. She's at a writer's conference so I probably won't hear back for a while."

"Well, she'll be able to fix things when she tells Keira it was her idea. This will all blow over."

"I can only hope. So how mad was Keira?"

Juliette shook her head. "I'll be honest, it wasn't pretty. She acted like the woman scorned. I mean, to be hit with so much stuff at once… you're the actual author, I live here, our relationship is platonic, your cousin doesn't exist… to her it was a bunch of lies on top of lies when in reality it was simply one big secret. Right now she wouldn't trust anything you say, that's why I told you to leave her alone for a while."

"How long is a while?"

"Hard to say. I don't really know her. Bella might be a better judge of that."

"Every additional minute is too long. I already miss her, Juliette."

"Stop acting like she's gone. She's not. You'll get her back."

"How can you be so sure?"

"You may have written a book from a woman's point of view, but I'm a woman. And a sensible woman like Keira wouldn't just throw away a guy like you."

Gretch peeked into the guest room and saw Keira snoring, finally all cried out and dead to the world. Between the emotion and the wine she was down for the count. Gretch gently closed the door, not wanting to wake her. The snoring continued.

She headed for the living room, grabbed Keira's purse and

pulled out her cell phone.

She saw Alexander on the list of missed calls.

Of course.

Keira wasn't ready to talk with him.

But Gretch was.

She tapped the phone as she stepped out on her balcony and closed the door. It connected on the first ring. "Keira, I am so sorry—"

"It's Gretch, Alexander. I'm using her phone."

"Oh. I, uh—"

"Keira's spending the night at my place. She's asleep so I thought I'd give you a call. Sorry to call so late, but I assumed you were up."

"Yeah, can't sleep. How is she?"

"Somewhere between pissed off and devastated. It hit her right out of the blue. It *is* a pretty wild story."

"Believe me, Bella and I didn't plan it this way."

"Yeah, I figured that out."

"So, should I call her? Drop by?"

"No, she needs to cool off. I've known her a long time, Alexander—"

"By the way, it's Alex."

"Right. Anyway, you may have noticed she's a very passionate woman, both at work and in her personal life. She's very logical at work, but when it comes to romance she's ruled by her emotions, and very often she needs help sorting things out when it comes to men. She went through a very bad breakup a while back. The guy really lied to her and ever since she has been slow to trust."

"And then she finds out she can't trust me."

"Look, this is different and you're not at all like the last guy, who was totally wrong for her. And it's not like you cheated on her with another woman. There isn't another woman, is there?"

"No, Gretch. The other person I was dating knew I was head over heels for Keira and let me go."

"Wow, that's pretty amazing. Anyway, let me work on her. It

might take a little while, but I'll get her to come around."

"Thanks, Gretch. And I really appreciate you calling tonight."

"I never called you, okay? I'm going to delete this call from her phone as soon as we hang up."

"Sure, got it."

"Look, Alex, I know you're a good guy and you're perfect for her. You're her Jamison and I'm assuming she's your Lexi. You had her floating through the office this week. I've never seen her so happy. And to be honest, I don't really blame you guys for hiding the sex of the author."

"Seemed like a good idea at the time."

"Well, you're an amazing writer. And any guy who can write with such emotion has to have a big heart. That said, here's the one thing you can do to help get Keira back."

Chapter 24

"Nice place, Alex." Bella looked around the apartment as Alex ushered her in on a Sunday morning.

"Right now it may as well be Alcatraz." Juliette headed down the hall in their direction. "This is my roommate, Juliette. Juliette, Bella."

The two women shook hands and exchanged greetings. Bella looked her up and down as they all took a seat on the couch. "Damn, honey, I can see why Keira was jealous. So, Juliette, you're the four-hundred-pound lesbian author who's afraid to leave the house?"

"I was in a previous life. Now I'm just the pathological liar who lives here who may or may not be in a sexual relationship with Alex."

Bella shook her head. "Guys, I am really sorry things got so far out of hand. Feel free to throw me under the bus. And then pick me up a change-of-address card from the post office because I'll be living there permanently."

"Hey, it was just as much my fault as yours," said Alex. "But, more importantly, how do we move forward?"

"You mean with the book or your relationship?"

He bit his lip and looked down. "Right now the relationship is more important."

Juliette patted his hand. "He was up all night, Bella. I can tell you he's got it bad for Keira and he'll be devastated if he loses her."

Alex locked eyes with Bella. "I'm already devastated that *I might* lose her."

Bella nodded. "I understand. By the way, what happened with Sizzle Girl?"

Alex looked up. "She realized I was in love with Keira at the photo shoot when Dash kissed her and I looked insanely jealous."

Bella furrowed her brow. "Who's Dash?"

"The hunk on the cover. He's the other guy Keira was dating."

"Wow. So she was dating that slice of beefcake while you were going out with the Queen of Sunblock."

He nodded. "Lauren told me to find out if Keira was my real soul mate while she's in Hollywood, that she couldn't share me. Or even have me if I was carrying a torch for another woman."

"Impressive. Both what she did and the fact that you picked Keira over the ultimate bikini babe."

Juliette wrapped one arm around his shoulders and pulled him close. "He's a special guy, Bella. He realizes beauty is more than just physical."

"Yeah I get that about him. I think I need to find more male authors who write romance." Bella studied his face for a moment. "So, here's what I'm gonna do. Tomorrow, first thing. I'm going to her office and take the bullet. I'm the agent, I basically created the ruse. Hopefully she'll focus her anger on me and cut you some slack."

Alex exhaled audibly. "That's all well and good, but you're not the one who's sleeping with her."

"I've known Keira a long time," said Bella. "Her last relationship ended badly, and it's a big step for her to trust a guy to the point she spends the night with him. Once burned, twice shy, you know? But Alex, you are so very different than the last boyfriend, who everyone knew was wrong for her. The guy cheated on her and really did a number on her head. I can talk to her, but you

248

need to leave her alone right now. It might take a while, but I think she'll come around."

He nodded slowly. "I'll ask you the same question I asked Juliette last night. How long is 'a while'?"

Bella shrugged. "Don't know. We're in uncharted territory here. Meanwhile, there's someone I need to call today. The one person who can really help get you two back together."

"Who's that?"

"Gretch."

Keira stared out the window as the pouring rain pelted it when she heard a gentle tap on the door. "I'm up, c'mon in."

Gretch entered carrying a glass of orange juice. "Morning, sunshine."

"Very funny."

Gretch sat on the end of the bed and handed her the glass. "Drink."

"Thanks." She completely drained the glass.

"Well, that's a good sign. Your appetite is still around. You get any sleep?"

"Yeah. Slept hard. I think all the emotion wiped me out. Bad dreams, though. I can't thank you enough for taking me in last night."

"You were in no condition to be alone." She reached forward and gently ran a hand through Keira's tangles. "So how you feelin', slugger?"

"Confused. Angry. Sad. It's like a badly written novel is kicking around in my head with the plot going off in ten different directions. I still can't believe all the lies. It's impossible to try and make sense of it all."

"Well, if you step back a bit and look at the big picture, it's not that bad."

"Not that bad? Are you kidding me?"

"You would feel a lot worse if you'd caught him in bed with

another woman."

"How do I know he isn't nailing some other babe?"

"Oh, come on, Keira. You know damn well he's not like that. Dash was. Alexander, no way. The guy's a classic Boy Scout. A girl like me can tell."

"How do you know?"

"I'm an expert, remember? Certain guys aren't wired to be players, and he's one of them. So, you gonna talk to him today?"

Keira shook her head. "I may never talk to him again."

"Oh, stop it. Look, you've been deceived, you're hurt. I get that. But he's the guy you've been waiting for all your life. He's your Jamison. And you're his Lexi. Geez, Keira, he basically wrote every quality you personally have into that character. You're his real-life dream girl. You're the girl he fantasized about."

"That's fiction. And in real life my dream guy doesn't lie to me."

"Not a lie, sweetie. More like a very big secret. Anyway, we'll figure it out. Meantime, you're hanging with me today. We're gonna go out and have a good time."

"It's raining."

"Supposed to stop in an hour and be a nice day."

"Gretch, I'd really rather stay in bed and hide. Can't we just binge-watch TV or something?"

"Sorry, not an option. Get your ass in the shower and get dressed."

"I don't have any clean clothes."

"You can borrow some of mine. You're skinny enough to wear my size."

"Yeah, but I'm a half foot taller. One of your skirts would barely cover my ass."

Gretch shrugged. "Your problem being?"

Keira laughed a bit.

"Oh my God, she actually smiled! We're making progress! C'mon, we'll go to your place and you can wear something that doesn't scream 'slut'. Which, in your closet, is everything."

"Then where are we going?"

"You'll find out. Now get out of bed, Keira Madison. And I don't wanna see any moping around today. You're still my kick-ass boss."

"Okay." She threw back the covers and swung her legs out of bed, then stopped. "You know what, Gretch?"

"What?"

Keira reached out and took her hand. "I think it's time you stopped thinking of me as your boss. And I'm no longer going to consider you to be my assistant. Because I think of you as a dear friend."

Keira stared out of the office window at her usual spectacular view of Manhattan on a sunny Monday morning, but didn't really see anything.

"You might not recognize Keira," said Gretch. "She's the moody sphinx behind the desk."

Keira swung her chair around and saw her assistant standing next to Bella. "Well, well. If it isn't my *favorite* agent." Her tone dripped with sarcasm.

Bella nodded. "May I come in?"

Keira gestured toward the chair in front of her desk. Bella sat as Gretch left the office and closed the door. "So, what are you pitching today? *Lying to Editors for Dummies*?"

"I deserved that. Come on, get it all out of your system."

"Oh, I don't think there are enough hours in the day for that."

"Obviously you're in no mood for an apology, so go ahead and tell me what a sorry sack of shit I am."

Keira stood up, hands on hips. "How the hell could you do this to me, Bella? My God, we've known each other for years and I've always trusted you."

She shrugged. "What can I say? It seemed like a good idea at the time."

"Lame excuse."

"Keira, I don't know what you want me to tell you. This was a

251

unique situation. I've never had a male client who wrote a romance. Put yourself in my shoes… how many editors would have even considered the book if I'd told them it was written by a man?"

"That's not the point."

"Like hell! That's *exactly* the point. My job is to get the best deal for my clients—"

"Your job is not to lie for them."

"Fine. But you know damn well half the editors in this city would have laughed at my pitch if I'd told them I had a great romance written by a guy. And don't deny that you might have been apprehensive as well. When I called you about the book I said I had a terrific novel by a debut author. There's no rule that says I had to tell you the sex of the author. Besides, it's an amazing book or you wouldn't have pre-empted it with a massive contract."

"But you guys could have told me after the deal was signed."

"You know damn well with everyone in this office knowing it the story would have leaked and it would have hurt advance sales. A lot of women won't buy a romance written by a male author. We needed to set the hook before the big reveal. The book comes out in a few weeks… did you happen to check the rank on the bestseller list this morning?"

Keira nodded. "Yeah. It's, uh, number one in romance."

"And the damn thing isn't even out yet! The rank is strictly from pre-orders! Jill is ecstatic. Now, can you imagine the great publicity you'll get when we reveal it was written by Alex a month after the release? Can you see all the dreamy-eyed women when they discover men can actually be as sentimental and emotional as they are? All the women who refused to buy a romance written by a guy who all of a sudden realize men can write the genre?"

"That's not the point. I got romantically involved with an author. That's conflict of interest to the tenth power. Do you know how that's going to look? I can already see the headline on the front page of *The Post*. Editor gives six-figure deal to author she's sleeping with."

"No one has to know that. And you brought the offer before you even met him. Besides, I think the headline would read *Romance Editor Finds Real Life Happily Ever After.*"

"Yeah, right. Well, I'm not sleeping with him anymore."

"Speaking of Alex—"

She put up her hand. "You mean 'he who must not be named.'"

"Oh, for God's sake, Keira, lighten up! Dammit, the guy is the best thing ever to happen to you and because of something *I* came up with, you're going to throw him away like a lousy manuscript. He is not even in the same ballpark with your last boyfriend, who, may I remind you, really did lie through his teeth and cheated on you with one of your best friends."

Keira's head snapped back like she'd been hit with a blow dart. "And thank you so much for bringing up that wonderful memory."

"I only do so to make you compare the two men. Look, I've been playing Jewish mother with you guys since that first day you met in the office. He calls wanting me to fix you guys up, you call me wondering if he likes you. Is she serious about this other guy? Is he really involved with the other woman he's dating? What's the real story on Juliette? I felt like I was back in high school. While I don't know him nearly as well as I know you, the words he wrote tell me he's what you've been looking for all these years. Keira, leave what you consider to be a lie out of the equation... look me in the eye and tell me he's not the best guy you have ever dated."

Keira bit her lower lip, sat down, and stared at her desk.

"Can't do it, can you?"

Keira remained silent.

"Keira, I've been married more than twenty years. Every couple goes through a rough patch. The ones that survive are those who accept the fact that their soul mates are not perfect. You can write 'em perfect in fiction, but in real life they come with flaws."

"I didn't expect him to be perfect. I expected him to be honest."

"Well, again, that's my fault. By the way, I dropped by his place yesterday."

She quickly looked up, eyes wide. "Yeah?"

"The man is devastated. He doesn't even care he's got a bestseller about to hit the shelves. All he cares about is *you*. He's carrying an Olympic-sized torch. Keira, I know you're hurt and angry, but try to forgive him. If you don't ever want to forgive me, fine, but please cut Alex a break."

"If I'm ever gonna do that, and that's a great big *if*, I'll need time."

"Don't take too long. Good men like that don't stay on the market forever. You know what's really amazing? The irony in all this."

"What irony?"

"You require every book to have a 'happily ever after' and you're about to take your own perfect ending and hit 'delete'."

Alex grabbed the phone and took the call on the first ring when he saw who was calling. "Hi, Gretch."

"This is Looking Glass to Red Leader. Operation Matchmaker is underway."

He chuckled. "Okay, there, Looking Glass. So what happened?"

"Bella was just here. Keira let her have it, but Bella read her the riot act about forgiveness and you being the perfect guy for her. Pretty good knock-down drag-out if you ask me."

"So you were in there with them?"

"No. I watched them through the glass and listened through the heating vent."

"Aren't you the devious little thing?"

"Hey, I'm Gretch. It's not just a name, it's an attitude."

"So how did Keira react?"

"There's a little crack in the armor. When Bella said she'd been over to see you, Keira looked very interested. Obviously wanted to know how you're doing. Couldn't keep up her angry poker face."

"She probably looks like a pissed off Strawberry Shortcake when she's mad."

"That's pretty spot on."

"So there's hope for us."

"Of course, Alex. Don't worry, I've got your back. When I get through with her she's going to be fed up with every man on the planet except you. There are many romantic tricks in *The Book of Gretch*."

"I can't tell you how much I appreciate it."

"No problem. Meanwhile, you working on that idea I gave you?"

"Yeah. It's coming along and I've got a friend who can make it happen."

Chapter 25

Keira was not at all in the mood for the publisher's annual office cocktail party. She forced smiles at all the agents, authors, and booksellers who filled the office, putting on a brave face when she simply wanted to be home in bed. To make it worse, the crowd was buzzing over the upcoming release of *Ring Girl* and the mystery surrounding the author who wasn't there.

She sipped her champagne with one hand while her other was occupied with a plate of bacon-wrapped shrimp as she saw Gretch approaching her with a hot guy in tow.

"Hey boss, wanted you to meet Tony from Readers Bookstores. Tony, this is Keira Madison, our senior editor."

The tall, dark-haired hunk smiled and nodded. "I've heard a lot about you, Keira."

"Hope it's all good. I'm sorry, you work for who?"

"Readers Bookstores. Small but growing chain out West. I'm not sure anyone in New York has ever heard of it."

"I'll be sure to check it out."

Gretch put one hand lightly on Keira's forearm. "Hey, boss, I gotta man the promotions table for a while."

"Sure." Gretch left and Keira turned to Tony, whose pale- blue eyes were busy running the length of her body. "So, what do you do?"

"I'm in sales. And I understand you've got a book coming out that is going to have people waiting in line around the block."

"We do. It's called *Ring Girl*." She pointed across the room. "There's a giant poster of the cover in front of my office."

He turned and his eyes widened. "Wow, beautiful girl on the cover."

"Her name's Lauren. She's also the spokesperson for Sizzle sunblock."

"Oh, right, the Sizzle Girl." He studied the photo. "Guess you changed her hair color."

"Well, the heroine in the book is a redhead so we put a wig on her."

"I see." He looked up at her hair. "If you needed a redhead, why didn't *you* pose for the cover?"

"Uh, I'm an editor, not a fashion model."

"Well, you should be." He moved closer, locking eyes with her. "You've certainly got the body for it."

Keira rolled her eyes. *Oh, geez. Get me outta here.* She looked around for an escape route. "Uh, excuse me, my publisher beckons."

She headed toward the bar, desperately needing a refill. Two men about thirty, one tall and one short, stood nearby leering at her as she reached the bartender and ordered more champagne. She heard one of them whispering.

"Check out the ass on that copper top."

Keira whipped her head around and saw the tall one smiling at her. She shot him the death stare. "And check out the ass standing next to me."

"Ooooh, she's a spitfire. I like that. How ya doin', Red?" He held up a cell phone. "Can I get a picture of you so I can show Santa what I want to find on Christmas morning?"

Her eyes narrowed. "Real clever. You the author of *Pickup Lines for Losers*? Or would it be *Cheap Come-ons for Dummies*?"

The tall guy shook his head while the short man moved closer and stared up at her. "Honey, now that you're here, I've got two wishes left."

She held her hand an inch over his head. "Sorry, you must be this big to ride. We wouldn't want you to get hurt."

"Geez, lighten up."

"Listen, boys, since this is a publishing office, you should consider me a sold-out bestseller. Currently unavailable." Keira shook her head, grabbed her drink, and quickly walked away.

Three hours and a ton of booze later the crowd had thinned. Keira headed for the safety of her office, all out of smiles and small talk. She simply wanted to grab her purse and go home. No sooner had she walked behind her desk than she heard a tap on the door. She looked up to see Tony, drink in hand, leering at her.

Oh, great. What a wonderful way to cap off the evening. "Can I help you?"

"Hey, Keira, wanted to thank you for the hospitality. Great party."

"Glad you enjoyed it." Take him down a notch. "Tommy, right?"

"Tony."

"It was nice to meet you. Have a safe trip home."

"I was wondering if I could get an advance copy of *Ring Girl*."

"Sure thing. I don't have any print copies right now but I can email you the manuscript. Leave me a business card."

"Just handed them all out, but I'll write down my contact information for you." He pulled a pen from his pocket, moved behind her desk, grabbed a sticky note and wrote on it. "That's the hotel I'm staying at and the room number."

He was now close enough for her to smell his overpowering cologne, along with the brewery emanating from his mouth. "Uh, all I need is your email address."

"Actually, I was hoping you might drop by and read to me."

She narrowed her eyes. "Get! Out!" She pointed at the door.

"Fine. Nice meeting you too."

Keira watched him leave, then sat at her desk and buried her head in her hands.

Gretch spotted Tony as he headed across the lobby toward her. "Did it go okay, Tony?"

"You owe me big time, cousin."

"Mission accomplished?"

He nodded. "Oh yeah. Hit her with a few of the sleazy comments you gave me. Pretended I was hammered. Your idea to spray this old sport jacket with bourbon really sold it."

"Yeah, that thing reeks."

He took off the jacket and tossed it in a nearby trashcan. "I was a classic drunk lounge lizard. Just like you asked."

"Good. Hopefully that will make her realize what she's lost. And what other single guys are like."

"Uh, excuse me?" He pointed to himself. "I'm standing right here."

"Not you, Tony. I know you're not that way. You're my favorite relative."

"Thank you. But it was pretty strange acting like a player. How'd Jason and Richie do?"

"Hit her with some seriously lame pickup lines I wrote."

"You really think this will make her go back to her old boyfriend?"

"All part of the plan. And there are many parts."

Keira flipped the light switch and saw Gretch getting off the elevator.

"Outta here?" asked Gretch.

"Been a long day. By the way, thank you soooo much for introducing me to Tony."

"Which one was Tony?"

"About six-two, short black hair, camel-hair sport coat. From that small chain of bookstores on the West Coast."

"Oh, him. Yeah, he was a hottie. So you liked the guy?"

"Hell, no! He hit on me in my office a few minutes ago."

"What'd you do?"

259

"Threw him out."

"You should have sent him to me."

Keira shook her head. "And damn, the cheap lines he used." She dropped her voice to imitate a man. "*You should be a model. You've got the body for it.*"

"Sounds pretty lame."

"Then he asks me to bring a copy of *Ring Girl* to his hotel room. Gimme a break. And, my God, it seemed like half the men out there hit on me with some sleazy comment. Had to use every snappy comeback I could think of. I was a damn loser magnet tonight."

"Well, boss, welcome back to the world of being single and unattached. If you're looking for a nice old-fashioned guy, it's slim pickens out there."

Gretch watched the elevator door close, then whipped out her cell and called Alex.

He picked up on the first ring. "Operation Matchmaker Headquarters."

"Looking Glass to Red Leader. Another crack in the armor."

"What did you do now?"

"Invited my cousin to the publisher's annual cocktail party to hit on her."

"You're fixing her up with another guy?"

"Of course not. I had him act like a total sleaze."

"Seriously?"

"And I had a few of my buddies from the old neighborhood hit on her with some seriously sleazy lines. But it all had the desired effect as she left here pretty disgusted. And hopefully that planted the seed in her mind of how great a catch you are."

"Remind me never to cross you."

"Hey, I don't play fair. But the stakes are high, so all bets are off. Everything is on the table."

"So, should I call her now?"

"Patience, grasshopper. I've got another romantic shell to launch in her direction."

"And what tactic in *The Book of Gretch* would that be?"

"Not gonna tell you, Alex. You need to maintain plausible deniability. But trust me, by Saturday night, she's going to be doing a lot of thinking about you."

Chapter 26

"I don't wanna stay long, Gretch. Let's just make an appearance and hit the road."

"Bullshit. This is Jenna's wedding and she works her ass off for you in promotions. You're staying. Besides, you always like wedding receptions. We get to do the Bunny Hop, the Alley Cat."

"Those dances are dumb."

"Yeah, but I end up with my hands on some guy's ass."

They checked in at the reception desk. A young lady handed them each a card. "Looks like we're at table twelve," said Keira. "Jill's already here."

"Hope there are some cute guys there."

Keira shook her head. "I just want some champagne."

They made their way through the crowded ballroom, beautifully decorated with white ribbons on each chair and red roses on every table. A huge four-tiered wedding cake sat next to the head table at the front of the room. A piano player filled the air with soft classical while the crowd buzzed, waiting for the bride and groom to arrive. They found their table, full with the exception of two empty seats. Both of which were next to men.

"Dibs on the seat next to the blonde guy," said Gretch.

"Fine, whatever." They took their seats and everyone exchanged introductions. The man next to Keira was named Rob, an attractive fortyish guy with close-cropped dark-brown hair, eyes to match and a lean face. He smiled at her as she adjusted her chair.

"Friend of the bride or groom?" he asked.

"I work with the bride. You?"

"Known the groom for years. Looks like he found a great gal."

"Yeah, Jenna's terrific."

"So you're in publishing too. What do you do?"

"Senior editor in the romance division." She pointed at Jill. "She's our publisher."

"Ah, so this wedding reception is a real life 'happily ever after.'"

"Yeah, guess so. So what's your profession?"

"Attorney. No lawyer jokes, please, I've heard them all."

"What kind of attorney?"

"Divorce attorney."

"Doesn't sound like fun."

"Sometimes I look at clients and wonder how they ever got married. But then I come to something like this and it gives me hope. I'm still a romantic at heart."

He locked eyes with her and she couldn't help but smile.

Two hours and three glasses of champagne later, Keira was having a decent time. Rob was charming, with a quick wit, and obviously interested in her. A far cry from the men who'd hit on her at the office cocktail party.

Gretch leaned over and whispered in her ear. "You seem to be getting along with your seat mate."

"He's nice."

"See, I told you it would help to get out. Still wanna leave early?"

She smiled as she sipped her drink, the alcohol having the desired effect. It was the first time she'd relaxed since… "Nah, I'm good."

The band finished a classic disco number. "Okay," said the lead singer. "We call this our ice-breaker dance. Get on the floor with

263

someone you just met today. Who knows, you might be sitting next to your future husband or wife."

Rob turned to her and cocked his head in the direction of the dance floor. "May I have this dance?"

She shrugged. "Sure, why not?"

He got up and extended his hand. She took it and stood up.

And found herself looking at the top of his head.

He looked up at her. "Whoa, you're a tall one. How's the weather up there?"

Like I've never heard that line before. "You want me to pick you up so you can find out?"

"I was just kidding."

"Hey, I didn't hit you with any lawyer jokes, so no amazon comments."

He leaned forward, putting his hand lightly on her forearm. "Would you, uh, mind… taking off your heels?"

"You gotta problem with tall girls?"

He shrugged. "No, but… you know…"

"Sorry, this girl comes equipped with shoes. You wanna dance, or what?"

The voice from behind Keira interrupted them. "Well, Rob, I see you're already stalking my replacement. And it's another ginger clone."

She turned around and found herself nearly looking in a mirror.

The woman was a skinny redhead, taller than Keira, about the same age, identical hair color, but with green eyes filled with fire as she glared at Rob. She turned to Keira. "Hi, I'm Jennifer, about to become Rob's ex-wife number three. He's going for the hat trick."

Keira turned back to Rob, folded her arms and widened her eyes. "You're *married*?"

The woman moved next to Rob, towering over him, and answered Keira while looking down her nose at him. "Oh, he didn't get to his usual line? 'My wife doesn't understand me.'"

"No, he conveniently left that part out. And apparently forgot his wedding ring as well."

Rob broke out in a sweat, surrounded by the two tall redheads. The woman turned and took Keira's hands. "Listen, honey, let me do you a favor and save you a lot of heartache. He cheats. He drinks and drives. He doesn't pay child support to his first two wives and doesn't bother seeing his four kids. And by the time I'm through with him, he won't have a pot to piss in. You can do better."

Keira turned to Gretch and grabbed her purse. "C'mon. We're leaving."

"I thought you were having a good time?"

"Meet me outside. I'll get a cab." Keira turned to the other redhead. "Thanks for the warning. And good luck in court."

"I'm gonna spend all his money on the stilettos he never let me wear. No more flats!"

Keira shot Rob a nasty look, then used her thumb and forefinger to form an 'L', the international sign for loser, and flicked it at him before storming out.

Gretch watched Keira power-walk across the dance floor and waited until she was out the door, then stood up. "That was perfect, guys. Really well done. Very convincing."

Jennifer exhaled and put her hand on her chest. "Whew. I've never played a woman scorned. So I did okay?"

Rob nodded. "You were terrific. I really believed you were going to divorce me. Or ready to kick my ass."

Gretch patted him on the back. "And you, with the great small talk for two hours. You sucked her right in."

"How was the part about me asking her to take off the heels?"

"Excellent! She hates when guys mention her height. Academy Award stuff."

"Thank you. But right now we'll both settle for a Tony."

"So when does your play open?" asked Gretch.

"In a week," said Jennifer. "It's so exciting that we both finally made it to Broadway in the same show. It's the ultimate for actors."

"I'm sure and I'll be there opening night. Thanks again, guys. You two really did a good deed today."

"Didn't feel like one," said Rob. "Let us know how it turns out."

Gretch found Keira tapping her foot with her arms folded next to the valet parking attendant. "You okay, Keira?"

"Cab should be here in a few minutes."

"Wasn't asking about the cab."

"I just wanna go home, Gretch." She put up her hand. "And please, don't try to drag me out tonight. I'm really not in the mood."

"Sure. I overheard some of that stuff back there. I understand."

"Men." Keira shook her head, then turned to Gretch. "Look, I appreciate all you've done trying to cheer me up this week, but I really need to be alone right now."

"Sure, kiddo."

Alex smiled as he saw Lauren's phone number pop up on his cell phone. "Hey, big-time movie star!"

"Hi, Alex!"

"So how's Hollywood treating you?"

"Well, it's different. The movie people are kinda plastic but the director is very happy with me, which is really all that counts. I'm amazed at how much I miss New York."

"Well, you're only out there for a few months."

"Might be longer than that. The star of our movie took a fall and broke a few bones, so we're shutting down for a month 'cause she's in a cast. But I can pick up some commercial work."

"Well, that's good."

"So how are things going with Keira?"

His face dropped. Alex told her the entire story, including their fabulous night together. "So right now, I'm not sure where I stand with her."

"Alex, that's horrible."

"But you were right, Lauren. Keira is my soul mate." His voice cracked. "And now I've lost her."

"I'm sure she'll come around."

"I dunno. Might take a while. Some of her friends are trying to get us back together, but she's pretty mad."

"Then I'm coming home."

"I thought you had some commercial work."

"You need help, Alex. I'm coming home. I'm going to knock some sense into that woman."

Keira slung her purse onto a chair in disgust and headed for the kitchen. She didn't even bother to get out of the dress she'd worn to the wedding.

She needed sugar. The ultimate comfort food.

Right. Now.

She whipped open the freezer door, but there was nothing inside but disappointment. "Sonofabitch!"

She was out of Haagen Daaz. She slammed the door.

"Fine. I'll have chocolate for dinner."

She headed to the living room and fired up the TV, loaded the *Die Hard* DVD. Keira needed to see the good guys win again.

She reached for the jar of chocolate she kept on the coffee table when she spotted the bag of licorice from the old-fashioned penny candy store. "Huh, I thought I ate all those." She grabbed it, her mouth watering for the classic confection. She smiled when she opened it, then stopped when she saw what was inside.

It was *his* bag. He had picked out all the round ones with the coconut and left them for her.

Her favorites.

"Damn, I wish you could buy just these."

She bit her lower lip as a single tear ran down her cheek.

Chapter 27

"Okay, birthday girl, ready for a great dinner?"

Keira looked up from her desk and saw Gretch smiling at her. "Damn, it's five already?"

"Yeah. Time flies when you're deep in thought while getting absolutely no work done. C'mon, let's go."

"Sure." She picked up her purse and followed Gretch to the elevator. It was a nice sunny day outside, and the walk to the restaurant in the fresh air would do her good.

"Oh, gotta make a quick stop at my apartment. Forgot your present."

"You didn't have to get me anything, Gretch."

"Bullshit. You're like a big sister to me. Shut up and take your damn birthday gift."

"Yes, ma'am."

Gretch turned the key to her apartment and they walked inside.

"Surprise!"

Keira jumped back as she saw people get up from behind the couch. But if this was a birthday celebration, it sure didn't look like one.

Bella stood there, offering a soft smile.

But what the hell was Juliette doing here?

She turned her head and saw the familiar weathered face dressed all in black with a white collar.

My priest is here?

Then it dawned on her.

This was no birthday party.

"Happy birthday, Keira," said Bella, wearing a serious look as she moved around the couch.

Keira's face tightened as Gretch closed the door behind her. "Uh, what the heck is going on?" She turned to the priest, studying his face. "Father Albert?"

"Have a seat, Keira," said the old white-haired priest, gesturing toward a love seat.

"Not sure I want to."

Gretch pointed to the couch. "Sit. Now." She glared at Keira.

One look at her assistant told her they weren't fooling around. "Fine." She sat as she glared at Juliette. "Juliette. How, uh, *unexpected* to see you again."

"I invited her," said Gretch, leaning against the door, presumably to keep Keira from making a break for it.

"So, I guess we're not here to play pin the tail on the donkey. No piñata either?"

Gretch folded her arms. "Keira, you can fire me when we're done, but I am not going to spend another damn day watching you mope around and stare out your office window because you're too friggin' stubborn to forgive someone you're in love with who truly cares about you."

"So this is some sort of romantic intervention?"

"Well, you don't have a drinking or drug problem. Unless you think we're here to keep you from eating junk food."

The priest smiled. "She tried that as a child, giving up candy for Lent. Failed miserably. Ended up in confession every week."

"Father Albert, how in the world did you come to be here today?"

The tall, lean priest leaned forward and folded his hands, his gray eyes locking on hers. "Keira, I've known you since I taught you

269

in the first grade and ever since your smiling face has been in the front row every Sunday, without fail. When you missed Mass two weeks in a row, I got worried you might be ill. You didn't answer your phone so I called your office. Your assistant filled me in."

Keira shot a glare at Gretch. Gretch returned a knowing smile.

Bella took a seat opposite her. "Keira, you know this is all my fault. You can't go on blaming Alex for this. I'm the one who is ultimately responsible and I feel terribly about how things have turned out. If you want to be mad at me forever, go ahead. But you are being incredibly thick-headed and probably throwing away a guy who seems absolutely perfect for you because of something I told him to do."

Juliette stood up and started walking around. "And you can hate me forever too if you like. But Keira, I've been best friends with Alex for years and I have never seen him happier than when he's with you. The poor guy is practically unable to function right now, he's so devastated at losing you. He loves you, Keira. I know he hasn't said it yet because he believes you should hold off as long as possible, but he does."

The priest started to speak but was interrupted by a knock on the door. Keira whipped her head around. "You invited him here?"

Gretch opened the door. "No. We're not gonna force you to see him. That has to be your decision."

Keira's eyes widened when she saw who walked in. "Lauren?"

Lauren smiled as she wheeled a suitcase into the apartment. "Sorry I'm late, guys. Flight was a little delayed."

"Aren't you supposed to be in Hollywood?"

"Our star took a fall and they shut down production for a month. I heard Alex was hurting so I came home."

Keira furrowed her brow. "Not sure I understand your connection to all this between me and Alex."

Lauren nodded, sat next to her and took her hands. "Keira, perhaps more than anyone, I know about his feelings for you. That's the reason I stopped dating him."

Her jaw dropped. "Whoa, hold on. You and Alex were seeing each other?"

Lauren nodded. "I'm the so-called 'other woman.'"

The realization hit her.

The brunette Alex had on his arm at the restaurant. With the Barbie-doll body whose face I couldn't see.

"You?"

Lauren nodded. "I got a clue he was hung up on another girl when I tried to seduce him and failed."

Her eyes became saucers. "Excuse me?"

"And then when Dash kissed you at the photo shoot I could see how jealous Alex was and realized *you* were the other woman from *my* point of view. Then at dinner that night I faced the competition and knew I had no shot. I could see how he felt and I had to set him free. That's when I told him to find out if you were his true soul mate. I can't share a man, Keira, especially if his heart belongs to someone else. And I already knew what a fine person you are. If you were a bitch I would have fought for him. Even though I wanted Alex I couldn't be mad at someone like you, someone who made him so happy. And someone who had given me a break as a book cover model. If I was going to lose, I was glad to come in second to someone like you."

Keira whipped her head around to look at Juliette. "That story you told me is actually true?"

Juliette nodded. "I knew you wouldn't believe it. But Lauren is an amazingly unselfish person."

Keira turned back to Lauren. "You actually tried to seduce him? And couldn't do it? But you're the Sizzle Girl. You can have any guy you want."

She shook her head. "Not this guy. He resisted. I put on the bikini from the commercial and basically gave him a lap dance but I still couldn't get him into my bed." Lauren's eyes suddenly went wide and her face turned red as she noticed Father Albert. "Oh my God! I didn't realize a priest was here. My goodness, this

271

is embarrassing. I am so sorry, Father."

He smiled and waved it away. "Young lady, if I wrote down all the stuff I've heard in the confessional and gave it to Keira, she'd have a book that would make *Fifty Shades* look like Jack and Jill."

Everyone laughed. Lauren turned back to Keira. "Anyway, he's in love with *you*, Keira, not me. Not anyone else."

"But you're the Sizzle Girl. You're ten times prettier than me. And you were just voted the most desirable woman in America by a national magazine."

"Obviously I'm the *second*-most desirable in his case. And from my point of view you're more beautiful than I'll ever be. Remember the first time we met at the restaurant and I told you how jealous I was of your hair? You've got those gorgeous turquoise eyes that are so full of life, and those cute little freckles. I got a good look at your personality when I waited on you at the restaurant and during the photo shoot. Every expression you have shows such an incredible life force, every movement you make has an energy that's off the charts. Your smile lights up a room. Your laugh is like a bunch of little bells. Your overall beauty blows me away. And you're so completely in control. I'd love to look and act like you. Hell, I'd love to *be* you."

"Now *that* statement blows *me* away."

"Keira, I wanted Alex but his heart belongs to you. You won, fair and square. You get the brass ring. I'll have to settle for being proud to know someone like him. And I'm being honest when I tell you he is the best man I have ever dated. The most decent, most unselfish, most generous. He's cute as hell and sweet as sugar. You can trust him around other women. I'm sorry to put it this way, but you're a damn idiot if you let him go. So, and pardon my French, get your head out of your ass and go back to him before it's too late." She turned to the priest. "Sorry again, Father."

"Again, I've heard much worse."

Keira exhaled her tension, trying to process what she had just heard.

The priest interrupted her train of thought. "Keira, you're one of those few young people who comes to my old-fashioned one-on-one confessions. Why don't you tell everyone how that works, since I'm sure not everyone here is Catholic."

"Father, they probably aren't interested—"

"Humor me."

"Fine. I kneel down in the little confessional, which is the size of a closet with a curtain for privacy, confess my sins, we talk about it, you give me a bunch of Hail Marys to say as penance, and I go to the altar and pray."

"And what happens when you're done praying?"

She shrugged. "I get up, bless myself and go home."

"Not what I'm looking for. So let me rephrase my question. What *has happened* to you after you've confessed your sins and said your penance? What is your status with God?"

She locked eyes with him, his look forcing the logic on her. She spoke in a soft voice. "I'm... forgiven."

"Sorry, I don't think everyone heard you."

"I'm forgiven."

"So if God forgives those imperfect souls he loves, what should we, as His children, do?"

"Dammit, Father, why do you always have to make so much sense?" Her anger began to dissipate as she locked eyes with the priest.

Gretch moved toward her while turning on the television. "See last night's news, Keira?"

"What has that got to do with anything?"

"Watch." She hit the remote and the screen filled with a shot of four New York City police officers at a ceremony as the anchor voiced over the story.

"Four officers were honored by the mayor for their bravery after being involved in a recent shootout. You may remember the gunfight that took place between two escaped convicts and

police one evening in Midtown."

The anchor continued reading the story as the video rolled in slow motion, showing Alex protecting Keira in the background. Gretch froze the video, tossed the remote on the coffee table, crouched down and looked at her. "He would have taken a bullet for you, Keira. He might have died. Or saved your life."

Keira stared at the screen, the video frozen at the moment the bullet hit the glass above them. She felt her emotions well up. Everyone was silent.

Gretch got up and walked back to the door. "And with that, your honor, the defense rests."

The priest leaned back and put his palms up. "Well, young lady?"

She exhaled as she looked at Father Albert. "Fine, you guys win. And you're right. I'll forgive him. I'll talk to him."

"That's all we wanted," said Gretch, now stepping away from her position guarding the door. Lauren smiled and gave her a quick hug.

Keira looked up at Gretch. "Do I still get my birthday cake?"

"As always, it all comes down to sugar with you."

Keira and Lauren took seats in a booth as the rest of the gang headed to a private room in the back of the busy restaurant. "I'll keep you company while they're setting up," said Lauren.

"Setting up what?"

She shrugged and smiled. "I'll never tell."

"So will you tell me who coordinated this full court press today?"

"I'll never tell that either. Let's just say it's a group effort between people who care a great deal about both you and Alex."

"I see."

"I'm so glad you're going to talk with him, Keira. Great guys are hard to find."

"Yeah. So, any prospective Mister Rights out there in Hollywood? I'm sure your dance card is full."

"Oh, please. I've been groped so much I need to be dusted for prints. Really, Keira, all the men out there see is Sizzle Girl. They're not like Alex. They don't see Lauren, just the girl in the bikini spilling out of her top. They don't realize that Sizzle Girl is simply a fantasy created in a studio for publicity, and I'm nothing like her." Hey eyes suddenly widened. "Speaking of publicity, nice article on you in today's *Page Six*."

"What are you talking about?"

She pulled a copy of the *New York Post* out of her bag and handed it to her. "Here, I picked one up at the airport. Sure miss this newspaper." Lauren's cell phone buzzed. She reached into her purse for it. "My agent. Excuse me, Keira, I have to take this. I'll be right back."

"Sure, take your time."

Lauren got up and headed for the back room. Keira unfolded the newspaper and flipped to the gossip page. Her eyes widened as she saw her photo and a headline.

ROMANCE EDITOR NEARLY LOST A REAL HAPPILY EVER AFTER

"What the hell is this about?" She started to read.

Starstruck Books Senior Romance Editor Keira Madison has been editing novels with a happy ending her entire career. But she almost missed her own a few years ago.
By now you know the story of bestselling romance author Alex Bauer and how he and his agent pulled the wool over the eyes of Madison to make her think the author of his first book, Ring Girl, *was a woman. What you might not know is that Bauer had fallen hard for the spunky redhead in real life while working with her editing the book. When Madison discovered the ruse, she was furious and broke things off with Bauer.*

Keira looked up at the top of the page.

The date was five years in the future.

This is a fake newspaper.

"I was devastated. Couldn't function," said Bauer. "I'm a writer but I couldn't come up with the words to apologize. Keira didn't trust me. I thought I had lost my true love. My life was destined to be unhappily ever after."

This is his apology.

She continued reading.

That's when Madison's assistant sprung into action, collecting friends for a romantic intervention to make the editor realize she had a good guy in Bauer. "Fortunately she gave me a second chance or I would never have ended up with such a wonderful woman."

So the guy who writes romance novels got his own happy ending. "I'm still just as much in love with her today," said Bauer. "Thank goodness she found it in her heart to forgive me. But that's not surprising, since she has the biggest heart of anyone I've ever known."

Just as she finished reading a waiter showed up at the booth and slid a chocolate milkshake in front of Keira. "Hey, I didn't order a chocolate shake."

"From the guy at the bar," said the waiter. "And it's not a shake, it's a malt."

"What guy?"

The waiter pointed to the bar behind her. "Back there."

Keira turned around to find her mysterious benefactor and was immediately hit in the face with something. She turned back and saw a straw wrapper on the table. Then she heard his voice.

"Damn kids."

She started to smile as she looked up and saw him peeking over the top of the booth, holding a straw, bloodshot eyes giving her a soulful look. A look that instantly drained all the anger from her.

A look that told her she couldn't live without him.

Every good memory, every feeling she had for him rushed back in an instant.

She wanted him back.

Right.

Now.

"Hey, Bauer."

"Hey, Madison."

"You always send shakes to women in bars?"

"It's not a shake, it's a malt. And no, this is my first time. A martini is much too cliché."

"I see."

"May I join you?"

She gestured with her hand toward the empty seat across from her. He moved around the booth and slid onto the seat, his shoulders hunched while ringing his hands. "Bauer, relax. I won't bite."

"Sorry. I'm a little nervous. I didn't know how you'd react."

"You're sitting with me, aren't you?"

His shoulders dropped a bit and he smiled. "Yeah. Thank you."

She tapped the newspaper as she took a sip of the malt. "Very interesting article in *today's* paper."

"Yeah, but I noticed you weren't quoted. The writer only got one side of the story. Sloppy reporting. I, as a reader, would be curious to know your feelings."

She smiled at him. "In this case, one side was more than enough. I think we can read between the lines, considering the outcome."

He locked eyes with her. "Listen, Keira, I'm really—"

"You know, we need to finish our editing on the book."

He furrowed his brow. "Uh, I thought we were done a few weeks ago."

"Not the real book, the one we were rewriting for fun in my

apartment. You remember where we left off, right? Lexi seduces Jamison and jumps his bones, makes him moan so loud the cops show up, wakes up on top of him, has her way with him again before breakfast. Great scene. I mean, damn, it was hot the way she just took him and he was powerless against her."

He instantly blushed. "Oh. That."

"Really, Bauer, you're a rookie at this but you should know you can't end a book in that manner. Get the reader back on the emotional roller coaster. You *do* know the big rule about conflict in fiction, right?"

"Which rule is that?"

"Things get worse. You must have the try-and-fail sequences. If the whole book was nothing but unicorns and rainbows, no one would buy it. The reader needs a rooting interest, wants Lexi and Jamison to get to their 'happily ever after'. But you can't just have her nail him a few times and write *The End*. As writers and editors we have to throw some obstacles in their way. Can't make things too easy. Anyway, I've been working on the manuscript."

"I see. So, what happens next?"

"Well, when last we left our story, Lexi had just found out something about Jamison that shocked her and she couldn't deal with it—"

"Keira, please—"

She put up her hand. "Let me finish, Bauer. Anyway, Lexi, who sometimes lets her emotions get in the way of common sense, gets very upset and lets her memory of a past relationship cloud her judgment. The reader knows what Jamison has done isn't that bad. I mean, it's not like he jumped into bed with another woman."

"He, uh, would never do that. Because he's head over heels for her."

"Exactly. And he's not a bed-hopper but an incredibly decent guy. But she's a redhead with a short fuse and a stubborn streak a mile wide. She won't cut him some slack. Deep down the reader knows she misses him terribly but she's got her heels dug in and won't admit it to the rest of the world."

"So Jamison decides to give her space even though he's devastated."

"Smart guy. He knows sometimes women need to be left alone. But what he doesn't know is that she's hurting as much as he is."

"Really?"

"Oh, definitely. She misses him like you wouldn't believe, but her anger is in the way of her true feelings. Anyway, after Lexi broods for a few weeks her friends trick her and she ends up at an intervention where they make her realize how stupid she's been. How he's the perfect guy for her and that she'd be a complete fool to let him go. How he was dating one of the most beautiful women in the world and still wanted Lexi, who doesn't see herself as anything special."

"She's wrong about that. And he's blown away that she was dating a guy who looked like Thor and chose him instead."

"That's because he's twice the man as the other guy. But don't interrupt, I'm on a roll. She realizes he's her true soul mate and needs to forgive him." Keira leaned toward him with misty eyes and dropped her voice. "And how *she's* the one who needs to apologize for not forgiving him right off the bat."

His eyes welled up. "I think Jamison would be shocked at that part. He doesn't think he deserves an apology. But is desperate to give her one."

She shook her head. "He doesn't need to. His eyes tell her how sorry he is. And so does what he wrote in a newspaper. The thing is, Bauer, as editors and writers we sometimes fall into a trap and try to create perfect people. But in real life we all have flaws and imperfections. If we want to create truly believable characters, we have to give them flaws, and have to make our heroine and hero accept those flaws. That's when the fictional characters become real in the mind of the reader and jump off the page. The characters have to be just like us."

"So in this case, Lexi is forgiving Jamison?"

"Absolutely. Because Lexi realized she's not perfect either. And because she's head over heels for him as well."

His whole body relaxed and he leaned back as he brushed a tear from his eye. "So, uh, what happens next?"

"Well—"

Gretch appeared at their table. "Okay, birthday girl— oh, Alex, what a coincidence that you're here!"

"Hi, Gretch. I was in the neighborhood."

Keira rolled her eyes. "Okay, guys, you can drop the act."

"What act?" asked Gretch.

Alex shrugged and put up his palms. "No clue what she's talking about. I came by hoping to pick up a hot woman with a chocolate malt. Amazingly it worked."

Gretch took Keira's arm and pulled her out of the booth. "Anyway, it's time to get this party started!"

Keira smiled as she wrapped one arm around Gretch's shoulder, leaned down and whispered in her ear. "I love you."

"I know."

Chapter 28

"Excuse me!"

The waiter had to yell to be heard above the laughter and conversation. Everyone quieted down.

"Much as we've loved having you guys, we're about to close, so unless you want to sleep here..."

Alex was sad to see the evening come to an end, but happy that Keira was back in his life. The dinner table held the aftermath of a memorable celebration: the remnants of a birthday cake, scraps of wrapping paper, streamers, balloons, cards, gifts, empty plates and wine bottles.

The most important memories were the smiles Keira had given him all night.

He'd held out the chair for her upon entering the private room. She'd immediately sat down and patted the seat next to her. "You're sitting here."

She really did want him back.

At one point during dinner he'd rested one hand in his lap. She reached over under the table and entwined her fingers with his, giving him a soulful look.

When Gretch lit the candles on the birthday cake and told Keira to make a wish, she looked at him and said, "It already came true."

Now it was time to proceed... how? He hadn't had a private

moment with her since they left the booth in the restaurant. Was it going to be hands off and take it slow again? All had been forgiven so quickly.

"Thank you all," said Keira, getting up. "A very unusual birthday, but one with a happy ending. Appropriate for a romance editor." She turned to him as he stood up. "Guess it's time for us to go home."

"Yeah." Suddenly his heart raced. He was a teenager asking for a first date, looking down as he shoved his hands in his pockets. "So, uh, when can we get together?"

"I just said it's time for us to go home. For you and me, the terms 'home' and 'us' imply the same location." She looped one hand around his elbow. She leaned toward him and whispered in his ear. "Your place or mine?"

"Well, then, in that case we need to swing by my place to get your birthday present."

"Why didn't you just bring it here?"

"Didn't know if you would want me around."

"I finally came to my senses. Now, can we try to forget the past few days and simply pick up where we left off?"

Keira placed two glasses of wine on the coffee table next to his cube-shaped present wrapped in red paper with a gold bow, then picked it up. "Wow, it's heavy." She shook it a bit. "And it's liquid. I'm guessing it's not jewelry."

He looked up at her from his seat on the couch. "Very perceptive. I thought about putting a snow globe on a chain, but it didn't seem practical for you to wear."

"Well, let's see what this mystery package is." Suddenly she turned, backed up toward him and sat on his lap. "Like to be comfortable when I open presents."

His heart rate rocketed as he supported her back with one arm. "You, uh, should have whatever you want on your birthday."

She licked her lips. "Don't worry, I will. Madison always takes what she wants." She tore open the wrapping paper like a kid on Christmas morning, then furrowed her brow as she looked at the old, tattered box. "A magic 8-ball?"

"Not just any magic 8-ball."

She took it out of the box. The black globe was smudged and had a few dents. "Yeah. An *old* magic 8-ball."

"The appropriate term is 'vintage'. It's made of glass instead of the plastic they use today. But it has unique powers. Got it from a gypsy fortune-teller who swears it only answers questions about love. So I thought it was perfect for a romance editor."

She turned it around and studied it. "I see."

"So, why don't you ask it a question? But remember, it has to be about romance and the person who gave it to you."

"Ah, there are rules. So I have to ask it about you and me?"

"Yep, or it won't work. According to the gypsy."

"Okay, here goes… how does the guy whose lap I'm sitting on feel about me?" She shook the 8-ball, then turned it over. Her eyes widened as the answer appeared through the ink.

Bauer loves you.

She turned to face him. "Where'd you get this?"

"Like I said, a gypsy fortune-teller. Ask it another question."

She looked back at the 8-ball. "Does the man I am with right now really think I'm his soul mate?" She shook it and turned it over.

You are his Lexi.

She looked back at him, her eyes getting a bit misty. "This 8-ball seems to be a bit biased."

He shrugged. "Hey, all I know is the gypsy said the thing never lies. Go ahead, one more question."

She looked at the toy. "Will the man who gave me this 8-ball always love me, even when I'm old and gray?"

You have his heart forever.

He smiled at her. "That gypsy was right, it never lies. Amazing, huh?"

Keira bit her lower lip, felt her eyes well up, put the 8-ball on the coffee table and turned to him. "How the hell do you come up with sweet stuff like this?"

"I'm a romance writer, remember?"

"Seriously, Bauer, you really love me? After all I put you through these past few days?"

"Number one rule of fiction, Madison."

"Huh?"

"Show, don't tell." He took her face in both hands, looked into her soul and kissed her. "That answer your question?"

She wrapped her arms around him and lay her head on his shoulder. "Don't need a magic 8-ball for that one." Her voice was so soft he could barely hear it.

"So, continuing our rewrite. I would assume the reader is happy about the turn of events that got Lexi and Jamison back together and we can proceed to the happily ever after."

Keira hugged him tight as she breathed in his cologne. "Uh-huh."

He wrapped his arms around her waist. "Well, now that Lexi knows how Jamison feels, don't you think he wants to know if she feels the same way? Is the reader waiting for her to say something?"

She looked up at him. "No, because of the aforementioned 'show, don't tell' rule. He should carry her to the bedroom and she'll *show* him how she feels. Words aren't necessary."

Alex smiled and lifted her as he stood up, cradling her in his arms. "So, she wants to be the one who's taken this time."

"I didn't say that. She commanded him to carry her to the bedroom and he must obey. She's still in charge. He's the transportation."

"I see." He started walking toward her bedroom. "So this isn't one of those books where the hero sweeps the heroine off her feet and has his way with her?"

"Nah, too cliché again, and Lexi isn't a formulaic heroine. Though the 'sweeping her off her feet' is literal in this novel. Since, ya know, she was out cold the last time he gave her a lift to the bedroom she doesn't want to miss out on that experience since it sounded so chivalrous. But Jamison doesn't mind letting her play the aggressive role since he had such an enjoyable night the last time, so he will surrender. Remember, he's still powerless against her."

"I think that will always be the case."

"Actually, in this story, it works both ways. He just hasn't realized it yet."

He entered the bedroom and put her down on the bed. "What now? Time for a clever line?"

"I think your shirt would look really good on me."

They lay there totally spent. Keira with her head on his chest, listening to his steady heartbeat, which was finally slowing down. She ran her hand across his stomach and threw one leg over him. His arm went around her shoulders as he kissed the top of her head. "Hey, Bauer, can I ask you something?"

"Good God, I can't possibly go again. Can you at least let me recharge till morning?"

She started to laugh. "Not that, silly."

"Good, because you'd wake up next to an empty husk."

"I'd better not. Breakfast is the most important meal of the day."

"So what did you want to ask me?"

"It's about that newspaper article. You know, the one from the future?"

"Ah, that one. What about it?"

"Well, in the article you were quoted as saying you 'ended up' with me. And since the paper was dated five years in the future, I can only assume through deductive reasoning that we are still together."

"You would be correct."

"So my question is… what constitutes 'ending up' together? In the future are we boyfriend and girlfriend, friends with benefits… or something more?"

"Considering the benefits I received tonight, it would definitely be more than friends."

"Hey!"

He gently stroked her hair. "Madison, I'm not commitment-phobic. If I'm still with the same woman after five years, by that time I will have offered her an exclusive lifetime contract at some point."

"Sounds like a publishing deal."

"I would pre-empt you so no one else could have you. Or even put in a bid."

"Think you've already done that, Mister. And 'at some point' would mean…"

"Sometime between today and five years from now."

"Is this 'lifetime contract' your way of saying there is a ring in my future?"

"One might assume that would be the case."

"Ah, how interesting."

"But it wouldn't be given in a traditional manner, such as getting down on one knee in a romantic restaurant like in *Moonstruck*. Or proposing in front of the Eiffel Tower. Much too cliché."

"Some clichés are good. As an editor I could live with either of those."

"Yeah, but as you mentioned, this is not a formulaic relationship. For you it would have to be something unique. But hey, I've got five years to come up with an idea."

She raised her head, looked at him, and thrust out her lower lip in a pout. "I gotta wait five years?"

"No, but you gotta wait. So who's powerless now?"

Keira ran her hand across the upholstery of the classic convertible.

The powder-blue 1957 Chevy with the tail fins was the perfect car for a night at the vintage drive-in. Even the name of the place was classic: *Passion Pit*. She breathed in the fresh air while waiting for dusk to become night so the movie could start. She couldn't help but laugh at her poodle skirt; he'd told her they were going to a fifties theme party and she'd gone all out, even putting ribbons in her hair. But he looked so damn good in a simple white t-shirt and jeans with the cuffs rolled up, she didn't care.

Alex returned from the snack bar carrying a tray of goodies and handed it to her, then slid back behind the wheel. "Got you what they call the 'throwback sampler' along with the popcorn. Goobers, Raisinettes, Cracker Jack. Just don't get anything on the seats."

"I'll be careful." She eyed the goodies, trying to decide which one to attack first. "Bauer, I love this car. Cannot believe there's a place that rents classics."

"Hey, it's a beautiful night with a beautiful girl, I needed a beautiful car. Besides, the owner cut me a break since I did a story on him a few years ago."

"You're never gonna run out of best-kept secrets, are you?"

"Probably not." He cocked his head toward the snacks. "That gonna hold you till intermission?"

"Maybe. Geez, I haven't had any of these in years."

He pointed to the box of Cracker Jack. "Wonder if they still put a prize in here?"

"I'm sure they do."

"You remember their slogan?" He started to sing the jingle. "*Popcorn, peanuts, candy-coated snack. Big surprise in every pack.*"

"How in the world do you know this stuff?"

"Reporters have a wealth of useless information. I should be a contestant on *Jeopardy.*"

"No kidding." She grabbed the box. "Well, dibs on the prize."

He laughed. "Sure, I can live without another pocket compass."

The sky darkened enough for the screen to light up with a Three Stooges clip in black-and-white. "Oh, cool, the Stooges!"

"This place really does take you back. After that they run cartoons and an old newsreel."

Keira opened the box of Cracker Jack while Alex grabbed the bucket of popcorn. The taste of the caramel corn and peanuts brought memories of her childhood. "I forgot how much I liked this stuff."

"Yeah, when it comes to snacks, older is better."

She talked through the caramel popcorn. "So, Bauer, you excited about release day?"

"Are you kidding? Of course! Though every author dreams of a book-signing."

"Don't worry, it's coming after the big reveal in a month. Considering the advance sales, you're gonna end up with carpal tunnel in no time." She reached into the box and felt some paper. "Hey, I found the prize! It's usually on the bottom."

"In other words, you don't have to eat the whole box."

"No, I still have to eat the whole box, I just got the prize early."

"You're so easily pleased, Madison."

She looked down as she pulled the prize packet out of the box. "Well, it's not a compass." She held it up and studied it. "Feels kinda heavy for plastic."

"You gonna open it or get it X-rayed?"

"Funny." She smiled as she tore the paper.

Her jaw dropped as she saw what was inside.

She turned to Alex, who was smiling at her. "Well, I figured, we have been going steady. And you didn't seem wild about waiting five years."

Keira's eyes grew misty, then she looked back at the diamond ring. About a one-carat emerald-cut in an antique silver setting. Her words grew thick in her throat. "Bauer, it's gorgeous."

"My grandmother's. She told me to save it for my best girl. She and my grandfather were married fifty years, so it's got good luck in it." She kept looking at it. "Well, Madison, you wanna see if it fits?"

She quickly handed it to him. "Put it on me."

"You want me to get down on one knee?"

"Not in a drive-in parking lot." She held out her left hand, keeping her eyes locked on his as her emotions welled up.

"Don't you want me to ask you something first?"

"I just held out my hand, which means I want it. Show, don't tell. Remember?"

He slid the ring on her finger. "Looks like a perfect fit."

"It is."

"So the answer is yes?"

"Show, don't tell. Again." She slid over, took his head in her hands and kissed him.

Then she didn't stop.

Until she heard the tap on the windshield.

Keira looked up and saw a burly, gray-haired cop standing next to the car, dressed in a vintage uniform, smiling as he held a flashlight. "There's a motel down the street if you two need a room."

Keira blushed. "Sorry, officer."

He studied her face. "Does your father know you're out late, young lady?"

She turned on her innocent little girl face. "I did all my homework, officer. And we'll be home by ten. I'm a good girl."

Alex snorted and she playfully slapped his arm.

She held out her left hand towards the cop. "Sorry if I got carried away, but we just got engaged!"

He nodded as he looked at the ring. "You two kids old enough to get married?"

"Yes, Sir."

"Well, okay." He then did the *I'm watching you* thing with two fingers, pointing at his eyes, then at Keira. "But I'm gonna keep an eye on you two and any canoodling going on in this car."

"We'll behave, officer."

"By the way, young man, this car is older than you are, so you probably don't know what back seats are for at a drive-in."

Alex nodded. "I do, officer. Today's bucket seats aren't exactly conducive to, uh…"

The cop dropped the act. "You two have a nice time. And congratulations."

They both thanked him.

Then the cop pointed at Alex. "And you treat her right. I've got your license-plate number."

"Absolutely, officer. She's going up on a pedestal when we get home and never coming down."

The cop moved on as they shared a laugh. Alex opened the car door.

"Where you going?" she asked.

He cocked his head toward the rear of the car. "Like he said, back seat. The place is called *Passion Pit*, after all. You gonna join me?"

Keira got out and moved to the back, sliding in close to him.

Alex put his arm around her shoulder as she held out her hand and looked at the ring. "Madison, you're missing the movie."

"What movie?"

"So, back to our rewrite. Is this a good 'happily ever after' to end the book?"

She scrunched up her face as she looked up. "Hmmm… ya know, it normally would be. But we do have one more loose end to tie up."

He furrowed his brow. "What loose end?"

"Ah, the reader will have to read one more chapter to find out."

Chapter 29

Keira beamed as she took in the long line that snaked around the perimeter of the bookstore.

Gretch patted her on the back. "Not too shabby, huh boss?"

"Not at all. Damn, this is amazing. I never expected a crowd like this."

Bella arrived and handed both a cup of coffee. "Who would have ever thought that not having an author available for a book-signing would be an incredible promotion."

Keira nodded. "I must say, this is a stroke of genius."

Juliette walked up and shook her hand. "Dream come true for an author, huh?"

"And an editor."

A young blonde reporter finished her interview at the signing table and headed toward Keira, then stuck out her hand. "Keira, I'm Jan Sullivan, from *The Post*."

"Nice to meet you." Keira handled the introductions.

The reporter glanced back at the table. "I see now why they call you Cover Girl. This is ingenious. I mean, having the actual cover model sign autographs."

"I can't take credit for it. The whole thing was Lauren's idea."

"Really?"

"Yep."

"How did you ever get the Sizzle Girl to do a book cover in the first place?"

"Lauren wasn't the Sizzle Girl when I hired her, she was waiting tables. Then her career took off and I was lucky enough to have her as the face of the book. Since her movie shut down for a month, she offered to do book signings until the actual author is available in a few weeks."

They looked over at the signing table, where Lauren was posing for a selfie with a blushing man in his mid-twenties. "Did you ever expect so many men to show up for a romance novel? I mean, half the people in line are guys. And a bunch brought flowers."

"I never expect *any* men to show up. But she's definitely the attraction. Once word got out that she would be here it became a literary flash mob."

"Think any of them will actually read the book?"

"Let's be honest, most are buying the book for their wives or girlfriends. But a few might check it out. Who knows, we might find a new batch of readers. Men can be romantic too, you know."

"Good point. Hey, imagine if you had the male cover model here as well. Damn, he's hot."

Keira shook her head. "Oh, he's not real." She felt Gretch give her a pat on the back.

"Too bad. I guess perfect men like that don't exist."

"Perfect is in the eye of the beholder. You want perfect, there's Lauren."

"Yeah, she's stunning."

"I wasn't talking about her appearance. She's a beautiful soul. One of the kindest people you'll ever meet. She did something personal for me I will never forget."

"Nice to hear. Well, thanks for your time, Keira, and best of luck with the book. Though it sure doesn't look like you need it."

"Thanks for coming."

The reporter left and headed for the waiting line, then started to interview a few of the men.

Keira felt a hand on her back and turned to find Alex next to her. "So, Madison, I guess this is a success."

"You might say that. By the way, did you catch the reviews in the morning papers? All of them were terrific."

"And you thought men can't write romance because their sex scenes only last one paragraph."

She furrowed her brow. "I never said that to you."

"No, but I heard you say it at a writer's conference last year."

"You went to one of my romance talks?"

He shook his head. "No, but I was waiting for a seminar on military thrillers and you were the speaker in the room before it got started. I got there early and was listening to you out in the hall. You saw me peeking around the door and invited me to come in."

Her jaw dropped. "That was you?"

"Yep. You told me to come in and join the romance revolution and I said I wasn't into a ménage à horde."

She slowly nodded. "I remember. But then you disappeared."

"You didn't see me but I listened to every word after that. When I got home I mentioned it to Juliette, how you said men should try writing romance because it's easier to break in. She made me dig out the *Ring Girl* short story and flesh it out into a novel."

Keira turned to Juliette. "Seriously?"

"Yeah, he came home disgusted about not being able to sell his military thriller. But he went on and on about the real cute redhead he saw who gave a talk on romance."

She turned to Alex. "Oh, really? So he thought I was cute the first time he saw me?"

Juliette nodded. "No, he thought you were 'real cute'. Actually he called you 'seriously cute'. He was smitten but very intrigued by what you said. And he thought you were funny as hell. He's always liked women with a touch of snark."

Keira eyes widened as she kept staring at Alex. "You were smitten way back then? You didn't even know me."

"I was. And you may also remember that when you spotted

293

me, you called me a cute guy."

"Oh, right. That I did."

"So maybe *you* were also smitten."

"Quite possible."

"And I think," said Juliette, "that subconsciously when he wrote the book, he patterned Lexi after you. You look exactly like the character in the book and have the same personality. In case you hadn't noticed, he has a thing for redheads. Fictional and real ones."

Alex blushed a bit. "But especially the real ones. So, Madison, basically you're responsible for me being here today." He reached out and took her hand. "And for us being together."

"That's incredible. Why didn't you ever tell me that before?"

"Hadn't gotten around to it. After all, you just found out I was the actual author."

"Well, I'll be damned."

"Madison, if you step back and look at the big picture, you made all this possible. You made me write the book, you made me fall in love with you, you made me propose. You wrote the script for your own 'happily ever after.'"

"I guess so."

"One more thing you said that day. 'The best men only exist on paper.'"

"Well, I was certainly wrong about that one. But you know what I always say, the most memorable characters jump off the page. In your case Jamison jumped into my life and became real."

"So did Lexi. I wrote my dream girl and she came to life."

"Awwww. Will you always be so sweet to me?"

He shrugged. "At least until the wedding."

"Very funny."

"So, now that all the loose ends are tied up, does this constitute a typical 'happily ever after' ending?"

"For the reader, yes. For us, the story is just beginning."

All chat, no narrative. Boring

294